WHEN EMBERS BURN

KESSAR

This is a work of fiction. Names, characters, places, and events are either the product of the author's imagination or used fictitiously.

Published by Arland Archives Press

Library of Congress Control Number: 2025927502

READER'S ADVISORY

This story explores themes of grief, psychological trauma, loss of identity, and prolonged harm,
including experiences of confinement and emotional manipulation.
Reader discretion is advised.

—To Spoon —

For every emotional support human who never saw themselves as heroic.

You steadied our storms and softened the world.

You listened when there were no words, and still understood.

You were the tether, the translator, the breath between battles.

You reminded us we were never too much.

You don't have to fight to be fierce.

Sometimes, love is the revolution.

— To Revin —

For every quiet one who was told they had nothing to say.

You shattered that silence with presence alone.

You showed us that voice isn't volume.

It is truth.

You don't have to speak to be heard.

CONTENTS

Remember: The only way to lose the mask is to become the person who never needed it.

PRELUDE

Ymir ruled.
Until the gods carved a world from his corpse.
They left the bones and kept the guilt.
His bones became stone.
His flesh, the land.
His blood filled the sea.
Men crawled from his flesh.
From his rot, the dwarves.
But something remained.
The Shadow.
It did not die.
It fractured.
It lingered.
It watched.
It shattered across the world.
Broken glass on the bones of creation.
A stain no god could purge.
And buried truth took root in the dark.

Chapter One

FIREFLIES & SOOT

Walk straighter. Elbows off the table. Obedience, Keothi.

She sat beneath the old tree on the ridge, staring down at the valley below. The river split the forest like a blade of light. Beyond it, the mountains hunched against the horizon, silent and uncaring.

The lessons scraped Keothi raw. She was in no mood for finery and false smiles, not this early. A cave's silence would be kinder than the stiff halls she was meant to command. The ancestors preach duty over desire. Even the gods expected her to preserve the bloodline.

But not today.

The forge sang to her. Hammer on anvil, smoke in her lungs, heat on her skin. Something she could shape with her own hands.

With a groan, Keothi thunked her head against the trunk, loud enough to scatter the birds. Wings sliced the quiet as they tore across the sky. She brushed bark from her dress and pushed downhill. The cold wind followed her, flattening the fabric against her legs.

The village walls rose ahead, built for protection, now a cage wrapped in stone and pride. The market's fresh baked goods and smoked meat greeted her before the Berserker on the wall even noticed. The Berserkers were the finest soldiers of her village, Irevandor.

She wove through the crowd, ducking beneath a fish hurled from one stall to another. A trader shouted prices, his voice swallowed by the clatter of cart wheels on stone. Timber halls pressed close above the stalls, roof beams black with tar and smoke. Her boots rang sharp against the cobbles as she forced her way through.

The Great Hall loomed ahead. Stone steps, worn slick by generations of feet, climbed to the longhouse where disputes flared and verdicts fell. The entrance had no doors, her father's gesture of open politics. Inside, the rafters echoed with bootsteps and worry, voices rolling through stone.

Obedience. Etiquette. Elegance. Her thoughts whispered a reminder as her steps slowed, forced to match the Hall's rhythm. She smoothed her dress, but it was the ember hair she wrestled with, slicking it back as if taming the fire she carried within her. She drew a deep breath, forcing the storm coiling inside her ribs to relax.

Her father, Halvar, stood near the throne, flanked by six advisors, bristling with news and worry. The rafters rang with gruff voices and tension. *Boars. Hunt. War.* The words snagged in her mind like burrs.

Children weren't meant for politics, but tension had a way of loosening rules. Maybe this was her moment.

To the side, her mother, Brynja, sat with a child in her lap, cradling a small arm with practiced tenderness. The boy's face was streaked with tears. A woman hovered nearby, concern etched deep.

Her mother worked quietly and calmly. The faint sting of herbs and iron filled the air.

Keothi approached soft and precise. She dipped her head. "Helga. Ragnik. Mother." *Guests first, then family. Always.* She grabbed the damp linen from the shelf, offering it without a word. "How can I help, Mother?"

Brynja's eyes flicked up, a mild surprise breaking her focus. "Willing hands? Mark the day." Her voice stayed level, as a smile ghosted across her mouth. "Hold this and speak plainly."

Keothi placed a hand on the loose end of the cloth. "I want to join Uncle Borin in the forge. He's buried in work. I think he could use the help."

Her mother glanced, cool and calculating. "Soot doesn't belong on dresses, Keothi."

"Yes, Mother. I agree." She didn't. "If I handle my etiquette lessons in the morning and work the forge in the evenings... the dresses stay clean."

Brynja tied the wrap with a final, decisive pull. "He'll need days to recover. He should stay home." She stood and handed the boy to his mother.

"Thank you, Brynja," the woman said, nodding. "Keothi, dear." She left with the child.

Brynja finally looked at her daughter. A sigh, soft as parchment turning. She brushed stray hair away from Keothi's eyes. "Ask your father because I know you've already thought this through."

Keothi rose, spine straight, each step precise as she made her way to the throne. Excitement successfully contained.

"The boars are shifting," one advisor said low. "Old ones say they only move like this when something stirs in the dark."

"Take your men and investigate," Halvar replied.

The men bowed and departed. Halvar turned, catching Keothi's approach with a subtle lift of his brow.

"Keothi. What blessing have you brought me today?"

"Father," she began. "I want to formally request permission to assist Uncle Borin in the forge." She gave him the smile her best friend tried teaching her. The one that always fooled people. Soft and perfectly measured. Close enough to real.

"And how will you balance your etiquette studies?" he asked.

"Mornings for study. Evenings at the forge. That way, per Mother's request, there's no risk of soot on my dresses."

Her father's brow creased, thoughtful. His thoughts seemed to be assembling with conditions and consequences.

Keothi didn't wait.

"You said I needed to become stronger. The forge can teach me things books and chores can't: discipline, strength, responsibilities."

His eyes narrowed. "Clever. Using my words against me." A smile twitched, grudging and proud. A soft chuckle escaped him despite himself. "Very well. Two conditions. Only if Borin agrees and neither duty is neglected."

Her grin almost broke through the practiced mask. She smoothed it. "Thank you, Father." Keothi stole a glance at her mother, mid-conversation, gesturing toward nothing in particular. She slipped unseen from the Hall.

Start at the Roots. Chop the Trees. Feed the fire.

Borin would never take her word. She had to show him. Not with scraps of wood, but with something he couldn't ignore.

She ran to the village's edge, to the woodcutter's field. Axes struck in rhythm, bark split with each blow. Stumps scarred the earth. Half-felled trees groaned as men dragged them away. An axe lay embedded in a weather-worn stump near the tree line. Keothi gripped the handle, muscles already bracing.

Barnaby lounged against a crooked birch, working a whetstone against an axe head, slow and lazy. "Oi, Runt! That axe is bigger than you!" Sawdust clung to his shirt and tangled in his hair. One of the Youngbloods, smug, splinter-brained, and always loud around girls with grit.

She yanked the axe free with a grunt. "Then it should be afraid."

Nearby, a coiled rope and iron hook sat discarded on a split log. She looped them over her shoulder.

"Sure you don't want to go back to the hearth, princess?" Barnaby asked with a cutting grin.

Keothi slung the axe against her back. "Careful, you might cut yourself on your own dull wit." Words like his always followed her. Always tried to chase her back inside to the hearth.

She stepped past him, into the woods. The world softened and the air cooled. Out here, nothing demanded, nothing stared. Trees didn't judge, they waited.

Start at the Roots. Chop the Trees. Feed the fire.

The fire in her chest wasn't a flaw. It was the forge. And it was ready to burn.

She knocked on a tree buried deep in the forest, hollow like her father taught. The tree loomed over her, bark flaked, roots exposed, dead, but defiant. It would burn beautifully. She remembered her father's lesson.

Cut one above, one below. Make it fall where you want.

Keothi set down the rope to the ground, twisted her grip on the axe. In the polished steel, her reflection stared back, shoulders squared, jaw set. Something was off. It blinked—slower than she did, a beat too late.

Her breath caught. The reflection leaned closer though she hadn't moved. Fire glimmered in its eyes, watching, waiting.

"What are you?" she asked the reflection, but no answer was provided.

It instead moved its lips with no sound. Her ribs rattled with three words, deep and certain. *Chop the tree.*

She gripped the handle tighter. The first blow rang out. Steel broke into the bark.

The reflection nodded once and vanished.

Keothi staggered back, breath hitched. The metal became metal again. A simple blade, a simple girl. Her stomach twisted as the strange vision clutched on tight. This wasn't the first time her reflection broke the rules.

She pulled a smooth ember stone from her pouch. Always warm, even in winter. She'd found it at thirteen, two years ago. It was buried in the cairn of trinkets during the Mountain Race.

Uncle Borin called it Dwarven Ember. An ancient burning cinder of the Old forge.

Sometimes, when she looked into it, she saw more than her reflection. She turned it in her palm now. It caught the light and in the heart of the stone, fire moved. It didn't speak. It never did. However, it watched.

Keothi placed the stone back into her pouch and gripped the axe. Each swing, slow and deliberate, carved a new notch against the tree.

She aimed below, continuing the rhythmic thwack. Her muscles shook, but her fire burned steady. A bird called overhead. Somewhere in her chest, the forge answered.

One final swing and the tree crashed down, splitting the silence like thunder.

Keothi sat against the log to catch her breath. The axe's steel caught the sunlight. Fire still lingered in its core, calm now. Approval rang through her bones.

She slammed the hook into the log. The bark resisted, then gave with a crunch that echoed in her chest. The rope chewed her palms as she looped it across her shoulders.

The forest exhaled. She did too.

One step. The strain bit into her skin.

Two steps. Her thighs trembled, fire in every muscle.

Three steps. The rope slipped, cutting into her side. She growled, adjusted, and pressed on.

Roots snagged and stones shifted. Pain dulled into rhythm. The forest floor gave way beneath her stubborn pace.

The clearing opened, bright and harsh. Her breath came hot and fast. The lumberjacks froze mid-swing as the little giant emerged, dragging her prize behind her. Even the wind seemed to pause.

Her legs shook with every step, teeth clenched. As she made her way from the trees to the village, faces turned. Eyes followed. A few murmured. "Is that—?" and "Did she—?" One logger ran up, offering to take the rope. She didn't stop, a silent refusal as she moved into the village.

The log scraped behind her, snagging on every seam in the cobblestone, a war drum pounding with each brutal step. Carts shifted to let her pass as the log screamed against the stones, every step a vow.

One step. Two steps. Almost there.

She turned down streets, ignoring the stares and offers. The log scraped behind her, each pull a groan torn from stone and muscle. Her lungs burned, the air like ash in her chest. Sweat dripped from her brow.

The forge loomed as the sun dipped, open on one side, its straw roof sagging over thick stone pillars. Smoke curled from the chimney, cinder fireflies rising into dusk. She didn't stop to watch. The fire inside her had work to do.

She dropped the log with a thud, then knocked once. For a breath, the ache in her back vanished. The forge exhaled, embers and soot drifting, a living, welcoming breath.

The oak door swung wide on its wrought-iron hinges. In the frame stood Borin, broad-shouldered, quiet, his face lined with soot as if stone itself had worn him down.

"Uncle, I started at the roots," she said. "I chopped the tree. I *will* stoke the fire."

A rare guttural laugh shook his chest. "Kindling." His eyes flicked to the tree, then back to her, shaking his head. "You will stoke the fire, eh?"

"Yes, I will."

"Callouses, burns, sweat, soot, and tears?"

"All of it. I *will* stoke the fire," she said more defiantly than ever. Her stare cut through every soot-dark crease of his beard.

"Tomorrow you begin."

Chapter Two

SILK & STEEL

The river split the village in two, restless as ever. It tumbled from the mountain's flank, driving bone-pale longships down its current, their sails slack in the windless morning. Trade vessels and war-bands drifted side by side, lifeline and danger braided into one flow.

Each hull bore Irevandor's mark: a mountain with an ember of fire resting at its heart. Only the subtle blackened pitch—visible to those who knew what to look for—marked whether the ship carried battalions or goods.

Keothi scrubbed dirty tunics that had personally betrayed her. Even the sun seemed to judge her. She sat at the stream's edge with a gaggle of Youngblood girls, yet another glorious morning of desperately trying to fit in among a chorus who knew how to be soft.

The Youngbloods, anyone under sixteen and not yet bound to a craft, got the grunt work: laundry, mending, goat-chasing if you angered the wrong elder. Even as a child, Keothi could never stop digging behind the task. Sure, someone had to wash these damned tunics, but why only the women? The washboard's screw was poorly smelted, the cooling uneven. She could fix it. Instead, she was expected to smile and scrub.

She sighed. Thoughts of the coming Trials haunted the base of her skull. When the Hunt and Hearthbind arrived, the Youngbloods would shed their title and take on apprenticeships. Signe the Seer, the Healer, the false Prophet had already decided Keothi's path: to become her mother, the Chieftain's Wife. Forever following in another's footsteps, never standing on her own.

"Keothi! Are the rumors true?" Elara called, curiosity sharp behind her smile, the one she had tried teaching Keothi to master. Her closest ally beamed, her blonde hair catching the sun.

"I heard it, the tree, crashing down in the forest!" another girl added, practically bouncing, an obvious exaggeration.

Two more clutched their laundry to keep it from floating away, whispering excitedly.

"Yeah," Keothi muttered. "I chopped a tree. It fell. End of story."

This morning's laundry had turned into story time, with Keothi the reluctant heroine of her own lumberjack legend.

One girl frowned. "I hear you're going to work at the forge?"

Another snickered. "What are you going to do there? Wash your uncle's clothes? Cook for him?"

Keothi sliced through the barrage. "I'm going to be a blacksmith."

"Isn't that a man's job? It's so sweaty and dirty..." One girl sniffed, nose wrinkled as she scrubbed a tunic against the washboard.

Isn't this also sweaty and dirty? She thought to herself.

"Come, girls!" a voice called. "Time for some mending."

Laundry didn't stop for learning. It just rotated. The younger girls traded in to give the older ones a break. Lessons in disguise, work repackaged as womanhood—a preparation for the Hearthbind.

The girls shuffled to the forest's edge. A basket of torn clothes sagged under the weight of sweat and sunlight. Keothi snatched a shirt with a ripped seam, always aiming for the easiest fix.

"Keep the loops tight and close," the instructor reminded the group.

Elara sat beside her. "Remember what I showed you," she whispered, holding up a sock with a gaping hole. "In one side, out the other, watch for your fingers. You always forget your right hand."

Keothi watched Elara's hands dance with the needle and thread, perfect flow. She tried to mimic it, only for the needle to betray her. "Ow, *dammit.*" She sucked the blood from her finger tip. The needle was too small, too delicate. A tool that was impossible to tame.

"She can swing an axe but not a needle," someone snorted.

Keothi groaned. The sun was not moving fast enough.

"If only you could be..." sighed Elara as her fingers danced.

"What? More wifely?" Keothi cut in. "When am I ever going to need this?"

Elara's needle paused. She didn't look up. "When you have a husband and children."

Keothi's eyes narrowed.

"Fine," Elara added. "Say you're alone in the woods. Your clothes rip. What do you do?"

"Be naked til I find some," she replied plainly.

Elara nudged her, half-scolding. "The Hunt and Hearth is approaching. We should find time to practice. For now, give me that." She took Keothi's shirt and mended the hem in seconds, her fingers moving with infuriating ease.

The morning bled by in pricked fingers and thread. Laughter, light chatter, all a facade for the slow bleed of becoming someone's bride by way of chores.

Until, finally, Keothi was freed from the cage of sun, thread, and expectations.

The forge welcomed her with soot and silence. The log still waited against the cobbled road, proof she'd done it. The forge didn't care how she smiled. It only remembered fire.

"Uncle, I'm here!" Smoke clung to her skin. Heat melted away the morning's ache.

Borin perched on the forge wall with a chipped mug in hand, watching her like she'd just dragged in a bear instead of a tree. "What exactly are you planning to do with that?"

"Stoke the fire." She beamed, the kind of smile that came with extra credit. Hopeful, a touch too proud.

His eyes flicked to the log. "And where's your axe?"

Her stomach dropped, right along with the axe she'd left behind in the woods. The forge heat whipped her cheeks raw with embarrassment.

Borin barked a laugh that shook his whole frame. "The lumberjacks trail a cart with pre-cut wood. I've already arranged for them to pick this up and take it back to the yard."

Keothi exhaled, part deflated, part amused. "Very funny, Uncle. I meant it."

"Oh, I know you did." He set his mug aside with theatrical solemnity. "Now that you've heroically brought down a tree, how about we do some real work?"

He gestured toward the forge. "Today, you're stoking the fire. Pay attention to the heat. The metal will speak. If you learn to listen, it'll tell you what it needs."

"Understood."

"So when I say 'more heat'..."

She cut in smoothly, "More wood, more air flow."

He gave a small nod, impressed. "Good. At least the court didn't manage to train that out of you."

"More like my mother teaching me the art of fine cooking," she muttered. "Maintain the Hearth, Keothi," she added, in her mother's pious tone, as if she was bestowed with sacred wisdom instead of dinner chores.

Borin's brow twitched. "The forge is a hearth. You can't burn one and expect the other to warm you."

"Yes, Uncle," she said, clipped, but not defiant.

"Start with the bellows," he said. "Ease it in. No frantic wheezing."

She nodded, gripped the lever, and gave it a good, confident pump.

The coal flared then died.

She blinked, tried again. Another puff. A hiss. The fire sputtered, then vanished back into its sullen glow.

"You choking it or stoking it?" Borin asked, voice dry as bone.

Keothi glared at the coals. "I'm...trying."

"Find the rhythm. Slow and soft."

She gritted her teeth, steadied her breath, and worked the bellows with a slower rhythm. Push, pause. Push. Wait. The coals stirred, slow as a beast dreaming of fire.

The ember caught.

A thread of flame uncoiled and licked the edge of the kindling. Then another. The heat changed, higher, tighter and alive. Keothi sat back, arms already sore. Soot streaked her cheek. Sweat tickled her neck. But the fire danced in the forge now, steady and rising.

The day blurred into motion, wood hauled, bellows fed, sweat stinging her brow. She watched Borin's hands move: confident and calloused, each motion precise. Words flowed through the bellows. The forge listened to him the way the court never listened to her.

The flames crackled in a foreign tongue daring her to translate. She needed to understand it: every hiss, every flare, a secret waiting to be earned.

Borin's voice poured years of silent knowledge into the flame. By the time the sword was finished, dusk had crept in. Keothi's arms throbbed from hauling wood and shifting coals. If the fire failed, so did the blade. So did she.

The far wall of the forge opened into his home. A single room warmed by the same fire that fed the anvil. A fine layer of soot covered everything. Stacks of dishes piled high. Clothes were in disorganized piles. It reeked of soot and sweat. But it didn't pretend to be perfect. That made it feel more like home than anything with her parents.

Keothi moved some old clothes from a chair and sat down. Her uncle handed her a mug, then dropped into his chair with a grunt.

"Excellent work today."

She smiled softly, thoughts racing as she tried to commit the day's teaching to memory.

"You look lost."

She chuckled. "Maybe the same look you always have."

"I know there's thoughts. Spill them, Kindling."

She leaned back, sighed, and raised the wooden tankard to her lips, letting the cold water steady the words. Outside, footsteps threaded between stacked homes. Each step silent and efficient, the village settling in for the night.

"Uncle. In a year, the Hearthbind trial begins."

He lifted his chin. "It does."

The sentence sat hot and heavy where it had been lodged in her throat. Staying behind, sewing clothes and cooking for the returning boys, rubbed against her. “I choose the Hunt. Not the Hearth.”

He watched her without surprise. A quiet, steady expression streaked through his soot stained cheeks. “What are you going to do about it?”

She tightened her grip on the tankard as if to tamp down a flare to stay loyal to her duties. “Smother the spark and do what’s expected.”

“The one who swings the hammer chooses their mark: tree, beast, or man. Every strike means something. Don’t swing unless you know why.”

Keothi held his gaze. Before even herself had put the pieces together, the words spilled. “I’m going to participate in the Hunt.”

“And how are you going to do that?”

It was true, no female ever dared to go on a Hunt. She chewed on her uncle’s question. “I need a weapon.”

Borin leaned forward, studying her as if weighing iron. “How are you going to get one?”

“Craft one?”

He rose without a word, disappearing into the forge's glow. When he returned, he placed a warm ingot in her palms, dense, glowing faintly.

“Craft one.”

Chapter Three

PRINCESS TO FIREHEART

Clang. The sound of a hammer on anvil split the morning air like a war cry.

Clang. Sparks danced against the red hot metal, angry and bright.

Clang. Keothi's hammer fell in rhythm with her breath.

She hunched over the anvil, the red-hot blade clamped in her tongs. The forge had once sung her uncle's song. Now, it sang hers. Since the thaw, she'd learned to bend fire to her will and twist raw metal into something with purpose.

Her uncle sat on the edge of the forge with a book in hand. A chipped mug sat on the half-wall, growing colder with every forgotten second.

Keothi's eyes stayed on the axe head she was shaping. Swords won glory. Spears won wars. Hammers were her family's pride. The axe was overlooked, versatile, and sharp; a weapon underestimated like the girl who wielded it.

"Master Borin!" said Trond, a Youngblood, as he ducked into the forge. His tousled hair was that of a boy who'd never known war. His eyes were too soft for the steel he carried yet he was the son of the Berserker's commander.

Borin flipped a page. "Didn't think you'd show." He snapped the book shut, nodding toward Keothi. "Ready, Kindling?"

She froze mid-swing, brow furrowed. "What's he doing here?"

"Finish up the axe. I've called for Trond's help." Borin swung his feet off the wall and rummaged through barrels of stashed gear. "You won't learn to fight by sparring only with me."

Trond frowned. "You're really putting her in? She's never been in the sparring ring before."

The tongs bit into Keothi's palm like Trond's hesitation. The forge hissed in answer, and she escaped them both. Four moon cycles and she was trusted to craft an axe head. In that time, Borin had trained her battle stances, and hammered the court out of her. Soot had carved into her brow. Sparring and war will do the same.

Borin laughed. "Then she survives in a real fight. Don't hold back, boy." He swung his legs off the wall and ducked through the open doorway into the soot-choked room beyond.

Down the lane came Bryjna, two bags in hand. She pushed through the low wooden door from the street and paused at the threshold. A soft smile touched her lips as she took in Keothi at the forge, still focused on her work. "Borin?"

From inside, pots and dishes clattered together. He hollered back, "Welcome to the forge!"

Her eyes flicked between Borin and Keothi. "The woods will tear at her. Beasts, men, and worse. She's still my daughter, not a blade for your rack."

Their voices fell quiet, lost beneath the hum of the village. Keothi tossed a nervous glance to Trond. His only answer was a shrug.

"Better she breaks under my hammer than shatter beyond repair in someone else's," Borin said.

The meaning was clear: pain now or death later. After months beside the blacksmith-prophet, Keothi understood his lessons. Yet a question rattled through her ribs, curling along her spine until it settled in the marrow. Something in his words caught—a whisper she couldn't name. Hunts weren't supposed to kill. So why did they speak as if they might?

Brynja exhaled, the tension leaving her shoulders with a sigh. She handed him the bags. "Bring her back in a week... and whole." Her gaze lingered on Keothi, streaked with soot and sweat.

◇═◆═◇

Two days from the village they stopped in a clearing. The hike had been steady, uneventful, filled with breaking twigs and soft scurries of unseen creatures. Elk trails split the underbrush, and a stream whispered nearby.

Keothi dropped her pack and knelt, the straps biting her shoulders one last time. Heat pressed against her back; sweat gathered beneath the collar of her tunic. She uncorked the waterskin and let the first sip cool the grit on her tongue.

Borin tossed down his own packs. His voice was flat, merciless. "Fists first. Begin."

Trond was busy setting down his bags, unpacking them. He looked to Borin, hesitating. He stood and waited, hoping the blacksmith would change his mind. With no words on the wind, his fist tore the air.

Keothi ducked, breath catching. This surely wasn't what he had planned, was it? "Uncle?"

Trond held back and waited.

Borin only folded his arms. "Fight."

"Back to the hearth, Princess." Trond's punch cracked her jaw, sending her reeling. The pain sang through her bones, cutting straight through her fear and hesitation.

Trond backed up, shaking his hand. "Shit...Didn't mean..."

"If you want to join the hunt, if you plan on surviving... Keothi, you'll have to learn to stand on your own." Borin leaned against a tree, his stare steady as hammered steel. "Trond, I heard you never let up on the other children. Don't you dare soften now. She will stand with you, spear and shield in hand, but only if she can stand first," he said with certainty.

Keothi spat blood into the dirt. Pain buzzed through her jaw. If her mother had dropped off the bags, if Trond was here instead of training for his own trial, then she needed to be ready. The sting sharpened her focus. She pushed herself upright, elbows tucked and fists raised. The next hit wouldn't catch her off guard.

They circled in a patch of churned dirt, morning dew still clinging to the grass.

Trond jabbed left, whistling past as she sidestepped. The right came fast and caught her mid-step, sending her to the ground.

Leaves tangled in her hair. The cold earth pressed into her bones. Still, the fire burned. She whipped her leg out from the ground, a wild, desperate strike. Her heel caught his thigh. Trond grunted, stumbling back and hitting the earth with a crack.

"Stop." Borin's voice cut the air.

Trond pushed up, chest heaving, eyes wide at her defiance.

Borin folded his arms, watching her drag herself upright. "You bent, not broke. Steel's the same. Soft first, then tempered. Every bruise is a lesson. Carry it. Don't fear it."

Borin's words stung hotter than the bruises. By dusk, her jaw throbbed purple and her ribs ached with every breath. Still, she stood at the fire while Borin pulled two hand axes from the pack and handed one to Trond.

"If you're going to claim the axe, you must learn both its weights, the heavy for war, the light for the belt. A weapon should answer your hand as easily as breath." He threw one at a tree and it struck with ease, the bark crashing under the blade. "Trond. Split it."

Trond hesitated, weighing the axe in his palm. Then he shrugged, drew a breath, and hurled. The blade buried itself in the bark, just inches from Borin's.

"Good. Kindling, grab the axes."

She yanked the blades free, sap clinging to the steel, and returned to his side without a word.

"Stance as we practiced."

Keothi gripped the handle, thumb to her ear, and let the motion carry her arm forward. The axe clattered against the tree, then spun off into the forest. A second throw. A second miss.

Borin set a hand on her shoulder. "By the time we return, you'll throw true. Remember, learn them all, but only one will ever answer your fire."

The day blurred with exchanged blows and lessons. As the sun set, the day's training turned into setting up the camp.

She carried a bundle of wood to the camp where Trond was busy skinning a rabbit. His gaze flicked up for a moment as his knife paused.

"Cheek alright?" Concern etched on his brow.

Keothi placed the wood next to the campfire. Smoke carried the scent of pine. Her left cheek throbbed where a knot of bruising had already risen. "Yeah, it's fine."

He set the rabbit aside and rose from the log, waterskin in hand. "You can hate me for hitting you."

"You didn't hit me hard enough to deserve it." She took a swig, the cool water coating her dry throat. "Is this how the boys train?"

A soft grin escaped him. "Aye, doubt you would survive our drills."

Borin emerged through the trees. "Going easy on her? Don't dull her edge, boy."

"Na, you'd see right through me." Trond sat back down, picking up the rabbit and knife. With a final tug and slice, he freed it. "Who's cooking, if we have no ladies here?" He smirked, glancing sideways at Keothi.

She rolled her eyes. "Lucky for you, my mother packed us enough spices to last. Give me that."

Morning bled into evening after evening, training, bruises, and laughter. Her arms steadied, her throws landed closer to the mark. On the fifth day, she sat against a tree on the edge of a stream. A cloth in hand, she dabbed at the most recent cut. A lucky shot from Trond's blade.

"Princess." Trond sat next to her, grabbing the cloth, his fingers brushed against hers.

Keothi groaned at the name. "That's enough."

"You're good at seeing where the weakness is, but you lack the patience."

She raised a brow despite herself. Across the stream, a deer stepped through the trees. It paused at the edge, scanning the clearing before emerging into the open. Lowering its head, it began to drink.

Trond pointed at the deer, settling into the ground. "You think that deer just walked to the river and drank?"

Trond leaned closer to her, cleaning the wound. Keothi's stomach dropped slightly.

"No, it paused, looked, and confirmed before it trusted," she finally said.

He nodded. "Exactly. So when we're sparring, when you go on your hunt, patience is as deadly as a sharpened blade."

The water from the cloth stung slightly, sending a chill down her spine. She lowered her head, held the silence of the forest between them. The calm of Trond's presence and the deer eased Keothi's inner fire.

For once, the silence with someone next to her didn't seem difficult to hold. The need to fill the quiet floated in the stream's ripples. The deer eventually skittered off back into the woods. He looked at her. His gold flecked eyes shimmered in the sun.

Her stomach twisted, as her gaze lingered a little too long. A scar on the side of his left brow caught her attention.

He tilted his head, grin tugging at his lips. "Do I have something on my face?"

Keothi's cheeks burned with embarrassment. She snapped her attention to a leaf off in the distance. She pushed up from the ground, brushing off leaves from her pants. "Come on, let's see what's next for training today."

Trond shook his head. "Anything you say, Princess."

Her heart skipped a beat for a second. The way he looked at her was different from the others. "Don't call me Princess, alright?"

A soft nod from him. "Alright, no 'Princess.'" He hesitated, eyes flicking to the mark on her shoulder, to the way she carried herself. "Fireheart. How's that one?"

Keothi shook her head, heat rising to her cheeks. Maybe this is what the other girls gushed about. "Last one to camp sharpens the blades!" She bolted into the trees, the sound of her heartbeat chasing her harder than his footsteps.

Keothi knelt in the underbrush, bow in hand, breath steady. A break in the canopy let sunlight spear the clearing.

She had been practicing the bow. All Berserkers perfected the skill. Swords tore at what was already too close; arrows struck before death could reach you. All go in, and all survive.

Tonight she'd hunt alone. There would be meat on the fire or nothing.

A rabbit eased from the tall grass, ears twitching, nose testing the wind. It hopped twice and took another look.

She steadied the bow and drew, breath held, the string whispering against her cheek. Pain flared along her forearm, but she fixed her gaze on the creature and loosed. The arrow flew wide by inches.

A twig snapped behind her. She turned, another arrow knocked before the sound finished breaking.

"Whoa." Trond crouched low, palms raised. "Easy, Fireheart."

Lowering her aim, she said, "What are you doing?"

"Helping."

"Aren't I supposed to do this alone?" Her gaze went back to the field, scanning for another to appear.

"Your arrow. Your shot. My steady assistance." His warmth pressed close behind her, fingers brushing her elbow into place.

"Do you know your hands are oddly too soft?"

Trond chuckled, "Focus. Watch the grass move. See how it bends? Let it tell you where to aim." His breath brushed her ear, the warmth of it stealing her next thought. His fingers guided and let her go. "Draw back the string..."

Another rabbit appeared. She drew the string back, muscles steadying despite the heat at her ear—then loosed too soon. The arrow thudded harmlessly into the dirt, scaring the creature off.

She glared over her shoulder. "You're too close."

"Or am I too distracting?"

She grumbled and knocked another arrow, ignoring the grin she could feel. A third rabbit, seems Trond was right. This was a good spot to hunt rabbits.

This time, he wasn't breathing in her ear. The wind still teased from the east.

A breath. A pull of the string. Release. The arrow flew, pulled to the east, and the rabbit dropped.

Trond clapped her shoulder. "There you go."

She spun, caught him in an impulsive hug. He was solid muscle beneath tanned skin, forged by years at the sparring pits. She stepped back as if he were the kiln itself, breath unsteady. "Dinner," she said, already moving toward the kill.

Behind her, his quiet laughter tangled with the rustle of leaves.

Chapter Four

THE STONE & THE FLAME

Nothing stirred in the early morning, save for the soft rasp of cloth over steel.

Keothi sat on the stool at the forge. A large two handed axe lay across her legs. From the street, some might have assumed Borin was at work until the sight of her, bent over the steel, gave them pause.

She polished the axe slowly, reverently. Each stroke, flawless. In the corner, a graveyard of misshapen metal glinted. A year of scars and ruined steel lay behind her. Now the axe sang beneath her hands.

The woods carved her into a hunter. Trond had softened her edges. When they returned, crafting her weapon continued. By day, Borin hammered her into shape. By night, Trond tested the seams.

Twisted steel meant not enough heat. Cracked handles? Wrong grain. Warped heads? Uneven cooling.

Every failure is a lesson learned. Her uncle's voice always came louder than the flame.

This time last year, she had pricked her finger with needles. Now, the forge burned her. Her time in etiquette classes had slowed as the Hunt and Hearth crept closer.

She paused her polishing, inspecting the axe head again. It looked perfect, but she remembered the one her uncle had broken in half with a single strike. A fracture, hidden inside.

Never trust the surface. Hidden flaws break blades and people.

She rose. The streets slept silently. In the yard, three dummies waited: straw, sticks, and bone. Her uncle had set them to help her prepare for the battle ahead.

If it can't cut through bone, it's not a weapon. It's decoration.

Keothi stepped into position. Hands placed with care, spaced just so.

Fear it, and you'll fumble. Doubt it, and it'll fail you.

She swung. Fast. Clean. The blade carved through the bone dummy with ease.

One clean cut doesn't finish the work. Look closely. A single chip means you start again.

She slid her finger along the edge. Still sharp.

Perfection.

"Two days," she whispered to the axe. "We will leave the gilded cage and slay our first beast."

The moon hung low, veiled in silence. Trial day had not yet begun, but Keothi's eyes snapped open, restless before dawn. She swung her legs over the edge of her bed and planted bare feet on the cold wooden floor, every movement deliberate. It was still a deep night, too early for doubt to stir, too late to turn back.

She sat clawing at the sheets, eyes pressed shut. Her heart battered its cage. This was the moment she would become a blacksmith or a wife.

The hearth had long gone out, embers glowing faint against soot. Crickets held the night together with their song. The village slept, waiting for the dawn of feasts and songs of the boys. A single question burned with her tears: would she return free to carve her own path or be forced to leave it behind?

Her uncle had trained her for this over the past year, muscle layered over bone, skills of survival and fights honed. Keothi would enter the forest alone. No mothers to usher her to the feast, no Berserkers to guard her step. She would take the Hunt without them.

If she was to shed the Youngblood title and take on a blacksmith apprenticeship, this was the only option. The truth hung sour and bitter in the air.

Acceptance or exile.

Tearing herself away from her thoughts, she pulled an already-packed bag from beneath the frame. The supplies within slipped past her parents in small, unnoticed moments. From her dresser's top drawer, letters:

One for her parents – to soothe.

One for Borin – to spare.

In the kitchen, she moved quieter than a shadow, snagging a muffin from the counter. A few well-placed crumbs would suggest a morning departure, not a nighttime escape.

She paused at the oak table, eyes on each carving. Generations had eaten here. Elbows, laughter, arguments worn into the grain. Swirls and dots edged the wood, the mark of the first carvers. In the center, her village's crest: mountain and flame.

Old stories said her mother's kin fled the mountain when the stones began to fall. Her father's line was already building by the riverbank. When they met, strength and patience found each other. From their union rose Irevandor, a village of fire and stone.

Tonight, she carried both within her. The flame in her blood and the stone in her spirit.

Her finger traced the edged lines of the table. An invisible character in her mind ran through the hills and jumped over logs. Long ago she would play as her mother hummed soft melodies over breakfast. Though the ladies-in-waiting could serve, Mother held fast to her own ritual: breakfast made by her hands before the sun climbed the ridge. *It is important*, she would say. *A family must eat together to stay together.*

Keothi kissed the letters and laid them near Bryjna's utensils. "It's important," she whispered, echoing the lesson.

Outside the small window, the moon had fallen low. Time to leave this life behind and find what tomorrow will bring. She straightened her pack, touched the crest one last time, and let go.

From the pouch at her belt, she pulled the dwarven ember. Focus snapped into place as her grip tightened. From its heart, golden chains uncoiled, catching fire as they rose. Flame ate metal, claiming it. Keothi held her breath, understanding the reflection. This wasn't heat, but a choice. *They won't understand, but I can't let them stop me.*

With her bag slung over her shoulder and letters left where they'd be easily found, she slipped through the quiet home into open chill air. The streets lay hushed, the village's usual clamor silenced. Even the baker's oven slept. No flying fish arcing through the market stalls, no shouts over barter.

At the forge, the cinder fireflies slept. Uncle Borin's snores rumbled through the threshold. Trond leaned against a stone pillar, arms crossed.

"Aren't you supposed to be asleep?" Keothi asked.

He rubbed his eyes and shrugged. "I don't need sleep. I needed to see you off."

She frowned, hopping over the short wall. "You don't need to see me off."

"As the son of the Berserker Commander, I do." His gaze followed her through the smithy. Her axe leaned against the wall, waiting. Beside it, two smaller axes, a dagger, a quiver of arrows, and a bow.

She side eyed him for a quick moment, adjusting her pack. "Is that all, Trond? Duty as a commander?"

"Caught me. I wanted to see you one last time with the title of Youngblood. When we return..." His voice trailed off, buried by Borin's snores.

She slowly packed the gear, holding her thoughts to herself. The hairs on the back of her neck stuck up. Nerves of the hunt. The cold air chilled her bones. Trond.

"Your uncle and I thought you could use more than an axe," he said. "Remember..."

"Yeah, I know. The string," she sighed.

Trond moved to her side, placing a hand on the side of the kiln. Choosing to seize the moment. "Blacksmith or wife. I'm interested."

Something in his tone, steady and sincere, caught her off guard. Her stomach twisted; her cheeks flushed before she could stop them. Something took over her. Keothi reached for him, fisting his tunic and pulling him into a kiss.

His hand came up, bracing her against the kiln. The forge's low heat pressed close, her heartbeat hammering against his. When he pulled back, a small smile played on his lips.

"You could find someone easier," she said.

"Yeah. But you're the only one who leaves scorch marks."

"Out of my way, Trond." She shoved his arm, a grin tugging at her mouth. The scent of pine and war lingered from him. When she returned, she could explore her feelings for him. For now, the apprenticeship needed her attention. The hunt needed to succeed.

He pushed off the kiln and watched her move with quiet pride. "Don't be heart broken if I don't return."

Keothi scoffed, shaking her head. She picked up the bow, removed the string with careful ease, wrapped it around the ember stone, and tucked it away.

"Last thing. Watch your left shoulder. You drop it," Trond said.

"Yeah, yeah." She slung the weapons across her back and started toward the road.

At the edge of the forge light, she looked back. "Good luck on your hunt, Trond."

"You as well."

His voice lingered behind her, soft and steady as the forge's dying flame.

Chapter Five

CACKLES ON THE WIND

The village vanished behind the curtain of trees. The forest consumed her. The further she went, her knees trembled under the weight of her gear. Her thoughts, however, finally free. They drifted like ships downriver, broken only by the soft scurry of unseen creatures.

One step, two step, crunchy leaf, bear.

Salmon. Spring. Flower.

Keothi twirled, arms out, lungs full, the scent of pine scraping her throat. The string of words was a silent game to challenge her mind beyond the limits provided by the village. The forest air swept her clean. The weapons clanged creating soft music in the wind. Trond's lips still teased her own.

She was free from the cage. She would return with a beast. She would prove she's more than a wife. The forest seemed to listen and answer with pine sap and morning frost, cool air threading through her hair.

She slowed. The first bird called. Then another. Sound layered on sound. A ripple of wings, the stir of brush, the far-off rush of the river as the world began to wake.

Keothi stood still, letting it rise around her. The hush before dawn became a hymn, and for the first time, she felt it: the living rhythm she'd been seeking.

The forest woke, and she woke with it.

She sank against a tree trunk, the bark rough against her back. The creatures greeted the light; she drank from her waterskin and listened. Peace settled through her, softening the tightness in her chest.

When the sun climbed, it was time to move. By now her parents would be stirring, finding the letters. Her mind flitted with images: Father barking orders, Berserkers already mounting up; Mother sighing, rolling her eyes, turning back to her duties.

Keothi rose and pressed deeper into the woods. Borin had told her of a place the Hunt no longer sought, a grove once favored by ancestors before the beasts learned their scent. It would take two days to reach. Time to move.

Trees brushed her shoulders; nettles stung her calves. Brittle leaves cracked under her boots. The afternoon breeze carried a new scent.

Smoke.

Faint at first, barely a thread of wood smoke beneath the pine and damp, but it was there growing with every step.

Keothi stopped mid-step, breath sharp. *Did they find me?* This far into the early morning, surely her father's army had found her. Followed her. Smoke meant torches and torches meant Berserkers. She pulled her axe, scanning the woods. Nothing but trees.

She hesitated, but she stepped forward. One foot, then another.

The scent curled tighter around her thoughts and the pine air. She followed.

Friend or foe. Prepare. Be ready to strike.

Deeper she walked, until a hut emerged through the trees. Cobblestone walls, a sagging straw roof, smoke coiling from the chimney in a slow, silent warning.

Keothi hunched down and watched. *Still the breath, hush the step, only then do secrets stir.* Nothing appeared. Her shoulders relaxed slightly knowing no one was on her trail. The curiosity in her burned for she hadn't known anyone to settle in the forest, especially this close. She cautiously moved forward.

A massive oak door with engraved wildlife mid-motion marked the entrance. Beside it, a herb and vegetable garden wilted behind a decrepit fence. From inside, dishes clattered in protest.

Knock. Knock. Knock. Keothi's fist met the door.

A crash. Ceramic shattering. Scrambling feet.

"Just a moment, dear!" An old voice screeched from within.

The door swung open. A gnarled hand, older than the Seer's, shot out and latched onto Keothi's wrist, yanking her inside.

Attached to the hand was a tiny hunched old woman, smaller than Keothi. Her white hair stuck up, storm-blown straw. "Oh it's you! I've been expecting you, you know."

The leathery hand burned cold against her wrist as Keothi pulled. It hung on, surprisingly tenacious, glued to her.

Uncle Borin's house was messy, this was chaos incarnate. A chicken coop huddled in one corner. Dishes stacked floor to ceiling, a ceramic monument to madness. Herbs hung from the ceiling rafters. A ladder leaned against a wall of shelves, that seemed ready to break under the weight of books.

They stepped over piles of stuff scattered across the dusty floor.

"Careful of the doom piles...Shoo!" The woman kicked bravely at the floral couch. Its ruffled hem erupted with a squirrel rebellion fleeing her assault. "Watch the squirrels, dear. They know when the moon's about to lie."

She dusted off her skirt and motioned toward a small, rounded table. "I'll get the tea, dear."

Every corner hid something new.

A wooden bird, a single nail piercing its beak, served as a bookend. Jars of twitching beetles lined a wall-mounted shelf, each labeled with a name in spidery script. On the couch, a doll with one glass eye stared back, mouth stitched shut with red thread.

A tea kettle screamed with a hiss of steam. The woman fiddled with it, pouring the contents into two porcelain cups. "Masks are hard to maintain. Freya's cat got your tongue, dear?"

"What is this place? Who are you?" A soot-smudged rag lay abandoned on the table. The rag scratched across her palm—rough, familiar, like the apron strings of home.

"Silly soot-hearted man, always leaving his bits about." The woman returned with two mugs of piping hot tea, smelling of mint and lemon. "I'm Satira, dear."

"I'm..."

"You're Lady Keothi—" Satira's eyes flicked to her hand, watching for the twitch. "Or are you Keothi of the Shadowforged?"

Keothi stammered, words catching thorns in her throat. The goddess, Freya's cat had her tongue, claws and all.

"Drink your tea before the Fates decide you're too slow."

"How do you know who I am, Satira?"

The woman chuckled, then pushed the cup up to Keothi's lips, gently, but insistently. "A berserker of stone, dearie." She winked, as if that explained everything. "Now, now. Ask too much and the world floods. For now, leaves."

Keothi frowned, but drank, against her better judgement. The mint and lemon left a whisper of the forge on her tongue, memory steeped in the leaves too long. At the bottom, a slosh of leaves clung stubbornly to the porcelain.

With a flash the woman whisked the cup away. She hummed, leaning into the window light, studying the tea leaves as they whispered an ancient story.

Keothi's gaze landed on a horse figurine, ceramic, cracked clean down the middle. She nudged it, gentle, curious. Her stomach clenched against the tea as it soothed her ache from the morning's hike.

A quiet breath passed between them. Soft rhythmic hums escaped the old woman.

Satira returned and placed the horse back in the exact same spot. "You're not a broken horse. You're just built differently."

Keothi's fingers curled into her palm, fingernails dug in. Something sharp and soft. "I… I should go," she said, the voice of a thread unraveling.

Satira spoke as if reading from an ancient scroll, though her hands were empty.

"Fire kindles a shadow.
A bear, cloaked in golden chains,
Screams beneath the weight of silence.
The masked shall feast,
And the forged shall choose."

"The mask is cracking. Left or right. Decisions may freeze. The one under the mask knows."

This wasn't just madness. It was patterned. Intentional. The chaos had an orbit.

Her heart beat harder than it should. She wasn't afraid. She'd been here before, in dreams, maybe.

"Golden chains? Shadows?" Keothi echoed, shaken. Then, louder, harder, stern. "Alright, I don't know who you are, and you don't know me."

Keothi stood, making her way to the door, stumbling on piles of junk. Her stomach turned, not from the tea, but from the feeling that Satira hadn't looked at her, she'd looked through her. The cool door knob attacked the warmth of Keothi's as she desperately tried to fling the door open.

"I know perfectly who you are, but do you know who you are? Hmmm?" Satira cackled.

This wasn't just eccentricity. This was prophecy wearing a madwoman's grin. Keothi flung the door open. Pine air slapped her skin, sharp and clean. Trees. Sanity. Anything but that haunted hut.

Behind her, cackled cries chased the wind. Masks cracked. Dolls split. Bears snarled. She ran. No direction but away.

The taste of lemon and mint clung to her teeth. Laughter clung tighter.

Roots blurred beneath her boots. Breath tore at her lungs. She ran until the fear dulled into ache.

The sun lowered, light softening from gold to ash. Her calves ached as she ran deeper into the forest. Her thoughts hadn't stopped running, even if her feet had.

Fire kindles a Shadow.

She stumbled into a clearing, flat, open, free of roots. Her Father used to take her out to spots like this, teaching her how to survive the woods on her own before etiquette studies took over.

No sleep, no strength. No strength, no kill.

She piled dried sticks and leaves, creating a small fire, letting the day come to an end. She needed the quiet, but the silence was no longer kind. The trees judged her now.

What was the mad witch trying to tell me? Why does it feel like I've heard it before?

A bear cloaked in Gold Chains.

She didn't understand it. Not yet. But her fingers clenched tighter around the ember stone. A beacon light kept her anchored. No haunted echo stared back. Only her and that was enough.

Somewhere, a branch creaked, but no wind stirred it. The shadows on the forest floor leaned slightly closer than they should have.

I'm tired. I need sleep.

She had left to slay a beast. But the real monster might wear chains instead of claws.

Chapter Six

Hunt. Track. Kill.

Keothi barely slept, just enough to make her body forget it hadn't. Quietly, she packed up camp. The prophecy itched at the base of her skull. A beast was needed today. Not answers. Not riddles.

Her boots sank into moss. Leaves rustled in a hush. Even the wind kept its voice down. Today's task was simple.

Hunt. Track. Kill.

She followed a winding slope down to a clearing brambled with berry bushes, thick with ripening fruit, and slick with dew. A good place for prey. Her father would've approved.

Keothi knelt beside a bush and plucked a few berries, their skins bursting sweet against her tongue. A perfect snack for an early morning. The taste pulled her backward in time.

She remembered a day from training with Trond. They slipped past her uncle to steal a breath of freedom in the woods. They found a similar bush and ate until their hands were strained purple. His soft and crooked smile hid behind the sweetness of the berries.

Her gaze remained on him for too long. Her boot caught on a rock and she slipped down a slope, straight into a freezing stream. The bow's string soaked through. Trond rushed to her side and helped her up.

From the memory she learned two things. Keep the bow string wrapped around the dwarven ember and Trond had a sweet side, like the berries in her mouth.

A rustle pulled her back. Heavy tracks pressed into the moss nearby, deep and fresh with morning dew.

She crouched, tracing one with her fingers. A clean trail.

Laying her gear aside, she slipped the bow from her shoulder and began to prepare.

She threaded the string through the tiny holes at each end, the needlepoint hours she'd spent sewing with Elara finally proving useful. The thought drew a wry smile as she tied the beaded knots and tugged the line tight, testing the strength. No snap this time.

A rabbit. A bird. Not enough. She needed something that bled big. A beast worthy to present to not just her father as a daughter. Instead, something to present to the chief as a warrior.

The snap of a branch cracked through the ambush of thoughts.

She rose slowly, pulling back the notched arrow. Steadying her breath, refusing to move, she waited.

From the underbrush, the bear emerged, massive, black, slow as a nightmare. Its paws made no sound. Its fur glistened with rain.

It hadn't seen her. Not yet.

Keothi notched an arrow and drew back the bowstring. A long and steady breath in.

Exhale and the arrow flew, striking the bear's shoulder. A second followed fast. Both hits made their mark. Not exact, but close.

The bear roared, staggering, yellow eyes scanning. Then they locked on her.

She dropped the bow and drew both hand axes from her belt.

The bear charged, slowed by the arrows.

She hurled one axe, then the other. The first missed as the beast veered; the second struck flat, spinning off into the clearing.

More blood. More fury. It roared, unrelenting.

She drew the axe. *Her* axe. The one she forged beside her uncle, shaped by her own hands.

They collided. The bear reared, a black mountain stitched with fury, claws high in the air.

Keothi darted left, hungry for the vein. She swung for its side. Blood burst hot across her hand.

A claw raked her back. She spun away. Too close.

Don't freeze now. The spars with Trond, the strength of Borin burned through her. She had to survive.

The bear bled onto the forest floor. Four claws on the ground. Teeth snapped. The axe screamed as she attempted another strike.

Slash. Step. Breathe. Rhythm before ruin.

They circled each other, a storm of claws and steel.

The bear's endurance lowered leaving a clear opening for Keothi to strike. A crack of bone. Her axe buried deep in its skull.

The bear stopped moving. It didn't die fast, but its rage didn't need breath, only momentum.

Keothi stumbled back, chest heaving. Blood, the bear's, her own, the forests, indistinguishable now.

She placed her palm on its broad, bloodied head. "Thank you for your sacrifice. Your death will nourish many. Your spirit will not be forgotten."

Her father's rule echoed in the silence: *A life taken must serve. Bone to blade. Flesh to fire. Spirit to memory. Speak thanks, always.*

She stayed still for a while. Let the quiet wrap her. Let the body cool. With what strength remained, she got to work.

The gutting came first, with practiced ease. Entrails were cast into the brush, scattered for scavengers. She worked in silence, the blade slow and reverent. Her hands were slick with heat and iron by the time she finished.

Strapped branches and rope pulled from her kit, she lashed together a sled. Crooked, but enough. It wouldn't last forever. It didn't need to. Only long enough to cross the ridge.

She heaved the bear's weight onto the sled with teeth grit and legs shaking. Axes and arrows she laid across its body.

By the time she stood upright again, the sky had gone gold around the edges. She looped the rope over her shoulder and began the long walk home.

Keothi dragged the beast through the village gates. The sinew-strapped sled groaned against the stone, its burden stinking of fire and blood.

Her body screamed now, every jolt snapping something loose in her ribs. The rope bit into her shoulder. Her jaw clenched tighter with every step.

She hauled the kill toward the Great Hall, where her parents waited with worry or judgement. Maybe both. Perhaps her mother would make a pelt cloak from the hide. Maybe that would be her answer. A quiet one.

Acceptance, stitched in fur.

As Keothi neared the market, the scent of fresh bread curled through the air. People bustled from stall to stall, fishmongers shouting, children laughing, metal clinking into hands.

The sled shrieked as silence rolled in, cold and slow.

One by one, heads turned. Eyes locked on the bear. On her. Whispers spread, quick as roots under stone.

"Is that a bear?"

"She's back."

"Gods be damned."

One step, two steps, let them stare. I brought a goddamn bear.

"Keothi?" Elara's voice snapped through the quiet. She ran. Skidded to a halt. Eyes swept over the blood-soaked tunic, the dirt-streaked arms, the sled. "Two days, Keothi. Gods, what happened to you?" She pulled Keothi into a corset-tight hug.

Pain lanced through Keothi's back. A hiss slipped from between her teeth. "I left letters…" she muttered.

Barnaby jogged up, joining them."Dragged it all this way, huh? Shame it's not bigger. Might've been worth the effort."

Blood pooled at her feet. Her legs folded, sharp and wrong. A deep pain rolled across her spine as the tension in her shoulders subsided. She had no more strength to stand upright.

Barnaby caught her, the rope slipping from her grasp.

Her mind blurred, edges dissolving like frost on glass.

"Whoa, easy," he said, gentler.

Elara's hands hovered over Keothi, unsure where to touch. Blood was everywhere. Tunic soaked, boots streaked, Keothi's hair matted to her skull.

"Gods, where..." She reached for the shoulder, then hesitated. Her hand shook as she peeled the tunic back. Elara's voice cracked. "Barnaby, take her. *Now.*"

It wasn't the bear's blood anymore.

Static buzzed in her jaw. The beat pounded in her skull, like the bear was still inside her.

Barnaby lifted her in silence, eyes wide. "What did you *do*, Keothi?"

The crowd blurred. The sky tilted.

She'd killed the beast.

But it had taken its share.

Chapter Seven

Dress the Wound, Dress the Girl

She woke surrounded in scent; crushed herbs, burnt leaves, something bitter beneath. The healer's home was filled with jars on shelves, herbs hanging from the timber rafters, and incense swirling through. An open fire crackled through the stone hut. A fire licked her spine. Her skin pulled tight, stitched with pain.

Her mother sat beside her bed, weaving a shirt. Fingers working as if trying to stitch the world back together. Her fingers danced, sending reminders of Elara's all those days ago on the river banks.

"Mother," she managed to get out.

"Keothi." Her voice was raspy, thick with concern. "Thank the gods, you're alive. I prayed to Odin to protect you, or to welcome you in Valhalla..."

Keothi shifted, trying to rise. Bryjna's hand stilled her. "Don't move. Signe will watch over you for a long while."

Signe the healer. She gifted roles to the Youngbloods and battled the fiercest killer, rot in the blood. Berserkers could rise from gut wounds, but once fever took hold, the Valkyries carried them away.

"What happened?" Keothi's lips cracked when she tried to speak. "I was on my way with the bear..."

Bryjna shook her head, tearful. "Keothi, the bear...It clawed your back. From your right shoulder blade down to just above your hip. They'll scar. They'll stay with you, my girl. As you walk your path in this life."

The words settled becoming a funeral shroud, stitched in flesh, tight with failure. *A feast of shame and I was laid at the center.*

"How long?"

"Five days," her mother whispered.

Five days in the dark. Five days without the sound of her own name. Now awake, watched over by Signe the false prophet.

Silence lingered between them, brittle and sharp as she processed the news.

"A scar like that... some men won't mind. Others will." Bryjna squeezed Keothi's hand. "We'll have to be careful what they see. What they know."

Each word pulled through her, sharp as a needle. No numbing, no mercy. Concern, not for her pain, but for the man who hadn't even arrived yet.

"Trond won't mind," Keothi said too quickly.

Her thumb traced the old scar from their sparring days. His strike was too hard, too deep. In the woods, with no one but the trees, he'd helped her bind the wound. Sometimes she'd catch his gaze lingering there, not with disgust like her mother feared, but with quiet admiration shining in those gold-flecked eyes.

"You know Irevandor relies on alliances and marriages. Trond would've been a good choice... if you weren't the chief's daughter."

The hammer on the anvil, truth striking metal. The village's needs burned hotter than her desires. She sighed. "Where's father?" *Anything to change the topic.*

"He had to leave for matters of alliance. He'll be away for a while..."

"Away from the great shame of a daughter." Keothi scoffed.

Her mother bowed her head and kissed her hand, silent. Tears welled, but never fell. "You know we love you, don't you?"

"Yeah... I know." The lie burned hotter than the wound. If they loved her, it was the kind that came with conditions. Pride polished into silence. "Mother, I'm tired. I need to rest." *And air.*

Bryjna stood from the chair, taking her sewing materials with her. "Rest, Dear."

Signe entered, a hog's brush dripping with amber resin in one hand, a lantern of pierced metal in the other. Smoke curled from it, heavy and sweet. Black, ragged robes dragged at her feet, bones on twine clattering against her chest. Her back bowed beneath years, forcing her ancient face forward. Rumors say she even gave the great-grandmothers their positions in the village.

Bryjna slipped past her, eyes full of fear and concern.

"The incense and the ancestors have her now," Signe murmured, her words brittle against the thick air.

Keothi closed her eyes, allowing herself to slip away from the pain of her back. Free from the suffocation of her Mother's expectation and false tears.

Her body rested. Her fury didn't.

The world came back in pieces: light filtering through cloth, the sting of a poultice, the tug of stitches by Signe's uncaring hands. The bitter scent of crushed herbs hit her nose before her memory caught up.

As she awakened, her uncle stood in the doorway, silhouetted by the sun. "Uncle."

He stepped in, quiet as ever. "The forge bit you." His voice was soft, but the corner of his mouth betrayed him, a rare flicker of amusement.

She winced as a laugh tried to escape. "Yeah, *'If you don't learn respect at home, the forge'll teach it the hard way.'* Isn't that right, Uncle?"

He nodded. "It taught you."

She shrugged. "Will it be a worthy trophy to carry around?"

He nodded again. "Yes, it will be. The axe held. Better than I hoped."

She smiled softly. "It did."

"And I saw you took some extra gear." He winked, keeping the secret between them.

"It helped. I will make it up to you." She paused, taking a moment to gain her thoughts through the pain. "How were Mother and Father?"

He shook his head. "Thick with concern."

"Did they blame you?"

His shoulders rolled back, not quite a shrug, not quite a flinch. "That's not your worry to carry."

She exhaled, wincing at the tightness in her side. "I left the letters."

"I know," he said, voice quiet. "You signed it like you were giving notice to a guild."

She smiled, just barely.

"But it worked. Your mother read it twice before speaking. Your father folded it like a death sentence." He glanced at her, expression unreadable. "And the one you left for me?"

"Did it help?"

"Helped me stay honest. Helped them aim their rage elsewhere."

"Good. It did its job then. Once I'm back on my feet..."

Borin cut her off. "The forge can wait. You can't. Rest now, Kindling."

The days passed, visitors came and went. She'd asked three separate times about the whereabouts of her father, and each time, the silence stretched longer than the last.

Two moon cycles completed before the wound was well enough, Signe released her from the hut and sent her home. Strict bed rest, but at least she could be within the comforts of her own home. The curtain dropped behind her. A chapter closed. Home wasn't healing, it was holding its breath

Alone in her room, Keothi unwrapped the bandages. The cloth clung before peeling free, revealing the scar beneath, jagged, ugly, raw meat stitched in white thread.

Good, she thought. *Let them see it.*

Four moon cycles passed. No word from Halvar. The days crawled, the nights longer. By the time the wound had faded to pale ridges, hope had begun to scab over until a ship's horn split the quiet. A sound she'd both longed for and feared. As Keothi began to wonder if he'd ever return, the door creaked open.

He stepped in with the scent of salt and smoke. The river hadn't let him go.

Keothi stiffened on instinct, but she held her ground.

Halvar looked at her. Not like the girl who killed a bear. Not like the one who forged her own axe. Just... a daughter.

Bryjna was there beside Keothi, smoothing her skirt. "Welcome home, Halvar. I've missed you." She kissed him lightly, a soft smile blossoming across her face. Keothi hadn't seen her smile since the hunt. "Shall I leave you two?" She glanced between them.

He shook his head. "No."

"Was the trip successful then?"

"It was."

The tension in her mother was released for the first time since the wound. Something was brewing.

Halvar turned his attention to his daughter. "How are you holding up?"

"Well enough, Father," she answered. "Still sore."

They embraced, his strength restrained fearing she might splinter. "Keothi. I bring news. We should go sit."

A silence stretched out between them. Full of words not yet chosen. Keothi leaned away slightly, trying to catch his gaze.

"I'm glad you're back," she said. "You've always been quiet, but... not this quiet."

He gave the faintest nod and raised a hand. "Keothi," he said, voice was iron wrapped in thread.

He gestured toward the dining room. The family sat together at the round table, carved with stories older than any of them.

Bryjna laid her hand on Halvar's and gave a quiet squeeze.

Keothi watched them both, her stomach tight. She searched her father's face for pride. Or forgiveness. Or anything warm.

Halvar cleared his throat, praying the gods might soften his voice the way they never had his hands. "You survived. That means decisions must be made." He clasped his hands on top of the oak table.

Her fingers twitched. Somewhere, Satira's laugh stirred dust in her memory. Keothi felt her throat tighten. *Maybe... just maybe...*

"I've arranged your betrothal."

The edges of the dining room turned white and for a moment, she wasn't in Irevandor. She was somewhere else. Even the forge-fire in her veins held its breath.

Then the burn began.

Chapter Eight

Honor's Toll

I *found you a husband.*

"I didn't get mauled by a bear just to be traded off like a sack of grain!" The chair fell, crashing to the floor. Keothi didn't notice herself standing.

No. She hadn't bled in the forest for this. She had done it for them, to be seen. To be understood. To be accepted.

Bryjna's voice cut through the tension, low and steady. "Keothi. Please sit. Just listen, temper that inner beast, if only for a moment." She didn't flinch, didn't plead. There was something in her eyes. "I beg you, Keothi."

That, *that*, stopped her.

Her mother never begged.

Keothi dropped back into the chair. The legs scraped like teeth on stone. "Talk. Or I'll go live in that cave I almost moved into at thirteen."

Halvar spoke next, his tone measured. "There's a bigger world out there, one we've been protecting you from."

"My axe clearly protects me," she shot back, folding her arms.

He didn't rise to it, simply continued. "We've been waging a quiet war for years. Vorik's father was a brute, cruel and loud. We kept him at bay with politics and patience." His gaze settled on her. "But now Vorik stands at our gates. He's quieter, smarter. Soft on the surface, but ambition coils beneath his skin, waiting to strike. He asked for you, Keothi. Not any daughter of the mountain, *you*. He's heard stories about the girl who killed a bear. He believes you're a legend wrapped in silk."

Confirmation tore under her ribs. Sharp and unyielding.

He didn't want her. Not really.

Just the Bear-Slayer. The silk-wrapped myth. Not the girl who returned home, but the legend who bled and who nearly died bringing it home.

Bryjna leaned in, offering her hand across the table, palm up. "The life of a Chief is a chess game. And we're all on the board." Her voice didn't tremble. "We didn't want this for you. But it's what the village needs. If we refuse him, he'll return with fire instead of flowers. The smile only masks the threat."

Halvar added, "We gave him a bride. But you? We're giving you an army."

Keothi's expression cracked, only a flicker. Enough.

"He brings with him a battalion of Shieldmaidens. Not courtly guards, real warriors. Women who've bled and buried sisters. You'll spar with them. Learn their language. Prove you're more than a story."

"Win them, and you don't just gain soldiers. You gain a shield wall. One that doesn't break. Not for kings. Not for gods."

"Protect your family. Protect your home. And walk out of this with a throne and an army, not a leash."

A pause. Something clenched in Keothi's chest. Her parent's words blended together as she attempted to make sense of the proposal. "Let him find someone else to wrap in legends and silk." She pushed back from the table, her chair groaning beneath the force. "I'll be in the woods. Alone with the scars."

Silence filled the home, sharp enough to bleed on.

Halvar's jaw tightened. For once, he looked older. "You can run, but your home will burn." He let the words hang, then added, quieter. "There's a battalion on our borders waiting for an answer. We have a full moon cycle."

The word landed with the weight of molten steel.

They had never lied to her.

Not once.

Not even now.

The weight of her village rested on her shoulders. She needed time. Space.

"You wanted a story? Let's see if I survive this one." The silence she left behind was louder than any shout.

From the hallway, as she reached her room, she heard them, trembling voices bleeding through the wood.

"She's not ready for this burden, Halvar."

"She brought down a bear alone, Bryjna. She's more ready than we ever were." A sense of pride hid beneath the words.

Keothi closed the door behind her. She didn't slam it, didn't need to.

The hearth barely breathed. The shadows had nothing to dance to.

She moved past the forge-worked shelves, a knife hanging near her bed, the window where the moon watched through frost. She wanted to scream. Instead, she packed silence between her teeth and paced.

She paused, turning. Her mirror grabbed her attention. Her reflection stared back, revealing the truth...

A single line split her reflection down the middle. Neither side felt right. One too wild. One too cold. But both were hers.

On one side: Firelight danced, wild and hungry, licking up the edges of her face.

On the other: the cold grey spine of the mountain loomed, unyielding.

She didn't blink.

Neither did the girl in the mirror.

Which side belonged to her? Firelight or stone?

Satira's laugh echoed behind her eyes.

Decisions may freeze. The one under the mask knows.

Chapter Nine

PULL AWAY FROM ME

Keothi slid her window open and slipped into the cold night air. The words *I found you a betrothed* followed her like blood from a wound. Cruel words. Cruel reality.

She needed to choose. Them or herself. Her boots struck the stone, punctuation on a fate already written.

The village slept beneath the moon. Trond's house sat near the barracks. She crept through the back garden and tapped on the window.

The world held tight like the scar on her back. Like the words in her mind. A second tap. The latch clicked. The window creaked.

"Keothi?" His voice was rough with sleep. "What are you doing out..."

She climbed in, cutting him off. "I needed to see you."

He didn't ask questions. Just pulled her close. "Gods. You're freezing."

"I've been promised to someone." The words cut her lips on the way out.

He didn't answer at first, choosing instead to sit on the edge of the bed, staring at the floor.

"Whatever we were, I can't carry it into this."

He laid a hand onto hers. A natural instinct. She pulled away from him, away from the bed. "Don't make this harder," she whispered. "You make it feel too easy to forget who I need to become."

Trond's voice strained, he rose from the bed. "When your laugh was too loud. When you wore two different boots to my father's harvest feast. You're not silk,

Keothi. You're fire. You're stone. Don't let them turn you into a crown with no spine."

Her breath trembled. "That's why I'm ending this."

"Let me stand beside you. Let me fight as your shield."

"I can't take you into what comes next."

The silence between them was brutal.

She paused at the window, every instinct begging her to turn back. "The girl you cared for was buried in that forest, Trond. This is who came back."

By the time she reached the river, her breath had turned to ghosts. The night swallowed the last of her hesitation.

She climbed into the hull of a long-dead ship, half buried in the mud where the drought had pulled the river back. Waves slapped the boards in a restless rhythm. Keothi drew her knees to her chest and let the dark hold her.

She wasn't ready to return home.

A knock on the side of the ship and a caring voice she knew all too well.

"Keothi, I heard." Elara's voice floated from above. A moment later she dropped beside her, quiet settling like silt between them.

A fish in the distance splashed. A wave broke on a rock. Ships down the river bed slapped against the docks. But nothing entered in the crashed ship except for the tender breaths of the girls.

"Trond told me. Said you left without a word, without looking back."

Keothi's breath turned ragged. "I can't do this. I don't understand how you easily manage."

"The village relies on us to continue. If we stop, then what will happen to the next generation?"

"Is this the only way to do it? Force us all to marry. Force us into a life not worth living?"

Elara sighed, picking at a loose splinter. “Iron melts. Do you think it chooses what it will be? Or does the hand shaping it decide?” She wrapped an arm around Keothi pulling her close. “I hope the metaphor hits,” she laughed.

Keothi trembled in her arms. “I get it. Just wish the gods had picked a different mold.” She stood from Elara’s grasp and paced the hull. “The village is threatened. War or me. I’m backed into a corner...”

Elara’s brow furrowed. “War?”

“Yeah...Fire or flowers my parents said.”

“If that’s true, then we need to start making plans.”

This stopped Keothi in her tracks. “What do you mean? We go to war?”

“Yes. It is now our duty to protect our home. As adults, it’s our responsibility to carry the burden.”

“Father did say to join the Maidens and decide how to proceed...”

A soft tap on the side of the hull.

“Elara, you in there?” Barnaby continued a series of taps.

Elara smiled. “Come on, Keothi. Let’s plan and cause some trouble.” She rose, holding a hand out.

Outside, a group of other used-to-be Youngbloods, now adults. A barrel sat on the ground, Trond sat on top of it. “I gathered the troops, Keothi,” he said. He hopped off the lid, pulled a knife from his belt, and popped the cork. “We’re drinking.”

Elara stepped forward. “Before we start, Keothi has a tale.”

Keothi’s stomach sank. She took a long breath, her eyes burned as thoughts raided. “Flowers or fire is what is facing our home. Either my parents accept or we all burn.”

This stopped the gaggle of boys and girls from passing around empty tankards. Low murmurs weaved between them all.

Barnaby pressed two fingers to his lips. The sharp whistle cutting through the barrage. “Keothi, explain?”

She shrugged. “Supposedly there’s a squad on the edge of the forest. We have a moon cycle to decide.”

Trond pushed off the ale. "Then we hunt."

Elara stepped in. "Don't be an idiot. If we go hunting, then we may get killed ourselves."

"Yeah, by either the squad or our parents," a girl sounded.

Keothi settled her breath as her mind traveled various different outcomes and paths. "I'm to be the Chieftain's wife, correct? Which means I'm the highest authority here. Anyone protest?"

Silence. Only the crickets and fish disputed the truth everyone knew and accepted.

"We need to plan and coordinate. That's the only way," Keothi added. "I will work my side, with the Shield Maidens as Mother and Father expect. I will be the dutiful daughter. You guys need to form a group."

"A rebellion," Barnaby said, a grin large enough to show his crooked teeth. "Very well. We'll work with each other, keep us all moving and alert."

Ale began to fill the empty tankards. The gaggle of young adults passing them around. A sense of pride and hope blanketed the night sky.

Trond raised his drink. "Protect the Fireheart."

Keothi answered, "Protect our home."

Baranby hollered, raising his own. "Sip sip, Motherfuckers!"

Cheers erupted and clangs followed suit as the wooden drinks met lips and ale was chugged.

They built a fire on the banks of the river. Someone pulled out a drum, a girl sang to the beat. The ale washed the sour taste out of Keothi's throat, replacing it with a bitter taste.

Another ale in hand, Trond placed a hand around her waist on the edge of the gathering. Her breath hitched as he pressed his lips against her cheek.

"Trond. I told you. This agreement amongst us all... I can't have you pulling me back to you. It will make things too difficult."

He spun her around, moved his fingers through her hair. "Pull away from me then."

Her body trembled as his voice calmed her mind. A tankard in hand, Trond in the other. Her thoughts raced. Her village's survival rested on her shoulders and her own. "Trond," she whispered.

"Just tonight, then I will wait for you." His lips pressed against hers. "The village will remain on your shoulders tomorrow. Tonight? You choose."

Her lips pressed to his, but her heart burned with the weight of tomorrow. For now, she let herself be held.

Just tonight.

Chapter Ten

GOLDEN CHAINS

She stood beside Halvar, not as a daughter. As an apprentice. The weight wasn't his alone anymore.

Stay or leave. Their survival or her freedom. The agreement of the rebellion steadied her mind.

A worthy sacrifice.

This was what being a shield looked like, too, not in the sparring ring, but here, in the quiet war of compromise. She listened with the light spark flickering behind her eyes.

"Sir, Master Roald and Master Ulfrik are at it again."

Halvar sighed. "Lady Keothi."

The men glanced between Keothi and Halvar, but didn't question their Chief. One said, "Master Roald has a fruit tree near Master Ulfrik's property. His pigs keep eating the fallen fruit. It's a dispute. Again."

Pigs eating fruit?

Keothi studied them. "What's been done in the past?"

"Population control of the pigs. Distribution of the fruit. Fines. Negotiations."

Keothi took in the previous attempts to resolve the matter, chewing on a solution.

"Plant fruit trees on Ulfrik's land. Move Roald's deeper in. While they grow, one pig per basket of fruit, until both sides forget why they were mad."

The two advisors tipped their heads and went off to set the order.

The day had unfurled like a fraying parchment: delicate, endless, threatening to tear.

Alliances for Marriage.

Funds for better housing for the Berserkers.

Roads requiring repairs.

As dusk settled, she turned to her Father. He nodded, approving of the hard days of work.

"I'm going to the forge to see Uncle Borin. If I'm needed, send someone to fetch me."

She left the hall, silk-clad and aching to burn. The forge called like a truth too hot to ignore.

The cinder fireflies crackled among the cooling coals, sending sparks that danced. She stepped into the forge's warmth, into her uncle's steady world.

"Kindling." Borin's eyes lifted, surprise flickering behind his weathered gaze. He rose and filled a pint of ale, the amber liquid catching the firelight. "Drink."

She took it in one long swallow, the ale burning her throat as it settled. Silence stretched between them, thick and unspoken, until she broke it.

"Why the forge, Uncle? Why not the council? Why not a warband?"

He snorted. "I like tools that do what I tell them."

She huffed. "Unfortunately, people don't work like tongs."

"No," he said. "But they burn just the same."

"So, I take it you've heard."

"I have."

She exhaled a long, bitter groan. "They want to chain me to a throne with a smile."

"Not all marriages are chains."

"Then why aren't you married?"

"Never met anyone willing to get soot on their dresses," he said with a crooked grin, raising his mug.

"You were never traded off like a pig at the market."

"Your parents mean well. They're trying."

She closed her eyes, tasting the truth in his words, ash on her tongue. "War nips at our heels, Uncle."

"It does."

"A wedding to temper the blade."

"Truth."

Her lips curled into a bitter laugh. A finger nail traced the grains of the tankard. "I heard about the Shieldmaidens my *'husband'* is sending."

Borin's eyes gleamed. "Fierce women warriors. Not as fierce as the Shadowforged, though."

A flicker of curiosity sparked behind her eyes. "Shadowforged?"

"Of the Stone, Keothi."

"What are you saying?"

He only shrugged, the weight of unsaid words pressing the air between them.

"I haven't told you about the Witch of the Woods."

"You haven't."

Her voice dropped to a whisper, haunted. "I met her. Crazed woman. Her cackles chilled my blood."

"I know."

She sat up straighter, the pain from her scar flaring again. "Uncle," she said, voice hardening.

"What did she tell you?"

Keothi recited the prophecy, voice steady but edged with doubt:

Fire kindles a shadow.

A bear, cloaked in golden chains,

Screams beneath the weight of silence.

The masked shall feast,

And the forged shall choose.

"What does it mean?"

Borin's grin hid something, but revealed nothing. "Means you're not done bleeding yet."

The forge's heat hummed around them, the silence thick with unasked questions.

Ask too much, and the world floods. The witch's words repeated.

The forge burned whether she slept or not. So would everything else.

Keothi dressed, straightened her spine, and made her way to the Great Hall. Her father was already at work, voice clipped but calm as he addressed Dafdin the treasurer.

"We'll see what funds we can allocate, but I'm not raising our people's taxes."

Dafdin bowed, sending a shower of parchment scattering to the winds.

"Morning, Keothi," Halvar said, glancing up. "Ready to get to work?"

"Yes, Father." Another day. Another mask. "What crises await us in the halls of power?"

He chuckled, trying to lighten the air, but the weight didn't lift.

Stubborn will. Careful compromise. Just another day in the gods-damned village.

Theft, hunger, land disputes, each one requiring her to weigh justice like iron.

Measured. Weighed. Decided.

Each issue came.

She listened.

The mask chafed with every passing hour.

Decision. Smile. Pretend to care. Slow death.

She smiled when expected, nodded when needed, but inside, the forge of her mind sparked against the silence of her shadow. Still unshaped. Still burning.

By mid-afternoon, her back throbbed with fire. The pain of her scar kept her focused and grounded. Reminded her what she'd already survived.

The final case: a land dispute. Two brothers, red-faced and loud, argued over a half-collapsed barn straddling their border.

"Split the land. Level the barn. Share the timber. And try to remember, you're brothers."

They grunted, nodded, and left.

She leaned back, exhaling. Ready to flee the hall like a fox from a snare. The cold ale and coals of her uncle's forge called to her.

Before she could excuse herself, a pale boy stumbled into the Hall. In his fists, clenched around a scroll sealed in wax. The wax seal bore a serpent crest. The paper smelled faintly of rosewater and steel.

"Message for Chief Halvar," he said, voice shaking. "Urgent."

Halvar broke the seal. His face gave nothing away as he read.

Keothi waved a hand toward one of the attendants. "Food and water for the boy."

The child was ushered away.

Without a word, Halvar passed her the scroll.

She read it once.

Twice.

Her lips pressed to a flat line. She read aloud.

To the Chiefdom of the Mountain,
His Majesty King Vorik sends greetings.
At sunrise on the third day, I shall arrive.
The Maidens of the Vale ride at my side.
Our swords are sheathed in peace.
My hand is extended in alliance, not demand.
May unity bind us, as the mountain binds stone to sky.
And may we stand together, unshaken, when the winds of war howl.
—King Vorik III

"Third day," she whispered. "Two nights. He gives us two nights to prepare for the parade and inspection."

Halvar nodded. "He moves fast."

"Eager to meet the Legend in Silk," she scoffed. "He wants to parade his gift. Inspect his prize. Confirm his alliance."

See if the silk hides a spine.

The Hall held its breath. Eyes darted between father and daughter. Between Chief and Heir.

Halvar gripped her arm, guiding her away from the crowd and into a quiet chamber.

"I won't let you do that to yourself," he said. "You're not a gift. You're not silk. You're a damn blade. You're my daughter. And the mountain does not trade stones for grain."

Then why does it feel like I'm being sold by the pound?

Keothi swallowed, the heat rising in her chest. "You say that now, but..."

"This isn't about dresses or ceremony. This scroll..." he held it up like it burned, "was a warning shot wrapped in poetry."

"So what do I do?" she asked, low.

Halvar's voice dropped with gravity. "You meet him. You watch. You listen. You find the cracks. And when the time comes, you decide if you'll wear the silk or burn it."

Keothi exhaled with an understanding.

The silk will hold. Or it will burn. Either way, she'd find the cracks. Be the one responsible for saving her kingdom through an alliance as Queen or be responsible for starting a war.

Chapter Eleven

BLOOD & DISCIPLINE

The hall crackled with tension. Keothi held her ground, breathing shallow under its weight.

She had worked at her mother's side, arranging the ceremony with precision. Balancing both her parents' roles demanded a focus she'd only ever known at the forge.

This kind of spectacle was rare. Weddings, births—even funerals—were rowdy releases, excuses to drown duty in ale.

But this?

This was theater.

And Keothi? She was center stage.

The familiar horn sounded through the village. The ship's arrival.

Bryjna asked, "Ready?"

Keothi shook her head, signaling no, but replied, "As ready as I'll ever be, Mother."

"Remember, we've got the full day planned."

Keothi nodded and recited the schedule in her thoughts:

Parade. Spar. Paint on a smile. Let them look. Let them think I'm tame. To her mother, she said, "All while you and Father balance the affairs of the village."

Her mother's voice was soft and sharp. "I know this is an impossible task for you. If you start to feel lost, ground yourself."

It was something her mother had been teaching her during morning breakfasts. Ways to subtly gather her wits beneath the unrelenting weight of expectations.

"Yes, Mother."

Bryjna sighed. "On with the show, then."

War drums thundered.

Her father emerged with his six advisors, forming a crescent at the foot of the Great Hall steps.

Keothi stood above them, flanked by her parents, the ancestral weight of their expectations pressing down.

Synchronized stomps shook the earth. Armor clanged in rhythm. The Shield Maiden song rose, iron-throated, relentless, uncannily close to the song of the forge.

Keothi wore blackened leather, not for show, for survival. On her right shoulder: a bear claw, etched deep, cradling her father's crest, the mountain and flame. A symbol of duty and legacy she had yet to shape into her own.

Her heart pounded against her ribs. A single thought rose with each beat:

Run. Run now. Don't look back.

The Legend in Silk.

The drums thundered through the streets, louder now. The rhythmic beats moved in perfect unison, until they came into view.

A battalion of Shieldmaidens filled two blocks, marching in flawless formation. Spears in their right hands, shields steady in their left. They moved with one heartbeat.

The line parted.

Keothi adjusted the fit of her armor, eyes locked on the parade. An army of warriors she hoped, one day, to join.

A large woman strode forward, flanked by two others who mirrored her every step. Leather clung to her broad frame; a sword hung sheathed at her hip. She moved like an unshakable avalanche in leather Every step deliberate. As she passed one of the Maidens, she struck the shield.

The woman did not move. The Commander's eyes never left Chief Halvar's. She halted on the fifth step, sword sheathed but presence drawn.

"Chief Halvar," she said. "I present the Shieldmaidens of Vaelrikar. I am Groa of the Ashenhilt."

She turned to face the battalion. With a sharp motion, she unsheathed her sword and lifted it into the air. Her voice rang out, reaching even the last ranks two blocks away:

"Hoora!"

The battalion responded in perfect unison, spears lifted high.

Three times.

"Hoora!"

"Hoora!"

"Hoora!"

Each chant matched the rhythm of a hammer on the anvil.

The rows of Maidens didn't waver. Their unity, the force of it, was overwhelming.

Keothi tugged at the black leather across her chest, fingertips brushing the etched bear claw. Her heart raced. Her mind screamed. But her body held motionless.

The mask stayed on. The village demanded it.

"Dismissed!" Groa commanded as the final Hoora rang out.

The army turned in a clean pivot on command. Spears lowered. Shields steady. The battalion marched toward the fields where their camp was already being prepared. The two women which flanked Groa stayed behind. Their expressions flat.

Groa and her two officers turned back toward the Chief and his family.

Halvar stepped forward. "Welcome to Irevandor. I am Chief Halvar. This is my wife, Lady Bryjna, and my daughter, Lady Keothi."

Bryjna and Keothi both tipped their heads in greeting as he spoke.

"Our home is your home. Welcome."

Groa sheathed her sword with a practiced ease. "This is Thorva and Kara. We're thrilled to be here."

Groa's face was carved from stone. Not a hint of warmth. Her tone was flatter than parchment.

"I understand I'm to spar with Lady Keothi," Groa said.

Halvar nodded. "That's correct. She's to join your ranks."

Groa ascended the final steps, boots echoing on the stone. She stopped one pace away from Keothi. "Step forward."

Keothi hesitantly stepped forward. Her heart kept pounding, but now the dread had risen higher, tight in her throat, strangling her voice. "Groa, it's a pleasure to meet you." Was that right? Too formal? Not enough?

Groa didn't answer. She studied Keothi the way a blacksmith studies ore, evaluating its potential, not its polish.

Without warning, she reached forward and tugged the edge of Keothi's leather armor, testing the fit, the give. Keothi didn't flinch. Compared to her father's tests of strength, Groa's inspection was almost nothing.

At last, Groa gave a simple nod. "To the sparring ring, then," she said. "I might be able to make something of you."

A light scoff escaped Keothi. *I might be able to make something of you...*

Groa pivoted with the same flawless precision as her battalion. "Follow," she commanded, no glance back, no room for question.

They moved as one. Keothi followed, fire in her throat.

Keothi flinched at the sudden shift. She glanced at her parents, eyes searching.

Halvar and Bryjna offered small, steady nods. Silent encouragement.

Good luck, their expressions said. Not that you need it.

They moved silently toward the fields beyond the village. Each step dragged her closer to what was certain death.

"What kind of metal are your swords forged from?

The three ladies kept walking, the only noise in the street was their boots on cobblestone.

"What is it like being a shieldmaiden?"

The silence stabbed back. She quit trying to break the three Maidens.

A sea of white tents filled the normally serene fields. This time of the year, it was a field of purple and yellows, lavender and dandelions.

Now: the clatter of arms, the sizzle of meat, the crack of splitting wood. The field was alive, and she was prey.

Which one is Vorik's tent?

A roped-off sparring ring waited, expectant and unmoving. Barrels of training and finely crafted weapons on the sidelines. Striking dummies already stood, waiting for the practiced strikes.

Groa unbuckled her sword, removing the sheath and all. She laid it on the wooden table beside the ring, kissed two fingers, and pressed them to the hilt, a quiet ritual of parting.

I should have done that with my axe. I wonder if they'll let me have my axe... or if I'll be forced to enjoy sword and shield or spear and shield.

Maidens gathered, one by one, forming a silent wall around the circle, waiting to witness the clash of Commander Groa and Lady Keothi. Groa pulled two training swords from a barrel, tossing one to Keothi.

Keothi wasn't expecting it; the training sword clattered to the ground. She bent to retrieve it, only for a shield to be tossed next, crashing beside the sword.

The crowd all laughed in unison.

Great. Making a real impression, aren't you?

She twirled it once. "Good weight. A slower temper, it'd sing."

She swung it once, too wide. A hiss of air. Too light. Not enough weight behind the blade.

A few of the Maidens glanced at each other, unsure whether to laugh or glare.

Groa provided no reaction, only commands. "In." She stood on the opposite side.

The silence stretched-tense.

Keothi stepped in anyway, heart thudding against her ribs trying to bolt.

She practiced with swords alongside Uncle Borin and Trond, but she always preferred the heft of an axe. Swords required finesse. She preferred momentum.

Shields? Dead weight. Delay. Besides, why have a shield? The purpose is not to get hit.

She adjusted her grip on both as she crossed the rope, the crowd closing in, eager.

Groa's voice cut through. "This is a sparring match. Three hits, we're done. Drop your shield, we're done."

Keothi's shoulders tensed. It was clear at this point. Listen. Act. Reflect.

Groa looked at Throrva and nodded. Thorva took control of the spar. "Ladies! We want a clean and fair fight today!" She paused. Groa's eyes narrowed, tracking their target. Right foot forward, shield off held in front of her chest, sword gripped to her side.

Keothi stood normally. Her sword and shield hung to their sides.

"Begin!" Thorva called out.

Groa moved with precision, sword high, blade a silver arc.

Keothi sidestepped, shield up, clang. The sword glanced off.

Swing. Sidestep. Lunge.

Breathe. Your survival depends on it.

No hits yet.

Step. Turn. Clash.

Groa struck like winter. Clean. Sharp. Inevitable.

Keothi rolled under, struck upward, not with elegance, but with feral memory.

She remembered blood: warm, alive; hers and not hers.

The weight of staying alive.

The Bear in her bones snarled. Yellow eyes gleamed behind her ribs.

She swung low. Steel kissed shin.

Keothi's point.

Groa spun, elegant and exact, blade arcing.

Keothi raised her guard, too slow.

Groa's shield met Keothi's ribs with a crack.

Groa's point.

Then came the boot. Hard. Ribs screamed in protest.

Groa's point.

No rules. Use everything.

Keothi grinned, blood in her mouth and fire in her throat. *Maybe...I might actually win.*

Ferocity against formation. Heart against heritage.

Her arm moved before her mind. The shield flew, a discus through air.

The shield struck Groa's chest, forcing her to stagger back.

Keothi's point.

Keothi charged, no sword, no shield, just the beast in her blood unleashed.

She slammed her shoulder into Groa.

The warrior crumpled. The crowd roared.

Keothi kicked the shield away.

Win.

Thorva's voice, cold as steel. "Match! Groa is the victor!"

Keothi blinked, stunned. "She lost her shield!"

"You threw your shield," Thorva replied. "You forfeited."

The crowd fell silent. Groa rose, brushing dust from her tunic, voice sharp as a blade. "At ease, Maiden."

The word landed like a brand. Not a victory, but a verdict.

Groa stood tall, blood at her lip, pride untouched.

Thorva didn't correct her. No one did. The rules chose who stood and who would fall.

Keothi looked around, searching for anyone to object. There was none.

The circle of Maidens began to stomp, in perfect unison. The earth trembled beneath their boots.

Groa met Keothi's gaze. Not with approval or pride, but something quieter. Recognition.

Keothi stepped back, heart hammering, lungs on fire. Around her, the stomps rang out like a war drum. But it wasn't their rhythm that grounded her now.

It was the scar on her back. The shape of her axe in her memory. The beast in her blood, still hungry.

If they want a blade, they'll get one. Not a sword, but an axe.

Chapter Twelve

THE DOLL DISPLAYED

T*ime to dress the Doll.*

The streets bustled with worry, interest, excitement whispered across the cobblestones.

Keothi returned home to find a bath already drawn. She scrubbed away the sweat and sparring dust, the silence of the bath clinging to her as she rose. She wrapped in a robe. Barely time to sit, a soft knock came.

"Come in, Mother."

Bryjna entered carrying two white boxes, each tied with golden ribbon. Her smile was soft, disarming. "How was the spar?"

Keothi groaned. "I passed. I'm a Maiden. However, I lost the spar."

"That's still a win. Learn to fight their way, but never let them learn yours."

Keothi blinked. This wasn't the woman who had once scolded her for slouching at tea. The mother obsessed with posture, propriety, and place.

What else have you been hiding?

"Who are you?"

Bryjna's smile tilted. "A wife is more than a bodice by the hearth, Keothi. She is the gamemaker. Husbands? Pawns." She glanced toward the door and whispered, "Don't tell your father."

Keothi stared, stunned.

"Children learn grace. Ladies?" She tapped a lacquered nail against the boxes. "They learn to be the unseen blade." Her eyes met Keothi's. "We all wear costumes. Some of us forget we're still in them."

Keothi chewed the words, trying to pinpoint which version of her mother had raised her.

“Now,” Bryjna said briskly. “These are from King Vorik. He requests you choose one for today. I’ll return shortly to help with your hair.”

She swept from the room, leaving behind the scent of perfume and the weight of secrets.

Keothi sat alone, with the gifts, the silence, and the question of who she was meant to become.

The first box: green velvet, gold-threaded lace, a bodice cinched for royalty, but familiar in style, village-born.

The second: blue silk, etched with silver floral patterns. Delicate and regal, fit for distant lands.

If she were to meet a king, she should play the role. Blue is the answer.

But, green would show she has honor for her home.

She chewed on her bottom lip trying to make the decision.

Queen.

It felt... correct. *Hopefully*.

In the kitchen, her mother waited, a hint of pride softening her stern grace.

“That’s beautiful! A queen in the making. Sit. Let’s do your hair.”

Her mother’s hands were deft, braiding an intricate bun. As the final twist set, a sliver of her scar peeked through, a bare glimpse of the claw, etched into her skin.

"With your hair up and that neckline... the scar shows." Bryjna mentioned softly.

Keothi sighed, "The girl that killed the bear."

"That's right, dear." She paused for a moment, letting the moment settle. “I’ll tell the others you’re not ready,” her mother said with a wink. “A lady shouldn’t be rushed.”

“I appreciate that,” Keothi murmured, returning to her room.

She sat. *Inhale. Exhale. Breathe.*

She shifted on the bench, eyeing the boxes. One now empty, one unopened. The braid tugging at her scalp. The silence pressed in. She glanced toward the mirror.

Her reflection smiled without her. The smile held no fear. This time it was porcelain-skinned and barely moved. A single crack splintered down the face, from temple to jaw.

Keothi didn't move. Neither did the image. For a moment, she couldn't look away. Couldn't blink. Couldn't breathe.

It knows.

A soft knock shattered the silence.

"Keothi?" Her uncle's voice, gentle, grounded, and familiar.

She blinked hard, tearing her gaze from the mirror. The cracked porcelain doll was gone. Only her own face stared back, too clean. Simply a trick of the light. Or something worse.

Borin stepped inside and froze. His eyes narrowed slightly. "You alright?"

She stood, too quickly, swallowing the knot of fear in her ribs. "Uncle." She moved into a hug. "You don't smell of smoke. Did you bathe?"

Borin was dressed in fine clothing, beard trimmed. Not a speck of soot was on him. "Your Father requested I join in today's festivities. I was asked to clean up..." He shrugged.

"After today, we'll both need to roll around in the forge." She teased.

With a soft chuckle, he stepped back, narrowing his eyes. "You looked... far away."

"I was." She avoided his eyes. "Just... nerves."

He didn't press. He'd seen that look before.

"How was the fight?" His tone was lighter, teasing but sincere.

"Lost by technicality." She shrugged. "Your training worked, though. Gave me an edge."

That pulled a smile from him, broad and proud. "Then every bruise was worth it."

"A few of them linger," she muttered with a small grin.

He laugh as his gaze dropped to the blue silk wrapping her body. "You look like someone who gives orders now."

She didn't smile this time, her eyes lowered. "I'm nervous, Uncle." Her voice was small. "What if I can't perform?"

He didn't answer right away. He studied her, then stepped closer, his voice low and firm. "Keothi… even shadows are born from something greater."

She met his gaze. There it was, the reminder that she was more than this version of herself. More than lace and posture.

"You're already standing in the fire," he continued. "And that's the truth of it. You'll either shape it… or you'll let it burn you down."

A sharp, trembling breath. Keothi took one last look at the ornate mirror. This time, it was only her. A small smirk, just in case and it was hers.

"Let's show them what they made."

The three returned to the Great Hall, now buzzing with evening festivities. Ribbons and flowers draped from the rafters. Four long tables lined the space, with a fifth at the front. Elara barked orders, directing decorations with a firm hand.

"Keothi," she smiled, as she snapped at someone. "That needs to go higher…" She sighed, turning back to Keothi. "Beautiful! Stunning!"

Keothi softly laughed, "Thanks, Elara. The Hall looks perfectly dressed up."

She shrugged, "It's getting there. It must be absolutely perfect. We have a King gracing our village!" She swooned.

Truth was, since Keothi became Queen bound, she hadn't seen Elara around much, if at all. "I know I've been scarce… the whole politics thing, I've been walking on eggshells. But tonight, let's be us again."

"I'd love that. Try and enjoy yourself, hmm?"

Keothi scanned the heads in the bustling hall until she spotted her father near the front, flanked by stewards.

"Oh and Keothi…"

"Yes, Elara?"

"Remember to use your Elara smile!" That same grin from long ago. Perfect. The two girls laughed, remembering their childhood lessons of etiquette.

"Father." Keothi walked up to him, he held out a hand. She grabbed it and he spun her around.

"My beautiful daughter! You're stunning," he beamed with pride.

"How's the preparations going?" Keothi asked, the words coming easily, a familiar rhythm of conversation.

"As planned, right on schedule."

"Anything happened this morning that I should know about?"

He glared. "What have you done with my daughter?"

"I guess it's becoming a habit..." A tinge of guilt hung on her words, momentarily forgetting her place as dutiful daughter.

He gave her a soft shake on the shoulder. "It's good to see the natural leadership in you blossoming. Now, a small change of plans."

"Oh? What plans are those?"

"A messenger came by. They said a King goes to no one, everyone goes to a king." He said sternly.

Disgusted by the sentiment, "Really?"

"Really, really."

"Wow. That's... something." It was a stark contrast to Father's open door policy. A gut punch. *Maybe I can influence King Vorik.* "When would he wish to see us?"

"As soon as you are dressed and ready..."

"And Polished," she cut him off.

He shrugged, "Elara and your Mother have the hustle and bustle here. Are you ready?"

"Do I have a choice," she chuckled. "Come on, we mustn't keep a King waiting, Father." She performed a perfect curtsy, thick with sarcasm and wit.

He let out a hearty laugh, matching her tone. "Come on, Queen."

Halvar rounded up his six advisors and Borin. Every single one dressed to the nines. A stark difference to the relaxed atmosphere among them all. Keothi led the group to the tent covered field.

"I only saw the sparring pit, I don't know where King Vorik's tent is located." Keothi admitted as they arrived at the edge.

"He'll find us," Halvar said plainly.

Two shieldmaidens arrived. Shields and spears ready. They turned into stone pillars once they approached. "King Vorik is expecting you. Follow us."

Swords. Pigs. Fire. Camp smoke. Canvas and steel.

Keothi adjusted her mask, mirroring the poise of the shieldmaidens. Her stomach churned. Good thing she'd skipped lunch.

They stopped before a massive tent. A fine rug spilled from the flaps, its edges muddied by boots. The entrance stood open. The shieldmaidens took their place on either side as a boy in royal livery stepped out and bowed low.

"Chief Halvar. Lady Keothi. Follow me, please." The boy pivoted in a manner that reminded her of the shieldmaidens earlier that morning.

Am I going to need to go to pivot school? She smothered a laugh.

The group exchanged glances and shrugs. Halvar and Keothi stepped forward.

Inside, the tent was split by a heavy velvet curtain. A throne, real wood, expertly carved, sat on a raised dais. Cushions of red velvet. A man lounged on it, head cocked.

Black hair, perfectly combed. A trimmed beard, soft and deliberate. He wore red velvet and polished black, every thread chosen to impress and intimidate. A silver crown perched delicately on his brow. His grey eyes wandered up and down Keothi's body inspecting his prize.

He lifted a finger, lazily twirling a circle in the air.

Keothi frowned. *Is he... Is he asking me to turn?*

The boy confirmed it with a practiced, deadpan tone: "Turn."

Her stomach tightened into a knot. She turned, slowly, letting the scar on her shoulder blade show. She spun back.

Vorik gave a satisfied sigh. "Next time, wear green. It stains slower. But the scar, now that was a good choice."

Her stomach coiled. Her breath hitched. She'd been right, he didn't want her. He wanted the myth.

He rose with the ease of a man who'd never been denied. His hand lifted, slow, deliberate, not asking permission, but as if he already owned the right. His touch was too soft, too possessive, making her skin crawl. He needed to work in the forge, not fondle women like prizes.

"Green eyes," he murmured, tilting her head. Keothi felt like a cow being inspected. "Shorter than I expected. But the bones are good."

He stepped behind her. A single finger traced the raised edge of the scar, pressing in, probing the seam as if it might come undone. His finger lingered, fondling the scar for a touch too long.

She flinched, instinctively stepped back. Then turned, wearing composure like armor. "King Vorik, I presume," she said, her voice flat. Every fiber of her being wanted to stop him from seeing her as livestock.

"Ah, the Daughter of the Mountain speaks."

Let him think I'm obedient. For now.

"We're honored to welcome you and your forces to our lands," she said. "We look forward to our kingdoms' alliance."

He smirked. "She does have fire, doesn't she?"

Halvar finally spoke. "She does. Lady Keothi is a Queen in making. Her spark will serve your court."

Vorik nodded. "That she will. I accept the trade."

He waved his hand like swatting away smoke. "Go. The Maidens await. Your kill is confirmed, not simply campfire stories." A pause, then colder: "This is no place for a Lady."

She glanced at her father.

His jaw was tight. Eyes unreadable. A subtle twitch of his hand. Once relaxed, now a fist at his side.

She didn't breathe until she stepped outside.

She'd walked in as a daughter.

She walked out as a warning.

Chapter Thirteen

DRESSING THE DOLL

She returned home. Didn't speak. Didn't breathe. Just shut her door and screamed into the pillow. It owed her silence.

She took a deep breath and calmed herself. *I need the forge. I don't care.* She rolled over, a quick glance at the mirror. The porcelain scarred doll stared back.

Her reflection watched with quiet judgment. That was all it took. Rage flooded back, sudden and hot.

"Ugh, go away..." She threw her pillow at the mirror.

The mirror tipped back, hitting the wall, but not breaking.

With all her might, she ripped the dress in half, forcing it off her. She grabbed her own clothes, stained with soot, and put them on.

She slid through the window, a secret being swallowed by a crescent moon and the judgment of stars.

Really? Is my scar all I'm good for? I should go to the camp, and stab him where he lay.

She kicked at loose pebbles, shivering.

Feeling my scar like that? Creep!

The village passed in a blur, homes, fences, the scent of hearth-smoke. Her body walked the path on instinct.

Ahead, the forge glowed faintly. The lingering smoke of the day hung in the air, thick and warm. It calmed her, barely. The beast within paced.

Uncle Borin's house flicked with firelight. He was home.

Damn. I hope he doesn't mind me starting the fire... I need to forge.

She crept closer. Voices.

Her father. With Borin. She froze in place.

What's Father doing here? This is mine. Go away.

She crouched beside the half-wall, hidden. Unseen. Just like Vorik wanted her.

She shivered thinking about him.

"Halver, she sees it. I don't know how long, but..."

"What did you see?" her father asked.

Keothi held her breath.

"This morning. I stopped by. She was staring into the mirror."

"That doesn't mean anything," Halvar said quickly. "Maybe she was... entranced by how she looked..."

"She's us, Halvar." Daggers shot at Halvar, with a sharp bark. "Don't deny it!"

A heavy silence, a simple heavy exhale from her Father breaking it. "Then we need to shape the world around her..."

"Halvar, she doesn't have Brynja to guide her. It's us or no one. And the visions? They're only going to get worse. I saw what that bastard did to her."

"You're right...but what can we do? Break the alliance and the Kingdom falls. Keep it..."

"And she becomes an object."

A long pause occurred between the two men.

Borin broke the silence this time. "Satira? We need to get out of here before..."

Satira? Does he know Satira? And why would he suggest her of all things?

"No." Halvar's voice was flat and unmovable. "You know it has to be her choice. Just as she chose to face the beast, so too must she choose this path. Satira will push. We can't force it, influence..."

"It won't appear." Borin's voice was bitter. "So what then? Let him keep breaking her? Strip her down until she forgets who she is?"

"The Shadow will take her, before the monster kindles her fire, and you know it..." said Halvar softly.

"And before the Shadow takes her, she'll save herself..."

"At least that's the hope," the two men said in accidental unison.

Keothi was torn. *Interrupt them. Flee to the woods. Stab the King.*

They said it... the witch of the woods also said it: *The masked shall feast, and the forged shall choose.*

It's her choice. Endure or... her heart sank.

Village. Fire. Battle. Graveyard.

She looked at the anvil, at the silent kiln hoping it would answer for her.

The coals were silent. Judgmental. Cold where fire once sang.

Once it roared with heat and hammer strikes. Laughter, sparks. Now, only hush. Only shadow. The silence screamed louder than the forge ever had.

That night, her room felt cold. The chill crept in through the walls, settled in her bones. Tears stained her pillow.

She didn't sleep.

She didn't forge.

Her hand twitched, clinging onto her blankets of furs, remembering the grip of the hammer.

The sun rose anyway.

Rude. Why do you insist on taunting me? She softly scolded the sun.

She planted her feet on the ground. A headache lingered from the cries the previous evening.

She rubbed her eyes, yawning. She looked up, the porcelain face staring back, not leaving. "What are you?"

A knock on the front door interrupted her slow morning.

"Come on in. I'll see if..." Bryjna had been interrupted.

Her door swung open. Groa and her generals barged in. "Up. We've got work to do." She stepped aside, and a parade of strangers stormed in.

"What's going on?"

Four ladies, all in simple garments, grey veils covering their faces. All looking at the ground. "Pardon, Mi'Lady. It's time for you to get dressed."

Groa interrupted the pleasantries. "Time to get to training. You will arrive at the Field at sun up. These ladies are here to serve you and only you. They are your Keepers." She paused for a moment. "Yo u will be presentable, at all times. Do as you're told. Don't ask questions. Understood, Maiden?"

She barely noticed they moved as one. Their breath, their silence, their steps, all moving as one. As if bound by thread.

"Ladies." Groa waved, and another line of Maidens marched in, trunks in hand. Each one held weapons of silk and lace. They rifled through Keothi's dresser, emptied it, and filed it.

Flashes of colors and textures. Keothi couldn't really see, her room was bursting at the seams with people. She groaned, "Groa. This is too early..."

Groa ignored her, but her hand wrapped around the hilt of her sword.

I wonder how far I could push her. Keothi chose to bite her tongue. Once her dresser was filled with who knows what, her Keepers piled in and stood still, waiting in silence.

Sternly, Groa said, "We'll be in the living room. Be quick."

Keothi fell backwards on the bed. Forearm pressed against her eye lids. Groans rumbled from her throat.

"Mi'Lady, we must get you dressed."

Her eyes twitched. At least she got to play with weapons. There's hope at least... Maybe.

Keothi rolled from the bed and the women all stripped her down.

"So, Keepers, huh?"

The women stayed silent, heads down, never meeting her eyes. One pulled a shirt over Keothi's head. Another did her hair in a simple bun.

"Do any of you have names?"

Silence. Another had her step into pants.

"You'll be Thread," she said to the one doing her hair. "You, who put on my shirt, Buttons. You with the armor, Knob."

Still no response. Just work. Keothi caught a glimpse of herself in the mirror, stripped down, arms half-raised. She was a doll. Four hands moved around her as if she wasn't there. A toy for them to play dress up with.

"The last one, you'll be Spoon." As the final unnamed Keeper slipped a pair of boots on. "You know I can tie my shoes, right?"

The girl paused, only for a moment. Her hands didn't stop working, but something in her eyes changed, as if '*Spoon*' had landed somewhere deeper than fabric and lace.

"Your fingers aren't meant for tying shoes, Mi'Lady," Spoon said softly.

Knob moved forward and slipped on the armor. Thread and Buttons snapped buckles.

"This has been fun, Ladies."

"Keepers, Mi'Lady," murmured Thread, her voice was dust on silk.

"Porcelain Sisters," she muttered under her breath.

Maybe Mother will be able to get them to crack.

Keothi moved to the living room. Groa and her goons were already there, still as statues. Her mother's gaze flicked to Groa, then back to Keothi, concern brushed across her face.

Keothi shrugged. "Training starts. Good luck with Thread, Knob, Buttons, and Spoon."

Groa shot her a look.

"They wouldn't give me names, so..."

"They don't have names. They are your Keepers." Her voice carried the frost of deep winter, sharp, stilling, the kind that silences whole forests.

"Then why do you have a name?" Keothi asked, honestly curious about the rules of her new world.

One of the Maidens stepped forward, and slammed Keothi against the wall. The house shook. Her forearm pressed hard into Keothi's throat.

Keothi's throat collapsed beneath the woman's strength. She tried to move, to push back, but it was fruitless.

Bryjna startled with a screech. "This house is not for your power plays!"

Groa didn't flinch. Didn't even blink. Bryjna just a fly on the wall. She stepped in close, voice smooth as broken glass. "You will bite your tongue, before I take it." She tapped the Maiden's shoulder. Instantly, the grip released. "Ladies," Groa said simply.

Keothi collapsed, coughing, air burning back into her lungs.

The parade of women moved toward the door, precise and silent.

"I'm sorry, Mother," Keothi rasped. "I didn't..."

Bryjna nodded, voice low. "It's alright. I know. Good luck out there."

"Keothi." Groa's voice snapped like a whip.

Training lasted until the light drained from the sky. Her arms trembled from the day's spar, her throat raw. When they finally released her, she didn't go home. She went where the air still remembered laughter.

Keothi leaned against Elara's porch rail, sweat still cooling between her shoulder blades. Her body ached in pulses. For once, the pain didn't scream, it hummed. A bruise on her temple, a welt on her shoulder, still better than silk and smiling for kings.

Children stampeded inside, Elara's mother snapped commands, a bedtime general wielding wooden spoons.

The door creaked open.

"You're skulking like a boy denied his hunt." Elara leaned in the doorway, sleeves rolled, flour on one cheek, smelling faintly of cinnamon and chaos. The sight hit Keothi like warmth after too many days in the cold.

"Not sulking. Just waiting to ignite," she shrugged. "Want help wrangling the pack?"

Elara snorted. "You'd start a war, not end one. Come on. Let's walk."

The gravel crunched underfoot. The night carried that brittle chill, the kind that made doors creak and trees forget their leaves.

"Your eye ok?" Elara asked as they slowed near the river bank. She stepped forward, grabbing Keothi's chin to inspect the wound.

Keothi pulled from her hand. "It's fine. Remember the time you tried skipping a rock, but you let go too late?"

A laugh exploded from Elara. "Your mother about had a heart attack."

"Still have the scar in my hairline too."

"Keothi... are you going to disappear on me? Go off to war, become someone I only hear stories about?"

Keothi didn't answer at first. Her fingers found the welt under her eye again. "The shieldmaidens are a nice change of pace. I may even have some ground with them. But, I don't think they'll see me like you do."

A fish broke the surface with a gentle splash, the only sound in the silence between them. Elara didn't look up. "I was promised to Barnaby."

"Do you want it?"

"I... I think so." Elara chewed her lip. "I mean, I want the life. The home. The warmth. The... quiet."

Keothi nodded.

"But I don't know if I want it with him. Not yet." Elara twirled her hair. "It's as if I was still learning the steps... then someone struck the drum and shoved me into the dance."

Keothi tried to picture Elara in a hearth-lit home, kids hanging off her, laughter spilling from the windows. It wasn't hard. But she could also see her friend sitting alone by the fire, waiting for a ship that never returned.

Elara sighed. "He's been given a spot on a warship."

"So a baby every voyage?"

Elara huffed a laugh, but it broke halfway. "That's the parents' plan. Barnaby and I... we're still talking."

A breeze moved between them. Neither one stepped closer.

Two girls. Two cages. One with velvet trim. The other bore a shield. Neither let you breathe.

Chapter Fourteen

THE CORONATION OF OBEDIENCE

The sun kept setting earlier. Or maybe the drills went longer. She couldn't tell anymore.

Training blurred into routine. Wake. Dress. Eat. Drill. Repeat.

Bruises and cuts blended together, never fully healing. Meals arrived too soon or too late. Even the Keepers came at different hours, as if time was another test.

Groa's voice was the metronome. Her silence, the rhythm.

Vorik's forces had taken root. Guard rotations crept earlier. Patrols spread wider. The village barely noticed.

Nothing was predictable anymore.

Today was no different.

Keothi stood in the center of the training circle. Her hand reached for the shield before she registered the command. Around her, the Maidens slammed their own into place, forming a ring of iron and silence.

Every muscle ached in Keothi. Her tongue sandpaper from thirst. Her stomach wanted to flee her body in search of food. She hadn't seen her family or friends in many moons. Honestly, everything blended together. Memory was a fleeting thought.

Her village counted on her to move forward. To continue to play the game. Exhaustion and pain tugged against her.

Thorva stood on the opposite side of the sparring ring, waiting, still as carved granite. Her blade gleamed like it knew how this would end.

Keothi struck the shield once, twice, three times. Each strike was heavier than the last. The weight was wrong, loose in the hilt, handle unbalanced. A show blade. Not meant to survive a fight.

Thorva echoed the rhythm, each strike a warning that vibrated through the ground.

They sprinted forward in unison, shields crashing.

Thorva's blade was faster. It swung low, striking Keothi's shield.

Keothi moved on instinct, but the general danced around her, too quick, too sharp.

Her blade striking Keothi's back. The pain tore through her spine. Another strike from Thorva, steel met shoulder, digging into a wound that wouldn't heal.

Keothi's lungs burned as she swung at the general, only to miss. Weakness took over, dropping her to one knee, the bear-claw scar flaring in protest. She wanted to fight, scream. Hurl her sword at Groa's smug face. But she had learned by now the rules don't exist. They're a lie. What's the point of fighting if she was going to lose anyway?

That was the single burning lesson. Spars. Food. Isolation. All designed to make her lose. In between the splotches of rust on her sword, the reflection stared back. Porcelain as ever. It always was now.

"Get up! Fight!" Groa commanded.

Her body didn't move. Her gaze remained on the cracked doll in the broken blade.

Maybe this is the crack Father told me to find. Let them think I've folded, so they never see the swing coming.

She wasn't weak, the fire still burned. Still, she was smart enough to know when they wanted her to fight. She was tired. Hungry. Her knees buckled and slagged. Her arms, brittle as spent kindling. Her spine remembered fire, but her body had gone cold.

She yielded, letting the sword and shield clatter to the dirt. She chose to stay down. Make them think they've broken her. Maybe then they'll ease on the beatings. Maybe then she'll be accepted into the fold of the army.

The chanting ceased from the rest of the Maidens. The ring quieted. The crowd's faces all twitched at once, too perfectly. They blurred, sharpened, blurred again, reality twitching on its string. Like someone behind the curtain kept adjusting the focus, testing the edges of reality to see what she'd notice.

A soft hum bled into the silence. Not breath, not voice. Like the hidden beat of a forge bellows, steady, unnatural, waiting. Then: bones cracking. Grinding. The sound scraped against her mind.

Groa's heel pierced the ring like a command line, driving into Keothi's ribs. The hum vanished. The crowd reassembled. The mask locked back in place as she fell over. The gravel pierced through training leather.

Blood streaked her temple. Groa's hand seized her, wrenching Keothi back into performance.

Their eyes locked. "Now you're something he'll keep. Scared and tamed. The Broken Legend in Silk." Groa leaned closer, breath brushing Keothi's ear. "Your family won't recognize you. Which means I've done my job."

Keothi didn't speak. She just watched Groa walk away, already measuring the weight of her fall.

"You've grown into what he needs, which means I've done my job. Take her."

Two maidens pressed into the ring. One kicked the shield and sword away. Keothi's eyes burned. Their arms looped under her armpits, forcing her to her feet.

That was the day the drills ended and the occupation began.

The weight of her own body was even too much for her to bear. The Maidens lined up. Beyond the tent-strewn field, Blades waited, an audience of steel. A Blade general sat on a horse, moving along the army. Groa led the Maidens forward. They all blended together, standing perfectly still.

Dust hung in the air, the only thing brave enough to move.

"Blades! Maidens!" the general sounded. "Do not falter! You know the drill!"

Swords all rang out. The Maidens began to move their own armor in sync. A song broke out. Soon the sound of feet marching matched the rhythms.

They dragged Keothi, keeping her in line with the Maidens. To the village wall that once was wrapped in protection and pride, now settled under the weight of new patrol schedules. The Berserkers no longer watched the gates, but Vorik's men.

As they passed the gates, in the streets the army veered off. All separating into different streets. Groa took to the cobbles. She moved like smoke. Her voice crisp and almost kind rang in between the timber halls. "We are here to help maintain order. To bring stability back to your lives. Cooperate, and you'll remain safe."

No shouting. No threats.

Keothi's people being pushed and shoved into their homes. Most were calm and controlled, but those who pushed and fought met their own force.

They moved to the Great Hall at the center of the village. Two squads of Blades carried large oak doors where they began to hammer them into the doorway of the longhouse. The clang against the hinges echoed through the square.

The maidens kept Keothi tight in their grasp, forcing her to watch the doors be put into place. Every strike was another nail to her ribs. She tugged at their grasp.

They kicked her knees, forcing her down.

One strike. Two. Raise the doors. Fall in line.

She hadn't heard any reports of the agreed upon rebellion of the young-adults, of her friends. She hadn't heard any reports from her family. Now children cried in the streets. Chaos disguised as order flooded the streets.

As the final hinge was nailed into place, Groa walked up. "He's ready."

Keothi was pulled back to her feet. Groa pivoted, turning to the door. She pulled on her leather chest piece, straightening it. The Blades who hung the doors, pulled against large wrought iron handles, opening them.

The fresh new hinges swung with ease. Perfectly tempered.

Inside, Blades lined the path from door to throne, forming a corridor of steel. Spears upright, arms parallel to the ground. They didn't flinch.

How long have they been standing there?

Flanking her father's throne stood twelve silent women in white silk dresses and bone-white veils. Their hands were folded. Their heads bowed.

Groa stepped to the side. Keothi's escorts pulled her to the front of the Hall, presenting her obedience to the King.

King Vorik sat slouched in the throne, the tips of his silver crown barely allowing her family's sigil to peek through. He rested his elbow on the armrest and swirled a finger.

The great doors opened once more. Light from the open doors barely reached the throne. Each pace forward swallowed more of her in shadow.

Keothi turned.

Borin. Halvar.

Dragged in. Chained. Bleeding.

Halvar roared, "Keothi!" His escort stuffed cloth into his mouth. Borin thrashed like a wild boar. Their eyes locked on hers. Unbroken. Alive. Desperately trying to pull against their own captives.

They didn't look at the soldiers. They didn't look at the king. They looked at Keothi.

She'd trained for months. Long enough to forget what quiet felt like. The fire in her surged, flooding her mind. Her fist clenched. The resolve finally surfaced.

She lunged with all of her strength. The maidens weren't prepared. Their grip released her. Keothi's gaze burned into King Vorik's. Jaw clenched. Ready to die for her village. In front of her father. In front of her uncle. She wanted his blood, she didn't care how she took it. Raw, animalistic instinct took over her.

One step. Two. Caught.

The Maidens moved, fast and wordless, slamming her to the floor. A boot drove into her gut. Another yanked her up.

"You'll be a Vessel," Vorik said lazily, gesturing toward the veiled women.

A hand rested on her shoulder. Her knees pressed into the stone floor. The veiled women weren't women. They were statues. The very thing she feared. *Conformity. Silence. Nobody.*

She snapped her head sideways, teeth sinking deep into a hand. Flesh tore from bone.

The maiden stumbled back, screaming and clutching her bleeding hand.

Keothi spat the meat at Vorik's feet. Iron filled her mouth. Blood dripped from her lips. Still pulling from the other maiden who clung on tighter. She shoved a knee into Keothi's spine, forcing her to the ground.

The woman's expressions never changed even as her comrade screamed, trying to stop the blood.

Vorik sighed. "Show them."

Steel eyes lined the corridor, witnesses to her undoing.

The second Maiden wrenched Keothi's head up, forcing her to look at the doors.

Her father and uncle were yanked aside. Blood trickled down their temples, bruising swelling fast around their eyes, breaths already ragged and desperate.

The doors opened again.

Two more Maidens entered, dragging a third figure between them. A disheveled woman. Hair unbraided, lip split. She struggled, snarling curses.

"Touch her and I'll flay your godsdamn face!"

She knew that voice. Even bloodied, even broken. *Mother.*

One of the escorts unsheathed a sword, pressing it to Bryjna's throat.

Keothi's hair was yanked to face the king.

"They always break after family," Vorik murmured. "You won't miss them. That part of you is already gone."

Keothi could have sworn one of the veils shifted some with a softened breath. A memory stirring beneath it.

His gaze flicked to the bleeding Maiden who had finally gained her composure.

"Take them."

Her family was dragged from the hall, back to the village streets, disappearing after the doors closed behind them.

"You'll stay silent," Vorik said. "Or someone else might bleed for it."

Keothi froze beneath the maiden's grip.

"Dress her."

One of the veiled women stepped forward with a black veil.

Keothi's breath hitched. *Not this.*

The veil dropped over her face. The clasp fastened tight.

She twisted, kicked, but there was no room to run. The months of unpredictable training had worn her thin. Her spirit raged, but this was coordination.

The silk smothered her breath. It tasted like death pretending to be soft.

Vorik descended the throne. Slow. Deliberate. He knelt, cold fingers catching her chin and forcing her gaze up. His touch was velvet stretched over iron.

Vorik's eyes, carved from cruelty, didn't blink. "Vessels are nameless. But you? You'll be catalogued. The world will know what I own." He let the pause stretch, his gaze locked to hers. "You are Yrsa. Fitting, a beast with teeth filed down, wearing a crown it will never touch."

The name dripped from his mouth, poison meant to linger. It clung to her skin, seeped into her bones.

He rose. Turned. Swirled a finger.

Blades stepped forward, seizing her arms.

"I will gut you like I did the damn bear!" she hissed. The silk swallowed the threat, but not the fury behind it.

They dragged her, heels scraping stone, all resistance and ruin.

Vorik watched, amusement curling at his mouth. "Your body's still here, swinging. But your name, your voice..." His smile sharpened. "Already *mine.*"

The word sank like a brand. Behind her, the doors shut. Before her, the throne burned brighter.

YRSA THE VESSEL

The court echoed his decree

And the world forgot her name

Part 2: Forged in Shadow

Chapter Fifteen

THE CLOSET & THE CANE

They dragged Keothi to the garrison, once the heart of Irevandor's armies, now stripped bare, bleeding purpose. Trunks crashed from the upper windows.

Keepers glided between the Berserkers, silent and inevitable. Soldiers herded them into the courtyard, outnumbered before resistance could form. Vorik's army stripped them of their fight.

The garrison had fallen, it belonged to the Keepers now.

The two soldiers escorting Keothi approached a Keeper in a light blue veil.

"Where do you want her?" one asked.

She didn't look at Keothi. Just pointed. "Second floor. Closet."

Chaos clawed at the walls, screaming through rising voices. No one knew where to look or who to look at.

Berserkers shouted at the veiled women. None of them answered.

The door slammed open. A massive man entered, sword and shield in hand.

He struck his shield with the hilt. The sound ruptured over the chaos like a bell tolling war. "Everyone out! This is Keeper grounds now. Objections? We can duel."

A Berserker stepped forward. "Gladly."

The large man grinned. "Men. Take him apart."

The Berserkers charged.

Keepers stepped aside, silent as ghosts.

Keothi's escorts held tight.

Vorik's men moved fast. Some Berserkers fell. Others were bludgeoned into silence.

At last, silence won.

They dragged Keothi upstairs. Her heels left a red streak behind them.

They shoved her in. Wood slammed behind her. She scrambled for the handle, locked. Of course it was.

"Settle in, Yrsa. You'll be here a while," said one of the soldiers, voice flat. "This door listens only to the Keepers."

A soft click of a chair scraped into place. The handle jiggled once. Then stilled.

She tore off the veil and let it fall to the ground. It curled on the floor, nothing left but shed skin.

The closet was empty, aside from the shelves.

Screams echoed from below. Metal clanged on stone.

The screaming stopped. Silence came to claim what was left.

Keothi slid down the wall. The shelves lined the wooden walls. Her throat dried.

A scraping sound startled her, wood dragging on stone. She stood.

The door creaked open.

A woman in a darker grey veil stepped in. Her features hidden behind it. She looked down at the black veil on the floor, then stooped to retrieve it. She held it out in offering.

"No thanks," Keothi muttered. She pushed past the woman, their shoulders colliding.

The Keeper didn't stop her.

Outside, the large man waited. Sword and shield at his side. Daring her.

"Veil," the woman said softly.

"No," Keothi snapped.

The man stepped forward and shoved her back into the closet.

The Keeper stepped out.

The door closed.

The chair scraped back into place.

Locked again. But not broken.

She stayed where they left her, cramped, starving, half-asleep in the dark. Her fingers searched the floorboards, tracing grooves like the carvings in her family's oak table. The swirls she once turned into forest trails as her mother hummed over breakfast. The grain here didn't lead her anywhere. Every trail dead-ended in the dark.

She slept. Was offered the Veil. She refused. Locked back in.

No food. No water. No sunlight. No warmth. The air stank of rot and dust. Hunger scraped at her bones. Her mouth tasted like steel. The count of the offer was lost in a haze of silence and dark.

She began to understand. Deny the veil, you deny yourself life.

The door creaked. The big one waited. The silk hung from the Keeper's hand, an invitation or a threat. Maybe both.

The veil hovered between them. Her vision blurred. Her stomach twisted again, sharp and wet.

She reached. Her fingers barely worked as they fumbled with the buttons. The silk slid over her face like surrender. Light as breath, heavy as the tongs she once held.

"Follow," the Keeper said, voice flat as dust.

Keothi obeyed. The thud of the man's boots and the faint crinkle of armor shadowed every step she took.

The garrison hall glowed with low candlelight. Rows of women in grey veils flanked the hall, hands folded neatly, bodies still. Their veils barely shifted with their breaths, as if even air feared making a sound. They looked less like women and more like statues waiting for orders.

At the entrance stood the woman in the blue veil. "Kneel," she said.

Keothi hesitated.

The man's hand twitched toward his hilt.

Her hunger howled louder than the part of her that wanted to resist. She knelt.

The blue-veiled woman produced a reed.

Whack. Her ankle.

Keothi flinched.

Whack. Again. Until her ankle aligned.

Then came her hands. Her spine. Her jaw.

Whack. Whack. Whack. Each blow welled with pain.

"Kneeling must be exact. Hands placed flat. Spine straight. Eyes down. Speaking is not permitted. Sound is not permitted. Thought is not permitted. Pain teaches posture. Posture teaches peace. Keepers exist to serve. Nothing more."

"Excuse me?" she muttered, stiff with pain.

CRACK.

"Self-reference is not permitted."

CRACK. The reed slammed her arm. She gasped. Another strike.

Again.

And again.

Until she returned to position.

"Posture must not falter."

Keothi did not speak again.

She remained.

And the silence became part of her. It wrapped around her ribs. It begged for food.

Any time she shifted, a passing Keeper gently moved her back into place. If the blue-veiled Keeper passed, the reed would come.

She began calling the blue-veiled woman Blue.

Soon the smell of food attacked her stomach.

A Keeper said, "Food." Keothi was guided to the dining hall.

A long table. Dozens of Keepers. The table was set.

The Keeper escorted her to a place at the table, at the center, flanked by two keepers on both sides. Keothi sat and pulled the bowl closer to her. She picked up the spoon as the rest of the Keepers settled in.

In the spoon were chunks of cabbage, chicken, and broth. It looked like more scraps of various foods. Keothi looked at the others. They all had plates filled with proper food. Chicken. Potatoes. Warm bread. A feast, really.

Keothi frowned behind the veil, scanning faces.

Blue came and sat at the head of the table. “Eat.”

The others began. No scrape of silverware. No slurps. No murmurs. Only silence.

“Is this all?” Keothi asked.

No response.

Her stomach ached. Her head throbbed. She picked up the wooden spoon and forced it down. The taste was... nothing. Not bland, absent, like the bowl had forgotten what food was. It dulled the hunger.

One by one, the Keepers finished. They didn’t move. Palms to knees. Eyes forward.

Until Blue said, “Rise.”

The chairs dared not make a sound.

Two Keepers remained. Blue among them. The reed was tucked away.

“Follow,” said the soft-voiced Keeper, the same one who first offered the veil.

Keothi stood. Her limbs ached.

They led her upstairs, not to the closet, but to a small room with a bed, a table, and a mannequin head.

Blue gestured. “Veil goes on the mannequin. Re-affix before breakfast.”

The three turned and left. She heard a lock on the door click into place.

Then they left.

Keothi tried the handle.

Still stuck.

At least there was a bed. And a half-full stomach.

She didn’t cry.

But something in her sagged.

She laid down. The mattress gave beneath her. The silence stayed. It always did.

Chapter Sixteen

The Silent Scream

Blue didn't speak again. She watched like a butcher waiting for the twitch to stop.

Days passed. The mush continued. The veil suffocated.

Keothi sat at the table, glaring into the beige sludge.

Something snapped. Something old. Something hers.

Enough.

She shoved back the chair. Rose, fists trembling. "I demand to see the king! My family!" She hurled the bowl at the wall. The crash shattered the fragile silence.

Blue's eyes lifted. She nodded.

The Keepers rose as one. They swarmed her. Dragged her to her room.

Locked her in.

Time blurred. Demands ignored. Mush. Veil. Mush again. Knees split. Silence held.

More days. More outbursts.

Always met with silence. Resistance. Control.

The walls began to breathe. Then press. Then bend.

Her mind blurred at the edges.

"Follow."

She was brought to the entrance. She knelt. Same position.

No reed. No correction. A simple habit and natural place to be. Keothi's breathing steady, head bowed.

A Keeper adjusted her arms, lining them perfectly, parallel to the floor. A silver tray was placed into her hands.

Porcelain cup. Empty pitcher.

Then they left. The Keepers floated around her, tending to their duties of pointless chores.

She remained, holding the tray.

As the hours passed, Keothi's arms began to tremble. Her muscles ached, desperately wanting to place the tray to the ground.

Phantom reed welts threatened her nerves. She hung on to the tray. Forcing her thoughts to become a friendly distraction.

The tray grew heavier. Though nothing was in it.

Through the cloth of the veil, staring into the silver tray. Her reflection frowned. A friendly welcome compared to the ghosts of the barracks.

The reflection nodded once. A silent agreement between the simple girl and not so simple reflection as her arms refused to stay.

Keothi once held a hammer that split mountains. Molded melted iron into tools. Breathed life into wild flames. Now, a tray trembled in her hands.

She closed her eyes. Tears welled behind the black suffocating veil. She whispered to her reflection. "I can't any more, Revin."

Her hands lowered. The tray fell with a crash, cracking the silence in half. Porcelain shattered, shards skittering across the stone. For a moment, it wasn't a tray. It was blood. A scream she stole from the silence. A moment she reclaimed.

Not a cry. Not a plea. Just rage, pure and marrow-deep.

Her body relaxed for the first time in months. Her mind released all of Groa's training. All of the rigid schedule and chaotic life of before.

Could she even remember her mother or father's faces? Uncle Borin's calloused hands. Elara's golden hair. Barnaby's dull wit. The only thing that remained from before is her reflection.

One she had named Revin during the months of training. Keothi hadn't seen anyone for ten days. The reflection had been the only one speaking to her. The only one who answered.

And even it stared back with eyes full of sorrow. Could a reflection cry? Revin reached out, but stopped at the edge of the tray and reality. The fire that once pulled at her ribs now was dull and empty.

The Keepers surged. Their silken dresses pour over her. Their arms braiding under hers to drag her away from the shards and her only remaining friend.

Keothi laughed, loud and wild, cracked wide open like the shattered pitcher.

They dragged her back upstairs. Her heels thudded against each step as she trembled with wild laughter. No one spoke. Shame hung behind every veil like smoke from a fire no one dared name.

The door closed behind the herd, leaving Keothi alone once again. She ripped off the veil, let it fall to the ground.

Fine.

She stripped the dress. Her skin clung to bone. The cold didn't bite, it devoured.

She tore the discarded dress into strips. Tied the ends into crude knots. A silken rope for the legend in silk.

The door clicked open.

A Keeper. Another round of kneeling, probably. It didn't matter what they wanted. The thing that mattered in this moment was freedom. Noise. Food. Life.

The figure froze. A hitch of breath behind the veil.

The Keeper lunged, tore the makeshift rope from her hands. She clung on, tugging against the rope. Weakness betrayed her and the Keeper won.

They left her shivering, exposed. No words. No blows. Just absence.

Another herd returned. Stripped the bed. Left her nothing.

Naked. Cold. Alone.

Silent. Starved. Cracked.

The stone disappeared beneath her. The cold faded. A new rhythm bloomed in her mind: steel on steel. Groa's voice. A ring of shields. Better here than there. Anywhere but there. Even if it is in the training fields with the Maidens.

Keothi stood in the center of the training circle, shield raised. Around her, the Maidens slammed their own into place, forming a ring of iron and silence.

Groa's lips moved, but it was Blue's voice that came out, clipped, commanding, and wrong. "You see the collapse? That's what silence earns."

Across the circle, Thorva, Groa's general, waited. A statue of stone, her expertly crafted sword sharpened and ready.

Keothi banged her sword against her shield, once, twice, three times. The distribution of weight was off. The blade was loose in the handle and worse, worn. A weapon for performance, not for battle.

Thorva echoed the rhythm, each strike a warning that vibrated through the ground.

They stepped forward in unison, shields crashing.

Thorva's blade was faster.

Jump. Lunge. Slice.

Keothi moved on instinct, but the general danced around her, too quick, too sharp.

Steel met shoulder.

Keothi fell to one knee, the bear-claw wound flaring in protest.

She wanted to fight, scream. Hurl her sword at Blue's smug face. But the sound wouldn't come. It had been trained out of her. Her voice had been silenced.

Her arms wouldn't lift. Her legs trembled beneath her. Her jaw clenched from months of silence.

Beaten. Tired. Snuffed Out.

She yielded. She chose to stay down, the fire had gone cold. The grip on her sword and shield released.

The Maidens led her forward.

Vorik's grin was a spreading stain. He looked her over, admiring his masterpiece.

She knelt in the Great Hall, flanked by a corridor of steel and soldiers. The world had shifted. Her mind was hers again, but her body hadn't heard the news.

"Look at that," he said, voice calm as poison. "A Vessel. Quiet. Obedient. Beautiful in defeat."

He rose, each step deliberate, indulgent. "Yrsa will sit tonight as proof. That fire can be tamed. That gods can be leashed. That all things, in time, kneel."

Yrsa. Yrsa. Yrsa. The word rang like bone on iron. Not hers. Never hers. But it stuck.

"You'll make others obey simply by breathing."

She wanted to scream, but there was no mouth. No sound. Just breath behind the veil. A name she never chose.

Somewhere deeper, between soot and silence. Behind the name: something stirred. The air thickened, syrupy with smoke and perfume. The world tilted sideways, it was glassy and wrong.

From beneath the veil, beneath the name, beneath the ash, it came.

And it whispered.

No.

Chapter Seventeen

My Dear Keothi

You were given a title: Chieftain Wife.
You were shown the truth: Dwarven ember.
I watched in awe.

Your fire raged with fierce resolve the tree crashing down.
You entered the Witches' Home. (She's friend, not foe.)

I watched the truth be threaded.
Watched the axe deliver the final blow.

I cracked, watching them strip you bare.
Dark nights, waterfall tears,
the silence, too loud to bear.

I watched.
I watched them smother your flame.
Watched you vanish.
And still, I stayed.

You knelt beneath Blue's boot,
your hands released cup and plate
The crash rang louder than any cry they stole.

Not a curse. Not a plea.
Just the crash.

Your weapon.
Your spirit.

Your flame.
Snuffed.
Not gone. Never lost.

They stripped you of the forge.
The cinder fireflies dimmed.
Mother. Father. Borin.
Names turned to echoes. Still, I held them.

Keothi gone. Yrsa born.
What was left?
A shell.

But you aren't alone.
You will endure.
The flame is not gone.
I remain.

I will relight your spark.
The cinder fireflies will glow again.

And when they do,

I'll no longer be your shadow.

I will be your flame.

Your axe.

Yours.

My dear Keothi.

Chapter Eighteen

THE LEGEND IN SILK

Yrsa stood in the throne room, stripped, renamed, and broken.

Keothi remained, buried beneath the shell they carved by the man she was promised to.

Vorik snapped his fingers.

Two soldiers stepped forward. They didn't need orders. The script had been written.

One gripped each arm, dragging her toward the stairs. Down they descended. Every stone step closer to a death sentence. A cell waited, just below the black mouth of the deeper dungeon.

One soldier opened the door. "Yrsa."

Keothi didn't move.

Calculating. Thinking.

Two soldiers. Two swords. Armor. Helmet.

Stairs. Battalion. Trapped. Caught. Killed. Tortured.

Now is not the time.

Yrsa moved forward. Behave. Fall in line.

The door slammed shut with a thunderous echo. A bed. A hole. A small slit for air and sun. Nothing else.

The cell wasn't hers. It was a display case.

She sat on the bed, legs hugged in, face buried.

Mother. Father. Borin. Elara. Barnaby. Trond.

So many names. So many she'd failed.

It was my fault. I wasn't enough.

Where did it begin? Maybe it was agreeing with her parents.

Not running. Not screaming. Not choosing another way.

Tears spilled, hot and silent.

I'm sorry I wasn't better. You trusted me. You needed me. And I couldn't fight.

Something stirred deep beneath her bones. Something sharp against her soul.

A soft poke on her shoulder. Lies.

A flick on her head. *Leave me alone.*

A pull of her hair. "Ow!"

The inner beast raged for a moment. Her head unburied, she looked around.

Empty. Just a lonely cell. A toy box.

Then. What? No. Can't be.

A featureless shadow flickered to life, zipping from wall to ceiling before settling in the center of the room.

Hands on hips. Back straight. Feet apart. Head tilted slightly.

Yrsa rubbed her eyes in disbelief. She blinked. Once. Twice.

It was still there. The air cooled around it, shadows thickened at the edges of the cell. Her skin prickled with fear and recognition in her chest.

"What are you?"

She crept forward. The creature zipped again. She tried to follow it, eyes darting, breath caught, but it always stayed one flick ahead. She sat back on the bed. It stood once more.

It drew a box in the air. It pointed to Yrsa and to itself.

"We...?"

It shook its head no. Box. Keothi. It.

"We're in a cell?"

It flicked her in the head. Black chains formed around its wrists. Box drawn again, fists pound against the air drawn box. Then waited.

"We are the same? My reflection?"

The chains vanished. It danced in place. A silent celebration.

She stared. She had cracked. Clearly. Imagining things. Talking to them.

Her Father's voice burst through, as though it had been waiting to ambush her. *The Shadow will take her, before the monster kindles her fire.*

She scrambled back, against the wall. "Alright, my family was terrified of you. So... shoo!" She waved at it like a rat. "Go away... I don't want you here. You're not welcome..."

It mimed laughter at her attempts. It held up two fingers, touching them to form a heart.

"Doubt it..." A cruel idea surfaced, sharp enough to try, and just hopeful enough to strike against the cold stone. "If you do love me, then you will get me out. Then. Maybe."

It zipped in a circle, wild and joyful, and vanished under the door.

Gone. Leaving her alone.

Maybe.

Hopefully.

Alone meant I haven't cracked.

Not alone means I'm free.

Neither sounded like salvation.

Left to be saved by my cracked mind. Like Borin's chipped mug: cold, forgotten, still holding poison.

Seconds bled into minutes. Minutes into hours.

Clang. Keys. Flood of footsteps flowed through the dungeon hall.

"Yrsa."

Two soldiers opened the doors.

Four Keepers poured into the toy box. They dragged a chair into place, its legs shrieking across the stone like something dying slow.

A whisper on a breeze: "Sit."

Yrsa sat. Tears had left salt roads down her face. The map of surrender.

One Keeper's hand settled on her shoulder, light, steady. The only thing in the room not moving. The first touch she felt in gods knows how long. The fingers gripped her shoulder, gently, lovingly.

The others worked around her, quiet and practiced.

Fixed her dress.

Tightened seams.

Scrubbed away more dirt.

They painted her face white and her lips red.

Replaced her black veil with a bone-white veil.

Her mind belonged to the King. Now the body obeys.

Stripped. Unnamed. Softened into something presentable.

Tamed into perfection. *His* perfection.

"Stand, Mi'Lady," A Keeper said, wrapping a golden rope around Yrsa's waist.

A leash. The final touch on his favorite doll. The illusion of grace, pulled tight.

The four ladies arranged themselves into a perfect, silent square. Yrsa in the center. Soldiers held firm on each corner. Groa appeared through the door.

She took the rope and stood before Yrsa.

No smile. No sneer.

Just the face of a woman who had learned to serve silence.

"The one he wanted most. The one that screamed the longest."

Crack. Shatter. Rotting dread formed in her chest.

Yrsa said nothing. Silence was louder than anything she could have spoken. They dragged her from the room, up through the stone throat of the dungeons, into the blinding hush of the Great Hall.

The air hummed with the coming festivities. A table near the throne, centered in the hall. The King's table.

Groa led her. "Up."

Yrsa stepped up to the empty table.

"Sit."

Yrsa sat.

Simple one word commands as if anything longer would be a sin.

Groa laid the golden rope around her.

The Keepers moved forward, and positioned Yrsa. Her left arm to hold her torso up. Her legs off to the side. Her right arm delicately over her chest. Every movement was slow, delicate, and ceremonious.

"Commit the position to memory, Yrsa. You will have moments of respite, but only to return to this position. Any other position—" Groa coldly left the sentence unfinished for Yrsa to finish the thought.

Beaten. Bruised. Punished.

She was provided a few moments to stretch and move. Occasionally the Keepers silently moved and stretched her limbs for her.

Servants carted food out and surrounded Yrsa's location with piles of food, boxing her in.

A ring of pies, sweets, roasted meats.

They did not seat her. They plated her. Scar towards the entrance of the Hall. Her face towards the wall.

Soon the guests started to pour in. Her moments of respite shortened to none. Soft rhymes of lutes filled the hall.

No sign of the cracked mind that had begged a shadow to save her.

The candles dimmed. The music played. The guests laughed. She remained a statue. Not silent by choice. But because there was no one left to speak.

Chapter Nineteen

The King's Centerpiece

King Vorik, was presented on a wagon, drawn by six blue-veiled Keepers. Their arms were painted in gold up to their elbows. All moved in perfect silence, perfect grace.

Draped in deep crimson and gold, he rose like a marionette pulled by divinity, arms flung wide in mockery of grace.

A King.

A God.

A showman.

Gods. You need an axe in your skull.

Keothi pressed her fingertips into the wood beneath her. A quiet ritual like her mother taught.

"Ladies!" Vorik's voice rang out, polished and theatrical. His voice smooth as lacquer. "Gentlemen! Loyal subjects and honored guests! Tonight, we celebrate a most... precious acquisition. New lands. New alliances. And... new trophies."

The crowd leaned in. His magnetism worked lured in the guests and his smile a gleaming unsheathed blade. Keothi's breath hitched. Cold air scorched her throat. A nearby noble smirked: cruel and entitled.

Vorik extended a hand toward the table and her. "May I present my greatest prize. The wildling girl. The beast-tamer. The bear-slayer herself."

Murmurs. Polite claps. She felt them all.

"She was a legend. Feral! Forged in soot and smoke. Even legends can be... shaped." Every eye laid upon Yrsa accompanied by a dry chuckle. "And now, look. Silk-bound. Wordless. Poised. The beast filed down... not gone."

Yrsa dropped her gaze. Stares chaining into her skin.

Vorik turned back to the crowd, smile sharpening. "Touch, if you dare. The bear hibernates inside her. She cost me blood. Coin. Patience. Please. Eat. Drink. Admire the craftsmanship. Trace her scars. Whisper your praise. She won't bite—unless you ask."

Yrsa snapped her teeth in the air. A trained bite. A quiet performance.

Laughter. Uneasy shifting. The clink of goblets.

Vorik's smile spread slow, smug. The master of well-broken beasts.

"Tonight," he said, lifting his goblet. "to conquest. To civility. To the art of refinement."

The crowd erupted. Dishes clattered. Keothi's throat choked on the scents of perfume, grease, and wine.

A feast of scent and sound.

And Yrsa sat, a stone statue, perfectly crafted in King Vorik's image. Caged in silk.

Keothi saw a shimmer, a shadow, moving against the grain.

Oh, perfect. My cracked mind, caged inside this body. How lovely. How wonderful.

The beast didn't sleep. It counted ribs. And waited.

Unwelcome fingers traced her scar. She flinched. Then stopped.

It's a room full of Soldiers and Maidens, and your girl's the centerpiece. On display. Guarded.

"Would you care to dance with me?" a deep gruff voice asked.

A softer and timid voice responded, "I'd love to."

Shatter the chains here, now? Dumb. Deadly. Not yet.

Laughter. Chattering. Clinks of goblets.

Wine spilled over her lace, turned it sheer. Yrsa's pale skin clung under the cold, soaked silk.

A spectacle. A doll. A plaything.

A privilege. A delight to play with Vorik's toy.

The shadow writhed in the rafters. An unspoken scream. It wanted out. Keothi kept it leashed. Barely.

Dishes crashed.

Voices rose.

"Oh Vorik, she's a beaut! Taming the wild ones...it's a gift."

Fingers walking the history carved into my skin.

The girl who killed a bear. Now they feed her fruit like a hound. A reward for staying caged.

Good girl.

A hand on her wrist. She didn't resist.

Keothi screamed behind her teeth.

Fire kindles a Shadow.

A sliced apple at her lips. Yrsa obeyed. The sweet fruit coated her tongue as the spilled wine assaulted her nose.

One bite. Two bites. A bear in golden chains.

A knife traced her leg. Not to draw a wound, but to carve fear.

The Masked shall feast.

"The men on the lines are pushing the wildlings back."

And the forged shall choose.

She mouthed to her Shadow:

I'm Keothi. They will fall.

One hand. Two hands. Tracing my scar.

The bear is here.

Seven blades within reach. Five hands that touched too long. Two fools close enough to bleed. One breath away.

They took the forge.

They did not take the fire.

The Shadow grinned in the dark. *Say the word.*

Not yet.

They're already bleeding. Let me. The voice begged. Keothi's fire refused it.

The night came to an end.

Scraps of discarded food clung to silver plates.

The guests were carted off to their homes.

Keepers cleared the tables: dutiful, silent, unseen.

One held out a hand.

Yrsa's legs bent stiffly, aching from disuse.

She rose on tiptoe, stretching for the rafters as far as she could.

The Keepers waited. The crowd thinned.

But deep inside... something was counting.

Waiting.

Clawing up the walls.

Her rope tugged. A reminder of the leash she wore.

"Come, Mi'Lady," said an unnamed Keeper.

Yrsa was led to the depths of the dungeon.

Keys. Lock. Trap. Dust. Sleep. Muscles.

She laid down.

The stench of spilled wine lingered in her nose: stale, sour.

Soft creak of a door. Footsteps.

Great. I'm tired. Go away.

Keys. Lock. Door.

The door swung open.

A Keeper stood there, eyes unreadable. Calm. Steady. Familiar. "Mi'Lady. Follow me."

Yrsa propped herself on an elbow, eyeing her with a silent question.

Of course he had more planned. Monsters always do.

The shadow drifted in behind Spoon, just above her shoulder.

Fingers miming a heart.

Keothi grinned.

Her cracked mind had actually come through.

She didn't bow. Didn't thank. She reached up, fingers slow, deliberate. And tore the veil from her face. Let it fall. Where it belonged. Among the scraps and bones.

Chapter Twenty

OBEDIENT COOS

Revin slipped beneath the cell door. What lay inside wasn't her Keothi, just a husk.

Cold. Cracked. Gone.

The person in there was broken, a ghost of hope, but no flame. As long as she remains closed off, she will never be free.

It's my job to free Keothi.

First stop. Her Mother. Bryjna.

Mother once held Keothi when no one else could. If anyone remembered who she really was... it would be the one who braided her hair while warning her to bite her tongue.

Revin zipped unseen, through the dungeon halls. Empty now, except a few soldiers. Their eyes stared forward, but Revin didn't trust unmoving things.

I wonder if they have names?

She slipped through the thick doors and down cobbled streets, weaving past shield maidens on every corner and the silent soldiers stationed between.

Citizens hid in their homes. Not daring to question the new rule.

She made it to Keothi's home, easy to navigate. Especially for a zipping shadow.

She slipped through a crack in an opened window into an empty home holding its breath.

Where's Mother? She has to be here...

Keothi. Yrsa. Identity. Mask. Self.

Revin remembered a loose board from long ago.

Bryjna complained of the consistent creak of a floor board in the hall.

Halvar chose to only fix the noise it made. "We'll leave it, but silence it," Halvar had said. "Just in case we need it."

Revin squeezed herself mouse-small and darted beneath the floorboards.

Letters. Folded. Stained. Forgotten.

She tried to pull one open, no dice. Her fingers, even shadow-thin, slid through the paper.

She hovered over one: crude wax, childlike, pressed with... a wooden spoon?

Her brow twitched. The top letter bore a bold seal. The aged wax pressed deep, as if carved into the page.

Revin's grin evaporated. These weren't letters. They were warnings.

She zipped out of the confined space, stretching back to her full height, eyes gazing toward the door.

Someone had to leave these letters. Quietly. Bravely. And someone had been meant to listen.

But no one did.

And now?

She paced back and forth, trying to piece together who could help. Revin clicked her tongue, half in awe, half in rage.

The barracks.

She turned immediately. King Vorik's soldiers and shieldmaidens lived in tents on the outskirts of the village. The barracks would have space.

Through the streets, toward the garrison. A high stone wall enclosed it, crowned by a wide, ornate archway.

Inside, dummies stood at attention, awaiting the deliberate strikes of soldiers who moved with meditative precision. Each motion measured, each blow a whispered prayer.

An eerie blanket of silence had settled over the garrison, a sure sign of a Keeper's presence.

Revin moved to the entrance, slipping under the doorway. A soft light of warmth. Veiled women floated, barely picking up their feet, careful not to make a sound. Their hands were all cupped, heads hung low.

She zipped around, trying to find any of Keothi's assigned Keepers. Spoon. Knob. Thread. Buttons.

Knob stirred a cauldron, Thread sewed in a rocking chair, Buttons wandered in slow, uncertain loops.

Spoon was in a room, with the door closed. She sat at a vanity, brushing her hair. It was short, easy to manage, easy to hide. The Veil rested on a faceless stand, kept wrinkle-free, waiting.

Spoon hummed softly. A silent lullaby. Her face was solemn, as she watched herself brush her hair.

A soft coo: "Spoon." She giggled at the name. It was easy to say, impossible to mean.

It was a name she was given.

A hesitant, clumsy, and rehearsed, "I." She hunched slightly. Her eyes darted, checking to see if anything happened. There were only candles flickering softly.

She set the brush down with reverence, eyes flicking to the Veil. "Apologies, but..." Her reflection held her gaze: wide-eyed curiosity, threaded with a trembling question she wasn't ready to answer.

With an almost pleading falling behind."I... am..." The words collapsed like dropped dishes. Courage hadn't stuck, but it had shown up. She shook her head. Not yet.

Revin knew. If there's any hope of finding Bryjna, reading those letters, she had to get Spoon's help.

It zipped to Spoon, interrupting the practicing of self. It twirled around the woman.

Spoon blinked once. Then again.

"You have... shape."

Revin danced in delight to be noticed.

"You've never had shape before."

Revin beamed.

A pause. Spoon tilted her head, studying her like a butterfly that might bite.

"...Alright. Is this a dream or a task?"

Revin held up a finger: one second. Pacing. Thinking. Then a leap, yes, the leap. That grin. She turned herself into an enlarged black bear. Exaggerated its steps, flailing around in the air.

Spoon giggled with a silken softness. "You're silly...are you trying to entertain me?"

Revin dropped the illusion, shoulders drooping. She crossed her arms, frustrated. Not understood. Not yet. She pointed at Spoon and to the window.

"Follow?"

She nodded. She put her hands together, to mime a please.

"Why are you praying?" She giggled. "Ok, I'll come with you... I need to put on my veil first."

Revin zipped around and danced playfully while she waited for Spoon to get dressed in her costume.

The world outside stirred a song she almost knew. The village remained eerily still as they made their way to the house.

Spoon's slow, methodical movements grated on Revin as they neared Keothi's home. Every attempt to urge her faster, a push on the shoulder, a nudge forward, was met with patient confusion.

Spoon opened the front door and slipped inside. She peered around. "Dark in here," she whispered.

Revin darted to the corner, pointed at a floorboard, urgent.

Spoon knelt beside it. "It's a floor... Do you want it swept?" She glanced around, already looking for a broom.

Revin poked her again, then shook her head sharply. She flattened one hand and mimed a hinge opening.

"Oh." Spoon nodded. "You want it opened? Why?"

Revin mimed running, feet pounding in place.

A shrug. "Alright." Spoon pried up the board. Beneath it, letters lay stacked and dust-covered. She opened one, brow furrowed, bottom lip caught in her teeth.

A flicker of recognition and guilt, shivered across her face.

"Lady Bryjna didn't see these, then," she murmured, mostly to herself.

She remembered the moment the letter had to be sent. Keothi's eyes hollowed. Fire raging behind them. Her arms trembled as the tray of tea slipped from her hands and shattered.

Revin jumped with her legs and arms out in surprise.

"What now?" Spoon asked, chuckling, nervous, shaky.

Revin slumped, head low. She raised a hand, opening and closing it slowly. *Read.*

Spoon flinched. The letters trembled in her hand.

"Um... Revin..." she whispered. "Keepers don't read." Her voice shrank further. "Keepers do. Nothing more."

Revin smacked her forehead, exaggeratedly. Then jabbed a finger at herself, then at Spoon, then turned an invisible page with such flair it was practically theater.

No words, just force of will and shape.

"Alright," she murmured, more breath than sound.

She flipped through the parchments slowly, reverently. Revin flickered behind her, peering over Spoon's shoulder. The excitement practically vibrating with hunger.

If Keothi could read, she could read. Her mother had sat her down at that kitchen table night after night, trying to help her learn.

The moment she saw the thicker page, the one yellowed by time and frayed at the edges, she surged forward. Revin tapped Spoon's shoulder and pointed to it.

Spoon opened it with the delicate care of long practice, letting the folds settle open like a blanket. She couldn't make sense of the marks, but Revin could.

The moment her eyes met the faded ink, memory broke through:

Halvar spoke with Bryjna, explaining the strange parchment. "Great-grandfather didn't build them to save us. He built them so the bloodline would survive. Even if it crawled out alone."

Practiced Understandings: The Great Hall. Where decisions are carved into the future.

Siren's Song: The forge. Where iron meets identity.

Unforgotten Hope: The Dungeon. The place of forgetting... where they put her. Where she waits.

Where the World Breathes: The wilds beyond the cliffs, wind-torn and waiting.

Mother's Warm Embrace: The Hearth. The Chief's home. The final shelter.

Revin buzzed like a spark caught in bark.

Spoon giggled. "That's... important, right?"

Revin nodded sharply, almost jolting with it.

"What now?"

She turned toward the hearth, layered with aged soot. Once filled with warmth. Her mother's laughter while she cooked. Morning breakfasts. A simpler time she hadn't realized she missed.

"Do you want soup?" Spoon asked, gently. "Are you hungry?" She rummaged through the bare cupboards.

Revin didn't respond. She crouched by the blackened bricks, hand hovering over the space behind the grate. A breath of air, barely there, whispered from a seam that had no right to exist.

She studied it, calm and focused.

A memory surfaced, tiny Keothi, reaching for the iron rod that held the cauldron. She'd tumbled forward, grabbed it, and her mother had snapped at her. Probably a mother's fear surfaced. But maybe...

Revin tapped Spoon and pointed at the iron rod.

"Not soup," she muttered, pressing the rod with a seriousness no child could manage. Stone scraped against stone with the sound of old bones moving.

The Hearth groaned, exhaling a puff of soot, an old breath held too long. The stone beneath shifted, revealing a narrow tunnel, lit only by the breath of air and the glint of mystery.

Spoon gasped. “This was never in the Keeper training.”

Revin melted into the shadows and slipped inside.

“Revin,” Spoon's voice echoed softly. "Revin," she called again, only louder this time. A shudder of discomfort in her tone. “Revin!”

She returned, and motioned *follow*.

“It’s getting late. Festivities require full presence.”

Revin hunched, a visual sigh. She tapped her foot, rubbed her chin in deep thought.

“Tonight, after the festivities, ok?”

She zipped around the room. She paused at the hearth and pulled the rod, to show she wanted Spoon to close the door.

Spoon nodded, “Do you want to go in first?”

She bowed low, becoming a knight pledging fealty, and vanished into the dark. The shadows welcomed their old friend.

I’m coming, my dear Keothi. And I’m not alone.

Chapter Twenty-One

Ash & Anvil

"This way, Mi'Lady." Spoon whispered, glancing over her shoulder as she led Keothi toward the far end of the dungeons.

Between two stone pillars, she stopped beside an old cupboard. With trembling fingers, she pressed a single brick.

The wall groaned, ancient and obedient. It slowly creaked open, dust-choked and hidden from time.

"Are you sure?" Keothi didn't understand, only that she was moving. No longer caged.

Revin flickered ahead of her, circling once, then pointing, decisive.

"Mi'Lady, follow," Spoon urged. "You must be quick. Revin will explain."

Spoon ducked into the dark. Keothi hesitated only a heartbeat before following, Revin slipping behind her, trailing smoke.

The air was thick with age and disuse. Each footstep stirred the breath of ghosts. Keothi whispered, "Where are we going?"

"Outside. Away, Mi'Lady," Spoon replied.

Keothi reached out, laying a hand gently on Spoon's shoulder.

The girl flinched as if a string inside of her had been struck.

Keothi froze, withdrawing her hand. "Okay. No more moving in the shadows. No more secrets. This needs to stop. *Now.*" Her voice climbed the edge of command, then collapsed. "Tell me. What is this? Where are we going? Why are you helping me?"

Her mind buckled, dropping to her knees. A sound hammered behind her eyes, a sharp, cold jab that sent a shiver through her very bones. She squeezed her eyes shut.

A sharp clickclickclickclick echoed inside her skull, behind her eyes, like an old memory trying to claw its way out.

That sound. Again. Where did I hear that from?

The tunnel twisted. A jolt. She blinked, and suddenly she wasn't underground. She was somewhere gilded, wrong, and distant.

Words slipped away. A whisper brushed the edge of her mind. The world buckled. Her stomach lurched. Air folded in on itself, thick and wrong. The smell of dust returned like a slap.

When her vision cleared, the tunnels had turned from the long forgotten escape passage to an adorned hall. A blanket of silence as figures floated around her.

A poke.

Keothi opened her eyes. The whisper, the revolting sound, was gone.

Revin stood next to her, anchoring her back to the ancient tunnels. The scent of dust was in her nose, but the air felt clearer, more real.

She mimed a pat on Keothi's head, motion, not touch. A heart formed in the air. A wave. Then two hands pressed together.

Keothi couldn't explain it, but she felt it. A pulse of urgency. Fierce, loyal, terrified love.

Spoon watched with concern, eyes pleading. "When you're free, your questions will be answered, Mi'Lady."

Keothi nodded, breath caught. "Alright. I'm moving...but." She hesitated. "I want my axe. Can we make it to the forge from here?"

"Yes Mi'Lady. But, you must be quick."

"Then we'll be quick."

They pressed on through the tunnels. The silence of her companions felt almost comforting. Revin zipped ahead now and then, scouting. Spoon clutched the ancient map pulled from the floorboards of Keothi's childhood home.

Spoon paused at a wall sconce, gave it a tug. With a low groan, the wall shifted, revealing a hearth. The scent of old soot hit Keothi immediately. The forge.

She stepped inside. It was unmoving. Abandoned.

The home was ransacked. Dishes held the ghost of old meals. A chair tipped on its side. Blankets half-pulled from the bed, tangled in dust. And above all, silence that had waited too long.

She crossed to Borin's old chair and bowed her head. "I'm sorry, Uncle. I will find you."

The chipped mug sat by the sink. His hammer lay untouched on the side table. Keothi made a makeshift bag out of the dusted blanket. She placed the hammer on it.

She ran her fingers along its handle, worn smooth. It didn't hum like it once did. But maybe it was just waiting.

She wanted to take the mug, but it would break. *I'll be back for you.*

"Mi'Lady," Spoon urged softly. "You must be quick."

Revin mimed a statue soldier, circling one arm, a warning: patrols all around.

The dread crept in. Keothi said, "You're right. Can you two look for anything hidden?" Her hand brushed the silk of the dress she wore. "I need to change... while you two search."

Spoon hesitated, fighting the instinct of undressing Keothi. "Mi'Lady..." and stopped herself.

Keothi shook her head. "I can dress myself. I need to dress myself..."

"Alright, Mi'Lady." She rummaged through the house upon request.

Revin darted through the quiet forge and out to the anvil beyond. Leaning against the cold steel was Keothi's axe, oversized, waiting. The one she forged with Borin. She returned, briefly morphing into the shape of an axe.

Keothi smiled, something tight and fierce behind it. "Perfect. Any soldiers?"

A small shake of the head. *No.*

She stepped into the forge. No siren song. Only memory. The kind that bites.

Fear it, and you'll fumble. Doubt it, and it'll fail you. Her uncle's voice, always clearest through the smoke.

Clear the ash drawer, he always said.

She knelt, moving without thinking.

Inside: A letter. A folded bear cloak. Clean clothes.

She froze. Stunned. She opened the letter.

Keothi,

If you're reading this, it is time to choose your path.

It's time you find your legacy.

When the sun stands highest, follow your shadow.

The Grove will find you.

The Ember Stone is the key.

The forge sleeps, but not forever.

If you've truly accepted this path, it will wake for you.

And it will test you.

I couldn't shield you from what waited in this world.

If we never meet again, know this:

I did my best.

And you, you've surpassed every hope I ever held.

I'm proud of the woman you've become.

—Your Father, always.

The cloak was stitched in her mother's hand, familiar and strong. The ember stone had been set into the clasp. The one she received during the Mountain Race. The fur, the same deep black as the bear she'd slain so long ago.

She clutched it to her chest, a lifeline to what once was.

It smelled of Mother.

Of Bear.

Of home.

Wordless, Keothi dressed.

Laced her boots.

Draped the cloak over her shoulders.

Lifted her axe. For a moment, it was too heavy. Memories surged—hammering the ingot into a double axe-head, sanding the handle smooth, wrapping it tight with leather.

She spoke the words softly, an oath to her companions, ancestors, and the Gods. "He forged a doll. Let's show him what I really am."

CHAPTER TWENTY-TWO

THE NAME WE KEEP

The group of three silent survivors sat in the woods, far from the village. A low fire flickered between them, warm enough for comfort, not enough for smoke to betray them.

They'll be looking for us by now. Stay on alert.

Spoon sat on the opposite side of Keothi. Her hand reached the clasp of the black veil, only to pause in the moment. Her fingers trembled, before a quiet sigh escaped.

Revin's head was in Spoon's lap. Seeing the hesitation, she gently shifted and leaned across to hug her.

"What's troubling you, Little One?" Keothi said, softly.

"Spoon," she whispered, trembling.

Keothi blinked. "Spoon? I'm sorry, do you need silverware?"

Spoon shook her head hard, pointing to herself. "No, Mi'Lady. Spoon."

"Spoon?"

"Yes, Mi'lady."

Keothi choked back a laugh, but the birds still took flight.

Revin whirled over to Keothi and flicked her on her head.

"Ow, what was that for?" She looked around.

Spoon stared at the dirt, gnawing her lip.

The weight of her emotion hit Keothi. "Ah. I'm sorry." She said seriously, "I understand. I was Yrsa. Supposedly..." She shrugged, "Did that monster name you Spoon?"

Spoon shook her head, "No Mi'Lady. You did."

Keothi's brow furrowed in confusion. "I did?"

"You gifted a name when there was none. And now—" Her voice broke, though a small smile hid beneath the veil. "It is retained. Before you were transferred to the Keepers, names were offered. You kept using them, even when they weren't permitted." She touched her chest lightly. "The first gift remains."

Keothi searched her memories. "I think I remember that... like I'm waking up. I wanted to have something to differentiate you four from..." Her thoughts trailed off.

Spoon looked at Revin. Revin nodded, like they could speak in silence. No words. No signals. They just knew.

"You... you were with the Maidens. For a while. Two months, maybe. Then they sent you to the Keepers. Most Vessels take four months. But you?" She winced. "You fought for three years."

She sat, stunned. Then the blinding rage returned.

"Three years?" The words barely reached her own ears. A breeze whispered through the trees, stirring the chilled air. Time held still like the moon in the sky. If three years had passed, then, "Where's Mother? Father? Borin?" she finally allowed herself to say out loud.

Spoon hesitated, sorrow dulling her voice. "I warned Lady Bryjna, but I feared it was too late. You were... close. To the end. The way they made the others."

Keothi looked up, skin cold. "The Vessel."

Spoon nodded. "They had almost finished."

"I need to find them..." Keothi's words were hollowed, tears clinging on.

Revin sat next to Keothi, holding her close.

"I'm Yrsa." The word stung. No. Not anymore. "Call me Keothi. Not Mi'lady. Not Vessel. Keothi."

Spoon smiled softly. "Alright...K..k..Keothi."

The sound was sharp as flint. She didn't flinch, but her jaw tightened. "Tell me about yourself, Spoon. Why help me?"

Spoon pulled a bundle of letters from her pocket, worn and weathered by time and hiding.

"You needed help," she said, her voice fraying at the edges. "Lady Bryjna was sick with fear. but she still fought with these."

She placed them gently between them. Each envelope sealed with wax: an X. An O. An exclamation mark. Symbols, not words. A private code. "It was a cipher," Spoon explained. "One she taught me. For when things went too quiet to speak."

Keothi's hand hovered over the letters, then traced a fingertip across the wax. "You cracked them, didn't you, Mother?" Her voice caught, half awe, half breaking.

She leafed through the stack, careful. Tombstones of wax and symbols.

All but one.

Its wax seal, marked with three carved lines, held strong. The other seals were chipped and faded to ghosts of color and time. But this one, still clung to its red, refusing to forget.

She broke the seal with trembling fingers.

My Daughter—

If this reaches you, then he has not destroyed all of you.

I know what they tried to make you. I know what they carved out of you. I also know who I raised.

He took my girl. He took my warrior. But he did not take my rage.

I will not stop hunting.

Let the stars mark this: I will burn the world to find you.

You are not forgotten.

You are not alone.

I am coming.

—Your Mother, always.

Keothi held the letter close to her, burying herself into the bear cloak she wore. Softly, into the world of silence. “Where are you, Mother? I need you and your strength.”

A branch snapped in the distance. Keothi tensed, snapping her back to the world, axe in hand, but it was just a fox. Still. Every sound meant something now.

Spoon continued. “You gave me a name. And Revin... she started forming too. Piece by piece. Like your spirit refused to go.” She sighed, with a softened smile. “Fingers to toes to her first sit. We comforted each other.”

Revin turned into a shovel and dug at the air.

“Revin helped bury you, to protect you.... Of all pain.”

Keothi was lost in the swarm of information.

Three years. Mother, Father, Borin missing. Her village? A strange shadow? A keeper with identity?

Keothi stood. Abrupt, sharp, a shadow cut free. The low burn in her chest flared into wildfire. The beast stirred. It wanted blood. It wanted him.

“Alright,” she muttered. Her eyes were as wild as the campfire. “Maybe I’m broken. But I’m not done. I’m going to find Vorik. I’ll mount his skull on a pike. Stay if you must. I’m done waiting.”

Her grip on the letters whitened.

“Keothi.” Spoon’s voice was soft, chewing on the words. “I want to help, but. Borin. Your Father. Your Mother. *You* need to go in prepared.”

Keothi turned her back on the group, not saying anything.

“You have been caged for three years. Not moving. Not living.” Spoon stood, and moved to Keothi, placing a loving hand on hers. “You need to gain your strength first. That letter your father left?”

Keothi squeezed her eyes shut, hoping to wake up from this nightmare. “Why are you helping? Why now? Why not back then? What’s changed?” The words cut sharp, Keothi’s voice laced with fire and betrayal.

Spoon folded inward, small again, but this time, everything came easier. “I wasn’t built to act. I was built to obey. It took breaking something inside me to even try. Your mother...” Her voice caught. Shame swelled beneath her ribs. A heavy breath. “I couldn’t. I was a prisoner too. Born, molded to meet everyone else’s needs. Their wants. Their desires.”

She let the silence settle. Her voice grew steadier, clearer. “When they took your name… something had to hold the pieces. I think Revin was the part of you that refused to die. Your shield let down, just long enough… to help you escape.”

Revin swirled around Keothi, trying in her silent, stubborn way to be a tether.

Keothi could hear the soft hum of something calling to her. “Fine. We find the IronGrove. We find my family. We put Vorik’s head on a pike.”

Keothi reluctantly sat back down, but her death grip on her axe never released. She needed to distract her mind. Somehow. Some way.

Her thoughts swarmed, grasping for any memory. Something solid. Anything.

The sound returned. Clickclickclickclick. Not from outside. Not this time. Inside. Behind her ribs. Her memory spasmed like a cracked reed.

Clatter. Tray. Blood.

Keothi dug her fingers into the earth until the dirt bit back.

A soft hand landed on her knee. Present. Real.

“Keothi?”

Keothi returned to the moment, the warm campfire. The trees and the sticks. “Yeah, I’m alright.” She smiled softly.

Revin looked at Spoon, signifying concern.

Spoon nodded in agreement.

A simple shake of her head showing now is not the time. Enough was said.

Keothi looked at Spoon, her gaze softening. "Want help with your veil?"

“The veil hides the Keeper,” Spoon whispered. “But I… I don’t want to hide. I don’t want to be small.” Her hand lifted to the clasp, only to freeze.

Revin curled closer to Spoon.

“When you’re ready,” Keothi murmured. “Your time. Your choice.”

Spoon nodded, eyes full of starlight and tears. “Together.”

Keothi smiled, a fierce aching thing she hadn’t felt in months. She turned to Revin. “You nudged me into that, didn’t you?”

Revin held up a thumbs, exaggerated and proud.

Keothi looked at Revin, something sharp behind her smile. "Revin... you kept me together." The words came as a confession, a tether snapping taut. "So... how are you here? What are you?"

Spoon studied Keothi's face. Whatever passed between the two, it was ancient and silent. She gave the faintest nod. "I think it's time."

Revin floated above the fire, the flames reflecting in the glass-dark of her eyes.

Revin danced above the flames. Her form bent, dissolved, reformed. A story unfolded in impossible shapes.

Spoon translated as the shapes twisted, the symbols etched themselves in firelight:

Some stories aren't told.

They're remembered into being.

Now that you have space to remember,

Let me tell you where you've been.

The words felt old. Not just spoken now, but from before as if they'd always been waiting.

The flames bowed low. Revin began to tell the tale of what was once covered to save Keothi's fire.

Chapter Twenty-Three

Until You Endure

The first crack in the mask let me breathe.
You were stripped of everything.
Every lash, every silence, breathed life into me.

A small woman stayed by your side.
She watched you. Cared for you.
I came to trust her. Know her.
We spoke in silence.

She wasn't afraid of me.
She let me be seen and stayed anyway.
And love, for you.

I did what I could to protect you.
I shielded your memories.
Hid them beneath the ache you couldn't name.
She fed you. Tended your wounds.
Together, we created a language of cues.
Eyes. Fingers. Breath.

Until the day they marched you to King Vorik.
The day they stole your name.

That's when I clawed to being.

In that stillness, I became myself.
I knew who I was.
I knew who I loved.

I swore to her, and to you,
I would relight your spark.
Guard it until you could bear its warmth.

Now you carry it.
You are safe.
You have endured.
The shadow can rest.

Let me hold you, not shattered,
but whole.
As you should've been.
As you will be.

Chapter Twenty-Four

THE IRONGROVE

Morning split the trees like a wound. Keothi crushed the last ember under her heel, eyes bloodshot, heart blistered. The Grove called. Vorik hunted. That was enough.

"Stay close," Keothi warned.

Spoon matched her pace without needing the order.

Revin glided beside them, silent as a dream, occasionally darting above the canopy to scout for any sign of Vorik's soldiers.

Keothi began a soft jog, finding her rhythm. Her steps quickened. A full sprint. Dirt and leaves flew behind them, a storm given form.

We don't stop. We don't slow. The Grove waits.

As long as we stay moving, we will find it.

The voice of her Mother rung the loudest: *You need to find your way. If their way doesn't work, make your own.*

Silence. Obedience. Masks. Pretend. Act.

Their way didn't work. It never had. Silence taught her nothing. Obedience only made her smaller. This path, this run, this wind, this fire.

She didn't need their path. She'd carve her own with an axe.

Nothing was going to stop her.

The Grove is real. I'm going to use it to end him.

Trees blurred past. Every step carved her further from what they made her. This was freedom. The wind lapped at their faces.

The hush of the woods was freeing, nothing like the caged silence the Keepers demanded.

The scent of pine and old ash clung to the air. Twigs snapped softly beneath her steps, and somewhere overhead, a crow cried once, then fell silent.

As the sun reached its highest point, Revin swooped down, and transformed into the darting silhouette of a black bear, limbs exaggerated, pointing hard toward the east.

Keothi came to an abrupt halt, instinctively knowing what Revin was saying. "Wait here, Spoon. Revin? Shield her."

Revin came to a full attention and saluted with the order.

Keothi hunched down and disappeared into the woods. Slow steady movements. Summoned by the Keeper's training. She slinked off till she saw light. She crept closer. Golden light flickered through the trees, not fire, not sun, but something older. Something watching.

Its yellow beady eyes watched her not as prey, but as kin.

Familiar.

Too familiar.

Weaving through the trees was a translucent bear walking to her. Keothi watched, unmoving. It was the bear she slayed so many years ago.

The same yellow-gold eyes. The same scar across its snout. But this time, no blood. No rage. Only... forgiveness?

It bounded over to her, and nudged her. She relaxed, confused. Translucent, yet solid. She hugged it as it nuzzled into her. It moved back towards the trees, a few yards off, and stopped. It looked at Keothi, waiting.

She shrugged and hollered for her companions. "He's not here to hurt us."

Spoon jogged over, Revin already twirling at her side.

Keothi crouched. "He wants us to see something."

The golden bear glided ahead, light flickering like molten amber across the bark. With every step, the forest thickened—trees towering, ancient, limbs interwoven into a ceiling of shadow. No sunlight made it through. Only the bear's glow lit the way.

Soon, their tops knitted together into a solid canopy, no sun pierced the woven black. A tree caught the golden light and reflected it.

Then another.

And another.

Keothi slowed, her breath quieting. She reached out and touched the nearest trunk. Though it resembled bark, it rang faintly when her knuckles tapped it. *Metal.*

She dropped into the Keeper's reverent walk.

The forest opened. The trees fell back and the forest changed shape.

A glade carved by gods. No seam, no flaw. A wound the world refused to close. Grass, soft and gold. A grove flooded in sunlight, as if the sky parted only here. In the very center, a single tree rose, a tower of green and bronze, its branches heavy with leaves that hummed in the air.

Keothi stood at the edge and smiled, something ancient tugging at her chest. "I think we found the Grove. What do you think?"

"Seems so. But... what happens now, Keothi?"

Keothi stepped into the Grove. Golden grass crunched under foot, then the world shifted. A soft blue hue fell over everything... The trees glowed with runes, ancient markings from the Gods themselves, a memory waking.

At the center, the towering tree stirred and straightened, standing watch over her.

"The doorway unfurled from the trunk like a wound, rimmed in golden runes. At its center: a symbol burned into the wood, the mountain and flame joined in a perfect circle.

Her family's crest.

Inlaid into the oak table where she'd eaten breakfast every morning.

Hammered into Uncle Borin's anvil

Carved into Father's seat of power, crowning the wood.

What is this place?

Revin swooped down in a blur, then morphed, offering a crisp signal. All clear.

"Thanks, Revin," Keothi whispered, as if afraid to disturb the quiet.

She moved to the door. A strange warmth pulsed from it. She placed her palm over the crest, oak and ash. The door swung open, beckoning her to come in.

The door pulsed with memory. The wood knew her. Knew her failures, her rage, her broken fire. She wasn't sure if this was a homecoming... or a reckoning.

Her hand trembled slightly. She drew a breath and turned. "I'm going in. You two don't have to follow."

Spoon smacked her arm with a frown. "Don't be silly. Here to the end."

Revin circled her, protective and glowing, a black ribbon against the blue light.

Keothi's gaze held with her companions. "If anything happens in there, if it even smells of danger, you run. My axe will protect me. You protect me by surviving."

Spoon crossed her arms. "I'm not strong like you... but I'm still here. That has to mean something."

"Spoon," she said gently. "Your strength is your heart, your mind. That's what needs protecting. If you promise to flee, I promise to return."

Spoon hesitated, arms tightening. "Fine. But..."

Keothi reached out, squeezed her hand. *I know.*

She turned to the doorway. The tree pulsed. The air waited.

She stepped through into the forge.

Chapter Twenty-Five

TRIAL OF REVELATION

Halvar and Bryjna stood before the throne, the great hall silent but for the breath of a thousand villagers. Halvar held a crown of twisted iron in both hands, no jewel, no velvet, only the glow of the forge, runes humming restrained thunder.

Before them, Keothi knelt. Her dress was a deep green threaded in gold, not a speck of soot touched it.

Soot does not belong on dresses.

The hall was full. Her people stood shoulder to shoulder, their eyes alight with awe.

She could feel a storm rise behind her: duty, pride, excitement, happiness. This was the moment she had waited for.

Her birthright. Her becoming.

Halvar's voice broke the stillness, low and worn. Every word rose to the rafters, reverberated, split into echoes. The truth came home late.

"Keothi of my blood. Daughter of smoke and fire.

When you were born, I whispered your name into the coals of the forge, and the flame did not recoil.

I believed the fire would shape you as it shaped me.

That if I taught you strength, you would be safe.

That if I taught you duty, you would be honored.

I didn't know the cost I was asking you to pay."

He turned to the hall, his voice carrying now, louder, not as a command, but a confession.

“This land has long known only one shape for a leader: Hammer-fisted. Stone-jawed. Crowned in the legacy of men who never wept in daylight. I led you that way. It is all I knew. But she...” He turned back to her, and his steel voice cracked.

“She made something else. She became something else. Not in defiance of our ways, but to remind us what they were for. The fire did not burn her. It named her. So I lay down this mantle. Not because I am tired. Not because my hands fail, but because I see now, she is the Chief we were waiting for. By ash and ember. By blood and blade. I name her Chieftain.”

He lowered the iron crown to her head. The runes dimmed as they touched her brow, as though settling into the hands of their true bearer.

Bryjna stepped forward in silence, her movements sure. She wrapped a robe around Keothi’s shoulders, soot-black, threaded in red, the robe of the forge. A legacy not inherited, but earned.

“And I will follow her into the fire.”

Keothi rose.

Her people stirred, breath held, the tide before the wave. Her six advisors stepped forward and knelt, fists to chest.

"What you speak, we strike.

What you carry, we bear.

We fall in your name.

We rise by your flame."

And so the flame bowed to its heir.

Keothi began to open her mouth to respond. Her shadow peeled off the ground, gaining form. It grew till its head touched the rafters. In a loud thunderous voice, it boomed, “NO! You were meant to rule yourself. Not their legacy.”

It picked up the crown off Keothi’s head. It melted in its palm into a pile of molten metal. It brushed the advisors like toys, knocking them to the side. It flattened her parents. They burst into clouds of soot, covering Keothi head to toe.

"Soot DOES belong on Dresses!"

The scene melted and disappeared. Keothi laid on the ground. A thunderous:

Clickclickclickclickclickclickclickclickclickclick

Scratched in her ear.

"You defied your parents.

You rejected your ancestral heritage.

You admitted your truth."

She didn't scream.

She didn't run.

She just watched the soot rain down.

A celebration bloomed inside a white marble hall

Columns held the ceiling aloft.

Long tables lined the room, over spilling with food.

Laughter echoed off stone.

Guests danced in celebration, each wearing a different mask:

— a plain black mask, silver specks across the eyes

— a vibrant one, feathered to be wings

— a slip of purple velvet, simple and soft

Music wove between them: lute and drum, a soft melodic rhythm honoring the occasion.

Spoon stood at the center, holding a tray.

On it: a single pitcher of wine. A single cup.

Her black veil lay snug against her face. Her dress was simple, black lace, clinging to her frame. Her eyes were small mirrors, reflecting the revelry. Her lips stitched shut in purple thread.

She stood unmoving. Frozen.

A table, nothing more.

Guests approached. They poured the wine and left.

She remained.

Wine bearer. Invisible. Furniture.

Then, slowly, she chose to lower her arms.

The tray clattered to the floor.

Wine splashed across jeweled boots and feathered cloaks.

A gasp rippled through the room.

Spoon reached up.

Tore the stitching from her lips.

Opened her mouth and a cloud of pale moths burst from her mouth. Smoke trailed their wings.

She spoke, her voice louder than the music, louder than the crowd, louder than silence. "I am Spoon."

No hesitation. No apology.

The room shattered into glass shards.

The guests, the masks, the ceiling, all crumbled into dust.

Spoon blinked and found herself once more in the chamber with Keothi and Revin.

She smiled sweetly, as if nothing had happened. "I'm Spoon."

Clickclickclickclickclickclickclickclickclickclick

"You are not a table.

Furniture to reflect others' needs.

You have chosen and accepted your Name."

Revin danced in place and Keothi giggled at Spoon's reclamation of herself.

"Nice to meet you, Spoon," said Keothi grinning. "That was fun, but let's not do it again, huh?"

"I don't know, I kind of enjoyed it," Spoon retorted. "We should probably go deeper, right?" She looked around: an empty black room with no doors, and yet, they could see perfectly well despite the absence of light.

They walked toward a wall, and it stretched. They kept walking. The room didn't move, but somehow, they did.

Somewhere ahead, something breathed and it was her own voice, just not yet spoken.

The Trial of Reflection — The Ideal Self

"Who did the world demand you become?
And who did you try to be?"

Chapter Twenty-Six

TRIAL OF RECKONING

Keothi sat on a shelf. The world had grown large around her. The room was simple—a bed and a dresser and toys scattered on the floor. Strings hung from her limbs, a crossed piece of wood balancing above her head. Her cheeks were rosy. Her smile painted on. Her eyes were plain and black as inkwells.

Mother stepped into the room, dressed simply.

She dusted the puppet, slow and deliberate, though no dust had settled.

She nudged Keothi a little straighter, aligning her on the shelf.

Then came the red paint. A brush. A careful practiced hand. Mother touched up the smile until it gleamed far too bright.

When she was satisfied, she stepped back, nodded once, and left Keothi alone on the shelf.

Father entered not long after.

He plucked the puppet from the shelf, the strings swaying with the motion.

On the floor lay crumpled parchment. He guided her hands, making her gather each piece and stack them neatly.

He swept her through the air, flying her across the messy room toward a row of dolls arranged in perfect formation.

He sat before them, positioning her at the front, building an audience of toys for her to perform to.

When the show was done, he placed her back on the shelf to wait in the quiet room.

Then came Vorik. He lifted the puppet high, studying her painted face with a bright, oily smile.

He lowered her to the floor and moved her through a graceful dance, one she had only ever watched during the feast-night

When the dance ended, he pressed her into a low bow.

He arranged her before the waiting dolls and directed her through a play she did not understand, a performance meant for an audience that wasn't hers.

When he was finished, he returned her to the shelf and left the room without a word.

No one came after.

She waited.

And waited.

There was now. There was not-now.

She remained still on her strings, waiting for the next hand, the next performance.

Revin drifted into the room, watching. She hovered before Keothi and waved.

The puppet didn't move. Didn't react.

Golden chains coiled around Revin's wrists.

Keothi blinked—a crack of confusion in painted stillness.

Revin gathered the scattered parchment and set it on the shelf. She swept the toys aside and lit the room on fire. Flames rose, bright and impossible.

Keothi flinched. A spark caught deep in the grain. It was small, but it burned.

A whimper cracked through her lips, a sound swallowed instantly by the choking silence.

A crack tore through the floor—up the wall, across the ceiling—splitting the world from top to bottom.

The room quaked under the weight of memory.

Keothi fell from the shelf. Her limbs splintered, the seams split wide.

Revin wrapped herself around the breaking pieces, holding them tight.

It should have been impossible. The doll was broken, after all.

But Revin flew into her heart.

And from the inside out, Keothi reformed. The scars were still visible, but no longer gaped open.

The doll stood. Not for a performance. Not for applause. But because broken things still rise.

Revin withdrew, leaving Keothi not patched, not masked, but rebuilt—scarred and whole.

Keothi looked down at the strings. Took each one in hand. She ripped them free, one by one.

Let them fall.

She faced Revin, and embraced her with everything she had.

"Thank you, friend." Her voice, this time, was her own. Her movements were her own.

Clickclickclickclickclickclickclickclickclickclick

"You received Warning

You ignored

But the one that you ignored

Freed you."

Keothi laid in a ball on a cot. She trembled, naked, bruised, scarred, ribs bare.

The room was familiar. No color. The size of a closet. No space.

The door was open slightly. The last Keeper who went in, didn't shut it all the way. Spoon reached out to the door knob, but hesitated. She looked, a sense of dread, sadness. She sighed, and did what she was trained to do.

She closed the door. The latch clicked like a sentence passed.

She returned the next day, a roll hidden in her pocket, the smallest rebellion she could carry.

Still the same room, empty of air, of color. Too small for a person. The perfect size for a Vessel.

Keothi lay curled on the cot, facing the wall, refusing any eye contact.

Spoon crossed the room anyway. She placed a gentle hand on Keothi's bare shoulder and offered the roll.

Keothi accepted it, ate it mechanically. Fear and sorrow held in her blackened eyes.

Soon, Keothi began to transform. Bit by bit, she folded into the shape they carved out.

She knelt when called.

She wore the veil without protest.

She swallowed her name like a stone full of nourishment.

She obeyed because disobedience had nowhere to breathe.

Spoon watched it happen, each day another thread cut from the girl she had been. Quietly, she stole a scrap of parchment from a forgotten officer's room.

In the dim hallway, she traced Bryjna's symbol. A simple exclamation mark. A memory carved in defiance, a lifeline disguised as wax.

Spoon walked to the front of the barracks. She paused at the door, hand on the knob, heart in her throat.

"You have nothing on me. I already broke free." The brass knob chilled her palm. Spoon bowed her head, breath steady despite the fear pressing hard against her ribs. "We can keep going through this memory, but I walk it with pride."

Clickclickclickclickclickclickclickclickclickclick

"You turned your back on your upbringing

You sounded the alarm when you knew she was gone

This was your awakening

Continue to walk the path"

The Trial of Reckoning — The Justified Self

"What did you do to survive?

What did you sacrifice to keep going?"

Chapter Twenty-Seven

TRIAL OF EXPOSURE

The stars and the moon lit the village in the depth of the night.

A younger Keothi wore soot stained clothes. She strolled the streets, kicking at pebbles, taking out her frustration and anger.

The scene froze, in midstep.

The scene cracked, but remained.

Present Keothi stood in this moment. She sighed, looking at her younger self. "I remember this moment. It was the moment I turned away from my first instinct. I should have gotten my axe. And killed him right then."

She dropped onto the cold cobblestone, facing the girl who didn't swing. "Because of that moment, I failed everyone. Instead of sacrificing my mind, I should have sacrificed my body."

Revin formed from the dark shadows. She wrapped her arms around Present Keothi.

"If I had acted then... maybe I'd be dead. But maybe they'd be free. And that's the guilt I carry."

Keothi could sense it.

You didn't choose this. But you lived through it. And that is enough.

Keothi let out a heavy sigh, "I know, Revin. Shall we?"

Revin stood, shifting into the axe Keothi had reforged a hundred times, chasing perfection she didn't yet understand. Not yet. But it was enough. She lifted it high above her head, and struck it down on the scene.

"I forgive myself for not acting because I am acting now."

Clickclickclickclickclickclickclickclickclickclick

"Perfect doesn't exist

We can try, but it only sets us up for failure

Learn from your past,

Try again."

Spoon sat curled in a cage no bigger than a bird's, adrift in an endless sea of nothing. Space stretched around her, colorless, soundless, cruel. Her knees pressed to her chest, spine bent, no room to breathe or move.

Before her, giant faces flickered into existence, women's faces, impossibly large, impossibly close, flashing in and out.

Each one a judgmental ghost, staring and unblinking.

Each one vanished before she could speak.

Vessel after Vessel after Vessel.

Each one lingered, long enough to burn.

She felt their pain. Saw their sorrow.

And knew, with terrible clarity, the part she'd played in the unmaking of themselves.

She felt the final thread of them snap, with her hands on the shears of the Fates.

Keothi's face emerged from the dark. Soft. Reverent. A slow smile blooming across features full of knowing.

"You are Spoon," it said, gentle as a lullaby.

Warmth radiated from the words. A balm against the endless ache. For a moment, the cage felt a little larger. Her body, a little lighter.

But the face began to melt.

Not fast. Not sudden. The waxed face dripped in slow motion. Eyes sagging, lips sloughing off the bone. The voice didn't scream, it just stopped.

And then there was nothing.

No face.

No sound.

Just the silence again. Pressing in. Always waiting.

A form began to take shape.

First, the movement of a hand, flickering at the edge of sight. Then half a body, slowly rising, assembling itself from nothing.

Until she was whole.

Revin.

She moved soundlessly to the cage and crouched, peering in with that strange, tender curiosity only she could make feel sincere. From her index finger, she sculpted a skeleton key, delicate, deliberate.

The lock clicked.

The door creaked open, and Revin slipped inside. She wrapped her arms around Spoon without hesitation, cradling her with the care of someone who'd waited too long to hold her.

Spoon melted into the embrace. Her shivering slowed. Her breath matched Revin's.

A long silence passed.

Then, barely above a whisper, Spoon exhaled. "I'm ready."

Revin stepped beyond the cage, and turned. She didn't speak, she didn't need to. She extended her hand, palm open, patient.

Not as a rescuer.

As a witness. As a promise. As a guardian.

Spoon hesitated, her fingers trembling toward that waiting palm.

To reach was remembrance.

To grasp was forgiveness.

To leave was not forgetting.

She took Revin's hand.

And the cage was not unlocked.

It was outgrown.

Clickclickclickclickclickclickclickclickclickclick

"You were blinded

Until a woman helped you see yourself

You received help while you were caged

Everyone needs help."

Spoon stepped onto solid ground or what passed for it in this dreamlike space. The cage behind her dissolved into mist, as if it had only ever existed within her.

The air was thick with static. The kind that buzzes behind your teeth before a storm.

Then, the clicks. The crunching and grinding of bone.

Clickclickclickclickclickclickclickclickclickclick

Keothi, Spoon, and Revin exhaled as one, three souls bracing, clinging to each other in the hush between battles. A breath held for themselves, for once.

Then the moment cracked open.

From the dark beyond form, it emerged: *Sigmantis.*

The voice did not come from a mouth. It came from everywhere.

"You passed the trials. You have one left. Me. Turn back if you are not ready to face the truth."

The Trial of Exposure — The Helpless Self

"When were you powerless?
What wound still bleeds beneath your armor?"

Chapter Twenty-Eight

I CHOOSE YOU

The creature dissolved into mist. In its absence, two doors emerged.

The first door was jagged iron, forged with handprints in the metal, as if someone clawed to open it from the inside. Inscribed into it:

TRUTH

The other was smooth wood, soft with moss at its base. Almost warm. Sunlight seeped under the crack. The word carved into it was gentle, almost apologetic:

FORGET

One burns, one soothes.

One demands. One forgives.

The promise settled bone-deep in Keothi:

Walk through Forget, and the Grove would release them.

No scars of what they earned in pain and revelation.

Truth offers pain. And through it, transformation.

Her lungs heaved like bellows. She knew the path. What she feared... was walking it.

Her hand reached out. Not to Truth. To forget.

Just to feel the moss, for a moment.

What would it be like to forget the plate? The silence? What would it be like to never need to carry the fire?

She pulled her hand back like it burned.

I've bled for these scars. I'm not giving them up

"Truth," she said, voice brittle. "There's something behind that door. It doesn't let you leave the same way you entered." Her eyes never left the iron door, glued to it. It seethed ancestral knowledge.

She felt a hand on hers, anchoring in the moment.

Revin pointed at the door labeled Truth.

"You two. Leave. I need to face this alone."

Spoon attempted to protest, but it was too late to hear her. If Keothi was going to do this, she had to do it alone. No long goodbyes. No heartfelt conversations.

As the door opened, it breathed a cold, dead, rotting smell. Once she stepped in, the door closed with a seal.

Her eyes couldn't adjust, didn't adjust. In here, there was no direction, no life, no light. It was pure instinctual nothing.

She felt the stone under her knees, smelled the rot of her doubt. She felt the roots, metal. The same as the tree outside.

Then it appeared. Something shuddered into form. A cuboid, unnatural in-between, hovered inches off the ground. Limbs jutted from its surfaces at impossible angles: too many elbows, fingers bent backward, twitching. They moved without rhythm, as if trying on gestures that didn't belong to them.

It pulsed, half-there and half-not, the world was trying to reject it, its outline trembling with the sound of splitting bone and breath held too long.

Fragmentation shimmered along its edges, the geometry itself refused to commit. The lines of its form stuttered, collapsed, reformed.

The creature reflected. Every flaw. Every mask. Every truth.

Then the sound.

Clickclickclickclickclickclickclick.

The sound of something trying to assemble itself, or maybe tear itself apart.

The noise threatened to split her skull. Threatened to bring Keothi to her knees.

The absolute dark fractured. Not into light, but into form. The suffocating nothingness seemed to collapse in on itself, re-shaping into the confines of a hollowed-out cave.

A dull, blood-orange glow pulsed from within the very earth, casting shallow, dancing shadows.

Everywhere she looked, roots burrowed through the earthen walls, their surfaces meticulously etched and carved, catching the faint, struggling light.

Her fingers closed, expecting nothing, finding steel. She looked down. An axe. The edge bore no mark, but it felt known to her bones. Both hands found their place.

Her eyes locked on her target.

She charged the creature with every bit of pent-up rage. Every fear. Every thread of her being. She brought the axe down.

I will slay this creature!

The blade went clean through, swinging at smoke. It crashed into the ground with a clang.

She didn't stop.

She hauled it up and struck again. And again. Until she was breathless. Until her arms shook. Until her rage had nowhere left to go.

The creature opened its maw.

The sound of plates and cups, breaking, falling, crashing, shattering.

Something inside her seized. Her knees buckled before she understood why. That sound, too familiar. It was a scar which pressed too hard.

Even after the shattering stopped, she remained, breath caught, body locked, the sound had nested inside her bones.

"Your uncle Kern had a similar fire," the creature said, plainly.

A silhouette of a figure appeared in the room. A man that was as tall as Uncle Borin and Father. He had the same red hair as them. Tattooed face. An axe on his back.

The figure's jaw opened, stretching inhumanly, down to his chest. With it the sound of a man screaming with insanity.

The creature before her washed away the image.

"The apple doesn't fall from the tree. I wonder if you'll scream like him. Or if you'll continue to be in silence. I don't need your silence, I need your pain. And that's easy."

The echo of a single plate crashed.

"King Vorik did all the hard work for me."

The sound shattered through her. She wanted to stand, to fight. Every instinct told her to. But she remained, chained to the spot.

"Kern screamed until there was no voice left. You swallowed yours."

She didn't move. Didn't respond.

"Borin and Halvar didn't dare face me. Face their truths."

The name clawed at her like it should mean something. But it didn't. Not really.

This creature was right. She wasn't fighting. Why?

"You know why."

Keothi pulled herself together for a moment.

"Yes, I can read your thoughts."

"Because I am your truth." said the creature.

"Alright. I'll stop." it laughed with the eerie **clickclickclick** crunching, scratching noise.

She used the axe as a crutch, to help her stand. She cleared her throat, and gathered herself.

"Enough of these games. What is the truth?" Keothi declared, burying every instinct to run.

"You don't know who you are. You don't want to know. You fear it. Fear yourself."

Keothi blinked, her mind stuttering.

The creature's voice kept talking, but the meaning frayed in her hands before she could hold it.

It sighed, "I thought you'd recognize the pattern... But mortals do struggle with pattern recognition, don't they?"

Silhouetted shelves appeared before them, in between them, images of Keothi's head all stacked neatly on the shelves.

It didn't need to be explained. She felt it.

A head for dutiful daughter
A head for the Elara-Keothi
A head for Chief
A head for bride
A head for warrior
A head for a doll
A head covered by a veil
A head of a bear
A head of a Blacksmith
A head for everything.

"You can't wear them all."

Keothi lifted the axe and tried attacking again, not caring. She fell through the illusion.

A sound of a plate cracking of laughter. "You lash out, but is there anything beneath the flame?" It barked the command.

"No one! That's your truth! You are no one because you are everyone. You are a chameleon, left to walk this path alone. To hide yourself."

Keothi felt it in her bones. She's been trying to appease everyone. Which mask was hers and hers alone? Which mask was crafted for herself?

She crashed to the ground shaking and shivering. The floor was warm beneath her, but it felt wrong, alive, like it could turn on her too. She pressed her hands over her face, trying to block out the creature's voice, its wrath, its truth.

"We've got plenty of time on our hands. This pain feeds me, makes me stronger. Let's play, Lady Keothi. Keothi the Barbarian. Keothi of the Shadowforge. Keothi the Wielder of IronMaw. Keothi the NameGiver. Keothi the Protector."

It opened again. She felt it all at once.

The crash of porcelain.

The silence of the room.

The breath she held.

The words she never said again.

The lashing of the reed when she moved.

The creature spoke over the crashing porcelain:

"Even now, you don't speak of it. You remember the crash. But not the scream you swallowed to cause it."

The memory hit her. "I never screamed after that day. Not even when..."

"You thought it would kill you to be you. You feared that your truth would be the match. That if you struck it, everything would burn."

Keothi, trembling, whispered back, "I was wrong."

Chapter Twenty-Nine

Let Me Burn

Behind her, a golden light unfurled, warm as breath. Bright as the bear that once guided her through the forest. The door opened. As it did, the crashing dishes started moving backwards, floating up instead of raining down.

A hand was placed on her shoulder. A soft whispering coo, "Keothi. You'll endure."

Spoon and Revin walked into the room.

Spoon stepped forward, boots echoing on the stone like a child's voice in a cathedral. The creature didn't flinch, but the shadows around it curled in. "You've had your turn. Now you deal with me."

The crashing stopped—sharp as a held breath. Keothi reeled, lungs tight, breath coming too fast.

Revin held her steady, silent as they watched this tiny, veiled woman face down a creature stitched from fear.

It recoiled. Not in fear, but... curiosity. "Spoon, is it?"

Spoon stood her ground. "That's right." Her words became daggers, "What's the truth you want me to face? You've got nothing to show me, because this isn't my fear. It's hers. And I'm here because she matters."

Spoon knelt beside her, back to the creature, shielding Keothi from its gaze "I can feel her, which means I'm in her trial. You have no truths to show me. Keothi, I know the truth is terrifying. But, deep down you know which mask is yours. Who you wish to be." She paused, letting the words reach her. "You won't be a failure. You won't be a disappointment. You won't be an annoyance."

Spoon linked her fingers into Keothi's. "I know who you are, Keothi. I've felt you—maskless, wordless, worth everything. And I'm not letting fear tell me otherwise. We face this together."

Keothi could hear the tiny woman through the onslaught of flashbacks. The terror surged, but Spoon's voice reached somewhere deeper.

"Even if the world can't see you." Spoon finished softly, "I do. I choose you."

Revin moved with slow certainty, her footsteps soundless. She placed a hand on Keothi's heart.

Slowly, she unfolded herself with resolve. The strength Revin offered her. The words Spoon provided. If they were willing to be there for her, help her confront the creature.

"There we go. Not every battle needs to be faced alone." She giggled.

Keothi stepped forward, the words weak at first, "I'm forged, I'm not Broken." The words shook her. Looking to the ground. Her chin rose. "You are Sigmantis. You have no control over me. I am Keothi. I forge my own path."

Each sentiment forced the creature to crack. It stammered, trying to hold itself together. "You think this will hold? A woman's words and broken memories? I am your truth, Keothi!"

Keothi squeezed on Spoon's and Revin's hands. She didn't need her axe at that moment. She needed her companions.

"If I disappoint my parents, so be it. If I fail my village, so be it. This path is mine. I'm not here to be your mirror. I'm not your doll anymore. I forge me. I am Keothi."

"You think that's strength?" it hissed. "Borrowed light? A child's hand? You'll burn for this."

Keothi smiled. Not cruel. Not scared. "Then let me burn."

With that final declaration, Keothi stepped into the creature.

Sigmantis let out a soundless scream, then burst into a riot of light and heat.

Flames licked the ceiling. Ash spiraled a storm-swept snow.

Masks disintegrated midair, unraveling into soot and threads of gold.

Expectations unspooled around them, torn from the loom of every lie she'd ever lived.

And when the smoke cleared, the cave didn't move once more.

In the center, where the monster had stood, lay a single object:

A mask, charred, cracked, the face of a bear forged in fire.

Keothi stepped forward, lifted it with reverent hands.

"This is me," she said softly. "I am the bear. forged in fire. Built to protect."

"The roots pulsed, veins of gold threading through bark like molten lightning. They unfurled through the soil, slow and certain—centuries of tension finally releasing.

With a low groan, the ground shifted, stairs formed beneath her feet, winding downward into the earth.

From below: a red glow pulsing, calling Keothi to its depths.

The scent of soot and old metal filled her lungs. The air trembled with the roar of a fire too ancient to die.

Keothi's body hummed with heat, not from the forge ahead, but from within her. Something awakened. Something ready.

One root lit up beside her, inscribed:

To Kern

A reminder:

We do not defeat grief.

We accept it.

We are not alone when we face the darkness.

Chapter Thirty

IRONMAW

The clatter of dishes echoed like ghosts as Keothi descended.

They carried the weight of what had passed, saying nothing. The silence didn't scare her this time. It anchored her.

The stairs were carved from ancient stone that thrummed with memory. Each rune bloomed with light as it awoke from centuries of sleep, whispering fragments of the forest's oldest truths. The stone vibrated beneath their feet, recognizing their presence. Below, the low hum of the forge-fires curled up the stairwell.

As they descended deeper, the mountain opened its throat. Caverns widened into a vast chamber carved by hands long vanished. The air shifted, becoming charged and reverent.

An ancient forge welcomed the silent warriors. Stone bellows, silent for ages, now hummed with breath again. Ember spirits danced through the heat-hazed air, swarmed by cinder-fireflies. The warmth wrapped around them, carrying memories of Gods and Ancestors.

Pillars etched with forgotten runes held the chamber aloft. Four great kilns glowed faintly at the corners. Anvils ringed the central firepit, calling for ten Master Blacksmiths to sing the siren song, hammer on anvil. The walls were worked with the care of centuries: reliefs of hammer and flame, battles long ended.

This was no mortal forge, this was where legends were born. Where identities were forged. It called to her, welcoming her home. It wanted to breathe again.

Spoon froze in place, trying to find the top of the cavern. Her head tilted till she was teetering on her heels.

Revin flew up to see if she could find it for her, disappearing in the vast mountain peaks.

As Keothi neared the forge, the ghost of distant hammering echoed from another age. The ring of mythic anvils, as if the mountain remembered the hands that once shaped gods' weapons.

Warmth rolled through the central fire pit. Filled with ember stones, each answered to Keothi's approach. The light leapt from one to the next until it found the cloak's clasp.

The stone burned as the others awakened. Heat radiated from it, alive with a pulsing heartbeat.

Startled, Keothi threw off the bear cloak. It landed silently, untouched by flame. Yet the clasp still pulsed with the rhythm of the forge's rekindled heart. Carefully, she bent and gathered it back up, holding the edges to avoid the smoldering clasp.

"That's Dwarven fire, what we buried in the mountain. What we bled for. Burning cinder of the Old forge. You don't cradle it... you build with it."

Spoon cupped her hands and shouted into the vast dark. "What is this place?"

Keothi stared down at the stone, her uncle's voice flickering in her mind. "Dwarven Ember." She hesitated. "I think... Dwarven caverns."

Her thumb traced the intricate edge of the clasp. "There's only one ancient being," she murmured, almost to herself, "that could shape stone with this kind of mastery. Not men. Not beasts. Only the old ones, the Dwarves. The ones who carved mountains into scrolls and whispered to fire until it listened."

Spoon tilted her head, confusion softening her voice. "Dwarves?"

Revin reappeared, circling overhead once before landing silently beside the fire, her head tilted in reverence. As if she'd always known this place waited for them.

Keothi didn't look up. Her fingers brushed the clasp as if it might speak.

"The Dwarves built the first forges," she said softly. "With thunder in their bones. They tamed fire, not with force, but with patience. They spoke to metal... called it by name before it cooled."

Her voice had slipped into a rhythm, half-chant, half-memory. "I heard it first during deep winter. The snow was threatening to bury the house. Father and Mother sat in their chairs. Mother's needle danced between fabric."

She paused; the Ancients spoke through her. Tears threatened to escape. "That's the first time Father told me of the Dwarves. I...I thought they were just stories."

She looked up finally, taking in the carved stone, the ancient forge that held back long forgotten spirits. "But now..."

The ground rumbled beneath their feet.

From the heart of the forge, stone began to shift. A slab rose from the center of the floor, smooth and deliberate. It lifted by unseen hands, glowing with fire-red veins, lava pulsing through the seams. Upon it lay an axe, broken into three pieces.

Keothi stepped toward it. Something in her bones pulled. She breathed, barely trusting the words as they left. "I think...it wants me to forge it back together."

Keothi stood before the ancient forge, the broken axe gleaming faintly on the fire-lit slab, three pieces waiting, watching.

The bear cloak lay crumpled in her arms, its clasp glowing hotter by the moment. She stepped toward the central pit, where coals lay dormant, black and cold. A single groove carved into the stone, thin and precise. A keyhole left by time itself.

She didn't hesitate.

Keothi took the ember stone from the cloak and dropped it into the hollow.

For one breath, nothing happened.

The mountain stirred. The fire remembered.

The coals didn't catch; they answered. Fire raced through ancient channels carved in the stone, igniting the kilns. The mountain's heart awakened. The bellows, untouched, heaved on their own, exhaling heat and fury into the room. Cinder fireflies burst into the air in a thousand swirling lights.

The chamber came alive with heat, light, and memory.

And Keothi was the center of it all.

Spoon and Revin stood back as runes flared to life on the walls, red, sharp, dancing flames. The same runes blazed across the axe fragments, each one pulsing. They, too, had waited for her to return.

The haft.

The blade.

The counterweight.

Each piece lifted, not by her hands, but by the will of the forge itself.

The blade turned first—broad, twin-edged, its crescent form catching the firelight as runes carved deep into the metal began to glow. The haft followed, darkened wood wrapped tight in worn leather, the grip shaped by hands that had bled for it.

They hovered above the slab, glowing brighter, as molten lines traced the seams.

The mountain grumbled low beneath their feet.

Ancient. Patient. Irrefutable.

"You don't cradle it; you build with it. Spoon, Uncle Borin's hammer, please."

Spoon knelt, opened the blanket bundle, and handed over the hammer. It had been passed down through the generations. Uncle Borin's, now hers.

The moment she touched it, the weight settled into her palm. It had been waiting. It sang back to her. Her hands found the old rhythm, Borin's rhythm. The one he had trained into her reflexes.

Now her fingers closed around the haft. It wasn't just familiar. It had always belonged to her. It had simply waited until she was ready to accept this path.

Her breath caught. She remembered his hands, rough and sure, folding hers around this tool teaching her how to listen to metal. An ancestral gift. A promise left behind in iron.

She raised it high and struck.

CLANG. The haft met the blade. Sparks hissed. The air thickened. Each spark a memory burned. Her father's steadiness, her mother's patience, her uncle's laughter.

Spoon and Revin stayed back, sitting on the ancient stairs, watching Keothi craft, mesmerized by the forgemaster.

CLANG. The weight snapped into place. The mountain breathed.

Flames licked the seams, runes sparking to life. The fire climbed the stone slab, warming the counterweight.

Keothi's heart thrummed beneath her ribs. Each strike a vow. Every scar a lesson. Every flame a promise.

CLANG. The forge roared. The axe awakened once the counterweight locked into place. The blade burned white-hot, then red, then ember-deep.

Silence fell.

The runes dimmed, but did not go out. They settled into a slow, steady pulse.

Keothi stepped back, trembling. The axe sat on the slab, whole again. Its edge gleamed with hunger: brutal and beautiful.

The forge's glow washed over her face. For a heartbeat, she swore it breathed her name.

She reached for it and the handle was warm. As her fingers closed around the haft, a distant sound of acknowledgement echoed through the forge. The voices of ancestors. Of forgotten Dwarves. Of the gods who once bled into this mountain's heart.

The forge did not test her.

It chose her.

The ancient cavern lit with blue runes, crackling to life, the stone exhaled after centuries of silence. The resurrection of the axe stirred something deeper than flame.

Keothi stepped back. The cavern breathed. Something stirred in the runes warm, familiar.

From the shadows...

Kern. The man from the final trial. He smiled, kind-eyed and proud.

"My niece... You've done what I could not. You found the heart of the mountain. You woke Moltrune. You brought fire back to the gods." His voice softened as his eyes fell to the axe, "and awakened IronMaw."

Keothi turned to the axe in her hands. Its surface reflected her face, war-worn, firelit, whole.

She whispered, "Kern? Who are you?"

"I was the first to reach Sigmantis," he said gently. "But I was not ready. I was defeated. You are the only one who made it through."

Keothi blinked, throat tight. "Why me?"

Kern chuckled softly, stepping closer. His golden light shimmered as if drawn from some deep ancestral fire.

"Because you do not seek wholeness to prove anything. You seek it for yourself. You walked through fire without flinching. And in doing so, you became the fire. You loved yourself even when broken."

He turned to Spoon. "You accepted."

Then to Revin. "You forged."

The warmth spiraled through her.

Grief and pride. Love and awe.

Molten gold through stone.

Memory. Myth. Fire. Self.

Kern looked once more to the axe. "The weapon you hold, Keothi... it is more than steel. It is a contract with *Reality*. You carry Sigmantis's truth now, deep in your soul." He met her eyes, solemn and bright. "You will forge identities with it. You will bring names to the nameless. You will strike with Strength and Truth, if you so choose."

The axe pulsed in her hands, breathing with her.

Keothi nodded, steady now. "Then I will wield it with my truth."

He smiled one last time, with peace and let the forge claim him, his golden essence pulled into the steel. Into the name. Into her.

The cavern fell quiet again, save for the slow, sacred hum of the fire.

"I think he waited for you." said Spoon.

She hovered near IronMaw, cautious, like it could whisper her name.

The three of them stood together. No longer lost.

Moltrune burned.

Spoon stepped toward the bed of ancient coals, the heat kissing her face, an old truth returning.

She unclasped her veil, the fabric that had hidden her softness, her past, her fear. Without flinching, she let it slip from her fingers into the flame.

"I don't need this anymore," she said, her voice steady. "I feel whole." She had wide eyes, a small nose, a mouth that always looked close to smiling, even when it wasn't.

The veil curled, caught, and vanished, no smoke, only a shimmer as the fire accepted it. She smiled, as the silk coil and burned away.

Revin spun with delight, wrapping herself around Spoon, a ribbon of shadow and laughter. Spoon laughed, real and unmasked, the forge itself had made space for joy.

Keothi stepped forward, IronMaw in hand, its runes pulsing. She looked at them, her unlikely sisters and nodded.

"We've bled enough. Now it's his turn."

Revin stilled. She raised her hands, eyes glowing with a quiet that trembled the air.

For the first and only time, she spoke. Her voice summoned the ancients of Moltrune.

The forge answered.

CHAPTER THIRTY-ONE

YOU'VE ENDURED

I was born in your silence.
I lived in your stillness.
And I rose in your fire.

My Keothi, you've endured.

You saved yourself.
You reclaimed your name.
You reforged your spark.

I was your shield.
Your axe.
The shadow that stood between you and silence.

I watched. I guarded.
I stayed.

But now,
You don't need me.

You wear your name like armor.
You walk in your own fire.

You are your own weapon.
You are your own light.

I am loved, but no longer needed.

And so,
With choice in my hands,
I choose to let go.

Remember, dear Keothi,
if your spark falters,
If silence rises again.
Then so will I.

The shadow will rise.
Your name will sing in Valhalla.
Your name will be carved into stone.
Your name will be forged in fire.

Because you endured.
Because you rose.
Because you are Keothi.

Revin turned to face Keothi. Her eyes shimmered, not with tears, but with completion. No words now, none needed. She had said all there was to say.

She reached forward and pressed her shadowed hand over Keothi's heart. Light flickered there, faint at first, red as ember she rose, warm as truth.

Revin smiled. Softly. Proudly.

She didn't fade. She released herself. She chose to go.

She unravelled.

Not in pain, not in loss, but a breath after the final show. A warrior's last exhale. A shadow stepping into light. Smoke coiled gently from her fingertips, rising in delicate swirls before dissolving into the warm air of Moltrune. The last of her shadow wrapped around Keothi's shoulders, a cloak being returned to its rightful owner.

Without another word, she was gone. But not lost. Never lost.

Keothi took a breath that tasted of ash and thunder.

Spoon wiped her cheek, then whispered to the empty space, "Thank you for guarding us." She turned to Keothi, voice steady, "Time to raise hell, right?"

Together, they ascended the ancient stairs, each step echoing with the strength of those who came before.

Stone opened into the sky. The IronGrove awaited.

Keothi stepped into the light, raised her axe high into the air, its runes blazing with fire-red resolve and screamed:

KEOTHI THE BARBARIAN!

The forest roared back.

And the world finally knew her name.

Part 3: A Flame Remembered

Chapter Thirty-Two

What Should've Stayed Buried

IronMaw pulsed along her spine. Spoon's quiet breaths matched the wind threading through Irongrove branches, steady and soft. Sunlight draped the clearing like it was holding its breath for her.

Her gaze lingered on the bark. The blue runes dimmed to a calm glow.

She had an axe. An ancient forge. Revin was gone. And something in her bones whispered: *Go deeper.* There is something more in there.

A soft hand brushed hers. "Let's stay here for a moment. Let the world settle."

Keothi's smile didn't reach her eyes. "Safest place in the world, technically. It's not like Vorik has a shadow, right?"

Spoon shrugged softly as they turned. The sentinel tree held the door with the Irevandor crest burned in the center.

With Sigmantis gone, the spiral stairs waited, heat bleeding up from below. Down in the forge, soot drifted in the glow of dying embers. Only the fading fires lit the room.

Five corridors split the central chamber. Each framed by identical stone: carved, ancient, patient.

"Which hall?" Spoon's voice stayed behind her.

She steadied her breath, studying each hall. They all looked the same. Each entrance was framed by thick pillars and weight-bearing crossbeams. Her eyes darted through the dark halls, not moving an inch.

The third corridor held a familiar heaviness to it. A blanket of silence, the same that once erased her name, filled the corridor. Her gut twisted as her gaze lingered for too long. When courage finally gripped her spine, she stepped forward.

"This way."

Their footsteps echoed as the light thinned. The temperature dropped, chasing away even the forge's heat. IronMaw's pulse quickened, soft at first, then insistent, as though the axe knew something she didn't.

At the end of the corridor, a narrow stair plunged deeper. With every step, the essence of the forge was devoured by the cold. Keothi's heart thudded with anticipation, recognition, and fear.

At the bottom waited a hall and a single arched doorway. Scorch marks spidered across the floor—carved deep enough to scar the deepstone's bones: **Virell & Nyrr.**

The names pulsed once, like dying embers flaring beneath ash.

Something moved in her marrow. A call with no voice.

Maybe her parents had been right. Maybe the hammer and anvil, the heat of the forge, weren't all they were meant to be. Maybe a child on her hip wouldn't be so bad.

Watching the child grow up in the Great Hall. Climbing the same mountain ridges. Completing the Hunt & Hearth Trial, face flushed with pride.

Maybe that life could be enough. Maybe it wasn't a trap at all. Just... the natural order of things.

A life laid out by the gods, approved by her ancestors, celebrated by her parents.

Maybe—

IronMaw twitched against her spine. Not once, but twice. The metal's pulse snapped her back, tore through the illusion.

Spoon stiffened beside her. "Keothi?"

Keothi stepped back, jaw locking. "We're leaving." She turned sharply, climbing the stairs without looking back. Spoon hurried after her.

"You know what that was?" Spoon whispered up the steps.

"No." She kept her eyes forward, the names burning her mind. "And I don't want to find out what I'll become if I stay."

Heat met them again as they rose into the upper hall. The forge air felt like a shove, pushing that cold desire back where it belonged.

"Spoon." Keothi braced a hand against the wall, breath steadying. "I'm leaving you with a witch Revin trusts."

Spoon's eyes softened, reading what Keothi didn't say. "Because of that room."

"Because of what it pulled out of me." Her voice dropped. "I need to take out Vorik. I don't know what it is, beyond the obvious. But that room? It's tied to him."

Spoon didn't argue. She stepped forward and took Keothi's hand, warm and sure. "You go break the world. I'll be here when you're done."

The journey to Satira's hut was quiet and punishing. The carved wall clung to her thoughts like soot, but rage burned hotter—sharpening itself into a dozen ways to kill Vorik.

The woods pulled back just enough to reveal the hut, as if even they didn't want to touch it. Echoes of Satira's laughter moved through leaves and trunks. It took every ounce of Keothi's courage to approach the oak door.

It swung open just as she raised her hand to knock.

The old woman stood in the doorway, straw-blown white hair jutting in every direction. Her eyes widened at the sight of Keothi. "In!" Satira barked, eyes darting past her shoulder.

She seized Keothi's wrist and yanked her inside.

Spoon followed close behind. Before the door could shut, Satira thrust her head out, scanning the treeline. Then she ducked in and slammed the door. "Keothi. What are you doing here?"

"Running an errand. Satira, I don't have time. I can't stay."

"That's not an answer..."

Light spilled from IronMaw's runes, shifting through a spectrum of colors. Dust motes drifted through it, catching each changing hue.

"...You opened it."

Keothi's brow furrowed. She leaned toward Spoon, whispering softly behind her hand. "She speaks in circles."

Spoon's shoulders shook with a suppressed laugh, her eyes flicking over the room's chaos. "I don't know, I kind of like her."

Satira squinted. "Wrong eyes are looking in the right places... and now you stink of something old. Like something that should've stayed buried."

"Enough riddles, Satira. Speak plainly for once."

Satira scoffed, folding her arms. "What is normal? Normal doesn't exist. Especially with that axe accompanying you..."

"I don't have time for spirals." Keothi's breath frayed. "What is this axe?"

Satira tilted her head, lips pursed. "Sometimes the forge makes things it shouldn't. Sometimes those things find people they shouldn't."

Spoon moved to the shelf and poked the doll with red stitching across its lips. A soft hum escaped it.

Keothi's brow knotted. A long sigh slipped out despite herself. "This here is Spoon. I'm leaving her in your care. We can talk about strange forges and whatever nonsense you're hinting at another time." The room pressed in with stories half-told. But none of it would matter if Vorik kept breathing. "Right now, I have a skull to claim."

Satira turned to the horse figurine on the table. Her gaze held on it until a flurry of words escaped. "I can't be certain... but the shadows aren't done. Whatever this is—echo, omen, leftover mistake—it's trailing you. Or you're drifting toward it. Hard to tell which..."

Spoon placed a hand on Satira's gnarled hand. "What do you mean something is trailing Keothi?"

Satira shrugged. "I need to check something. A very old record."

Keothi shook her head. She needed a place deep in the woods. Quiet. Forgotten. Where the hunter could become the bear. Where the hunted became the teeth. Where the silence waited to bite back. “If something wants me, it can get in line.” She turned, placing a hand on the door knob.

“While you two figure it out, I’m going to go hunt. Spoon?”

Keothi’s gaze remained on the door; looking back at Spoon made her stomach twist in knots. She couldn’t explain it, but she knew they hadn’t separated in three years. Spoon had helped Revin and in return, helped her. She was there when Sigmantis threatened to keep her locked away. Spoon was the only person who hadn’t left her to be devoured by the silence.

And she was about to leave her to the mad woman in the woods. What choice did she have? She didn’t know who else was out there. She didn’t know their loyalties. All she had was herself, Spoon, and a woman who chose isolation over civilization.

Spoon smiled softly. “Go, Keothi. I’ll be here when you get back. Maybe we’ll have answers.”

Chapter Thirty-Three

Where the Fire Asks Nothing

The wind carried the subtle grind of cartwheels and distant voices, drawing nearer. Sunlight peered through the leaves above, but down here, the air was thick. It stank of old leather and sweat, a scent more reliable than any scout.

The underbrush rasped softly as she shifted, thorns brushing leather, a nettle sting blooming against her forearm. Overhead, a raven gave a low croak. Even the insects had gone quiet. The forest was listening.

Keothi didn't move. Not yet.

Stillness had saved her once before, when she'd watched an entire patrol pass a few feet from her face, blades red, eyes blank. She'd learned prey that breathes too loud gets carved. Silence was survival. Silence was war.

Her breath came shallow and steady. These woods had shaped her in isolation, every root and hollow, every bird call. She sank deeper into the concealment of the undergrowth, becoming one with the shadows. Every muscle in her body tensed.

IronMaw pulsed against her spine, alive with lust and hunger.

"The Vessel's been striking harder. We need to be careful out here."

"Aye, but we've trained for this. She's sat on a shelf, gathering dust."

"I really think we should've taken the upper path."

"And risk another damn pit trap? No thanks."

One scoffed. "Just saying. She's not normal. We've seen what she did to Captain Borsk."

She stepped from the shadows and hurled her axe, a whispered curse turned deadly. It split the helmet and the skull beneath it in a single, brutal whisper.

Lambs to the slaughter. Training won't protect them from hunger.

Keothi surged from cover, her voice the promise of ruin. "Who's next?"

A quick count.

Five.

That'll do.

She grinned, "Hel's got your room ready. Fresh sheets and everything."

Vorik's men weren't bound for Odin's high halls. Helheim would remember them instead.

Drawing a second axe from her hip, she hurled it straight into the cart driver's chest. The thud of impact was thick. He crumpled backwards, reins flying, horses whinnying in panic.

A soldier broke from the formation, sword raised, fear and fury twisted across his face.

Keothi unsheathed IronMaw, a hiss of steel daring him.

He charged, but not fast enough.

She sidestepped and swung. The axe tore his chest open. Bone cracked.

Blood painted her, a warrior reborn in war. The rage didn't ask questions. It answered with blades and blood.

Another came at her, swinging wild.

Her shoulder ached from the last swing. Didn't matter. She'd bleed gladly, if it meant fewer of Vorik's bastards breathing her air.

His blade clanged against IronMaw, a shriek of steel on steel that rattled through the trees.

She twisted, hooked her axe under his guard, and tore the weapon from his hands. It spun into the undergrowth with a traitor's clatter.

His eyes widened, shock, fear, a flash of regret.

She brought IronMaw down on his shoulder.

The crunch of bone echoed.

He dropped, wailing, trying to hold together what was already ruined.

Keothi stomped a boot into his chest and yanked IronMaw free with a wet, sucking crack.

The last shudders of life faded beneath her heel.

Two remained.

They froze mid-step, horror blooming across their faces as they stared at the carnage.

Their bravado withered. Primal fear bloomed.

Swords clattered to the dirt, useless toys being abandoned. Hands rose in surrender.

She dragged IronMaw's blood-slick edge across the nearest corpse. She slung the axe across her shoulder. Dark drops fell from the blade to the leaf-strewn ground.

"To your knees."

They dropped without hesitation. Shoulders hunched, eyes locked on the blood-slick axe in her hand.

One stammered, "V-Vessel, we're on King Vorik's orders..."

"King Vorik's?" Keothi laughed, raw and jagged. "You mean Argr Eldus-Fifl? The coward by the fire, too scared to burn himself? Too hollow to forge anything real?"

She chuckled again, no joy, just rusted venom. "Strange. Looks like you're on your knees, not on orders."

She stepped forward, crouching low, IronMaw gleaming between them, daring her to strike. The axe throbbed faintly in her grip.

Her voice dropped low. "Now. Tell me what I want to know."

They shared a wide-eyed glance, sweat crawling down their temples, mouths opening and closing like stranded fish gasping for air.

Keothi sighed. "Always surrounded by idiots. And not even the useful kind."

She studied them, every twitch, every flicker of resistance. A predator weighing the effort it'd take to crack bone.

"Where's your bastard King? Speak or I'll milk it from your bones."

Her tone was soft now. Deadlier for it.

A soft, melodic coo drifted from behind the cart, strangely out of place.

A veiled figure stepped into view, gliding across blood-spattered earth, not paying attention to the bodies around her.

"Mi'Lady," the girl said, voice smooth as oil. "I have information I can share."

Keothi's attention snapped. "Ah. Someone useful."

She knew that veil.

A Keeper. Seen only when they were needed. So why here? Why now?

The guard on the left twitched, seizing the opportunity of distraction and lunged. Blade flashing.

Keothi caught his wrist mid-strike, twisted, and drove the dagger back into his throat. It slid in clean, then stuck. He choked. Spasmed. Dropped.

She faced the second man, voice flat with disbelief and genuine curiosity. "Tell me, was that bravery or brain rot?"

His twitching fear and confusion provided her the answer.

"Excellent." She glanced at the Keeper. "Come here."

The girl approached, silent and smooth as flowing silk. Her foot slipped on a puddle of blood. She flinched at the acrid stench.

"What do you know?" Keothi asked.

"Your raids are being noticed," the Keeper replied. "I joined this caravan to find you."

Keothi narrowed her eyes. "Using self reference, huh? That's not normal."

"Mm." The Keeper slid a folded letter from her robes. "I was sent by the Mother."

Three diagonal scratches marked the parchment. The same one carved into her back.

Keothi's breath hitched.

Mother.

"I must return," the Keeper said. "The letter has details. She's on the wind."

Keothi tucked the parchment into her vest, expression unreadable. "Then the wind better brace itself."

She turned to the last soldier.

"You'll live. Tell them the Bearbarian haunts. And it hungers."

The first raid had been clumsy. Hesitant. Now the rage growled. It burned. It defined.

She was becoming something else. Claws that cut. Steel that remembered. Shadow made flesh. Instinct given voice.

Each raid carved her deeper. Each kill erased the girl she used to be and closer to the spirit of the bear, forged in fury.

She loaded what she could from the cart: food, supplies, clothing. Then turned without another word, vanishing into the forest.

The blood didn't slow her.

The Keeper didn't stop her.

The soldier dared not follow.

She moved like a phantom through the twilight, blood still clinging to her skin, the iron stink of violence refusing to be shrugged off.

Nestled deep into a hill, she moved the twig-braided gate from the entrance and slipped inside.

The cave's silence welcomed her as an old wound might, aching, unavoidable. It pressed in, heavy as guilt, smothering the echoes of screams and steel.

Each breath in the cold cave pressed heavy. This was the life she chose.

An old campfire lay dead in the center, cold ash staring back.

Off to the side, some food and rations. Nearby, scavenged gear from her latest raids. Each item told a story: brutal, efficient, blood-earned.

She peeled off her bear cloak, blood and sweat clinging to fur. She hung it on a jagged rock jutting from the cave wall. The cloak had become her disguise. Her wild self, her rage, her armor.

The bear cloak hung heavy with memory. A home stolen. A silence never answered.

Keothi laid IronMaw on the ground, kissed two fingers, and pressed them to the bloodied blade. Her eyes closed. Moltrune still lived in her bones, heat, metal, questions unanswered.

A forgotten memory, a distant echo of a forge-fire, briefly illuminated the darkness behind her eyes before fading back into the shadows she now inhabited.

With flint and tinder, she coaxed the flames of the cold fire back to life. It crackled and awoke with slow hunger. Twitching shadows danced across the cave walls telling stories of the ancestors.

She grabbed a rabbit's leg and held it over the fire. Firelight caught on the Dwarven ember in her clasp, shaping her reflection in its curve. No sign of Revin. Just a smudge of soot near the cave mouth.

The warmth from the fire seemed to push against a knot of guilt leaving Spoon.

Spoon softened rooms through existing. She would've smiled through this blood until she couldn't. The chaotic kindness of the witch was a place of safety.

The cloak stared back at her, silent, heavy with judgement. Every fold, every matted patch of fur, seemed to accuse her, to question the savagery she now wielded.

Her voice was rough, a desperate plea to the silence, an argument she'd had with herself a thousand times.

"She would have slowed me down."

Then why did you accept the letter?

Keothi growled at the questions. They were relentless, insidious whispers, interrupting her peace.

She leaned in close to the fire, eyes scanning the sparks. The flames could consume the letter, silencing it forever. Live in blissful ignorance. She wouldn't need to live in false hope.

She held the letter inches above the flame, taunting the fire with an easy meal.

The fire owed her answers, but offered none. It only provided consuming warmth.

But the letter might.

She broke the seal. The wax cracked sharply in the quiet cave.

My Dear Keothi,

I could hardly believe the stories.

A raging bear, haunting the woods.
Find Maren of Saltvik.
She's the key to understanding.
And Remember:
The rage will call itself freedom.
But it will rot you, if you let it.
We'll find each other soon.
Mother

Her fingers hovered over the ink, the familiar slant of the handwriting dragging old ache from deep places. The forge whispered. The forest listened.

"Maren of Saltvik. Never heard of her. But if she's got answers, I'm coming..."

The thought of leaving her self-imposed exile, of stepping back into the intricate web of human interaction, was a bitter pill to swallow.

Yet, the promise of answers held a powerful, undeniable pull. The forest had been her sanctuary, her training ground. But the path forward led out of the shadows back into a world she'd sworn to abandon.

Chapter Thirty-Four

Names Burn Hotter Than Fire

Saltvik reeked of brine, rot, and lies. Even the gulls warned her to stay away. Salt and fish guts thickened the air. Streets slick with brine and the morning's blood. Boats bobbed like tired dogs in the harbor, their nets sagging heavy to dry.

Keothi didn't know what Maren meant to her mother. But if she'd been worth scratching into the letter, she was worth the risk.

She left the bear cloak in the cave, choosing a grey cloak instead. Every step into Saltvik forced her into a costume she thought she'd burned.

She hadn't stepped into a village since the tunnels. Since Spoon's soft hand found hers in the dark. Not her mountains. But the fear? That tasted familiar.

Erland had forged cranks for Borin once, in the days before the war reached their doorstep. Whatever loyalties he held or didn't, meant nothing. Keothi would pay the price, if the path pointed to Maren.

First stop: Ale.

The thought of cold, bitter liquid cutting through the grim taste in her mouth was a sharp, insistent pull.

The tavern nestled on the main muddied road. The wench behind the bar wiped down the counter with tired hands. Brown hair, a beige dress, simple in every way.

"Welcome in. Meat pie and ale?"

Keothi sat at a table in the back, chose a shadowed corner, back to the wall. "Please."

A wanted poster clung to a post, crude lines, wild hair, and a jaw too sharp to mistake.

Yrsa: Keothi scrawled underneath.

She shifted, adjusting her hood, and placed three coins on the table.

The wench set down an overflowing mug of ale and a full meat pie, snatching two coins. "Paid too much, lassy."

The door opened. Two men stepped in, black leather and clean steel cutting through the sawdust air.

Keothi tensed, but forced herself to look like a traveler with nothing to fear.

"Is Erland still around?"

She scoffed. "Old Erland? Yeah, he's still kicking. You'll find him at the forge."

A drunk patron hollered, "Oi! Woman!"

The wench rolled her eyes. "Enjoy, eh?" She turned toward the man. "Cool your tits, Amund!"

She left Keothi to her meal.

One of the soldiers leaned against the counter. "Magnihild, any word on the girl we've been searching for?"

The wench shrugged, filling two tankards with ale. "Still nothing, Rolad. Have some ale, on the house." She moved the tankards towards the man.

He picked one up and sipped, slow and deliberate.

Magnihild's gaze flicked to Keothi, brief, but enough. A warning, or a goodbye.

Keothi buried her face into the pie, adjusting her hood.

Rolad took the two tankards, lifting one in her direction. "Thanks. Keep your eye out. She's dangerous, hit a caravan the other day."

"Will do."

Keothi swallowed the last bite, kept her head down, and left before the steel turned her way.

Outside, the wind bit harder or maybe that was fear trailing her shadow. The cool air carried the forge's siren call. The rhythmic clang of hammer on anvil echoed, the language she once spoke with blistered hands.

Drawn through twisting streets, she stopped behind the forge's door and watched.

The forgemaster's focus was a dance in fire and steel, the hunched shoulders, the arc of his hammer, the raw power in each strike. A memory she hadn't dared touch. The smell of hot iron tore into her, a longing she swallowed hard.

She stepped forward, voice low and sharp. "Forgemaster."

The hammer paused mid-strike. He glanced up, eyes narrowing. "Eh?"

"Sorry to disturb you. I need your help."

"Gods be damned..." He looked her up and down, spit steaming in the forge air. "If you're who I think you are, this is suicide. Come. Quickly."

Erland led her through the back and into the stables. A lone horse grazed, indifferent to history shifting in its presence.

"Keothi, it's too dangerous for you here." He peered out the stable door. Concern shadowed his eyes, deeper than she'd seen in years. "Borin once told me you forged a belt buckle so fine it made him cry. That true?"

"I've got the scars to prove it." She held out a finger, a small, puckered burn, proof she once belonged to something.

He chuckled dryly. "That's a blacksmith's mark for sure. What brings you here? This place isn't safe."

"I'm looking for Maren." She rubbed the side of the horse's head.

His face shifted. "Maren? Gone, a smear on the books. What do you want with her?"

She pulled the letter from her pouch and handed him it.

"You didn't hear this from me." He glanced toward the door, then back. Words slow, heavy. "A long time ago, when you were maybe six, we were raided. The King came to Saltvik, demanded rations and bodies."

A gull screamed overhead, sharp as memory. The horse's chewing was quiet but steady.

"Maren stepped up. Her brother was about to be forced into the King's forces."

Keothi's eyes narrowed. "The King's claws reached that far back?"

He nodded once. "Aye."

"Why hadn't I heard?"

He scoffed. "War and politics ain't for children."

Her brow furrowed. "You clearly didn't know my parents."

"Or maybe you don't," he said, a bitter wink. "Secrets burn hotter than any forge, girl." His gaze held hers, sharp and challenging.

She let it go with the salted wind. "Why would my mother want me to know about Maren?"

He shook his head. "The Gods only know. But if you want answers, her brother Osmond is down at the docks."

"Thanks, Erland."

"Be safe out there, alright? If you find your uncle..." His voice trailed off, heavy with unspoken fears.

She didn't press. Just nodded, stepping out. She followed the road down to the fisheries.

Closer to the sea, life bustled with purpose. Nets slung from boats unloaded heaps of flapping fish. Men shouted over the cries of gulls. The ground underfoot was slick and uneven.

A well-dressed man sat at a table near the warehouse, quill poised, gold gleaming beside the ledger, baiting thieves. A line of villagers waited their turn. His crisp tunic and polished boots seemed out of place amidst the rough labor.

Keothi tapped the shoulder of a tired-looking man hauling crates. "I'm looking for Osmond."

He barely turned, jerked his chin down the docks. "There," he said, eyeing a young man wrestling with a net of fish. The man's weariness was etched into every line of his face.

The net bounced loose into a waiting bin, and the man's grin was bright and quick as lightning caught in storm clouds. A brief, genuine flash of joy in a harsh world.

"Thanks," she said, and made her way down.

"Osmond?"

He yanked again on the net, his focus remained on a rope. "Aye?"

"I was hoping to ask a few questions. If you've got the time."

"Depends who's asking." He hopped off the boat and landed beside her, wiping brine onto his trousers.

"A stranger looking for information. About Maren."

He froze. The warmth bled out of his face until only the stark white of fear remained behind his eyes.

"Oi!" he called over his shoulder. "Taking a break!"

Without waiting, he grabbed her arm, and led her away from the bustle, toward the shadow of stacked crates.

"What do you want with Maren?" The name was barely a whisper, as if speaking it too loudly might summon something terrible.

"I was told you might know something," Keothi said. She didn't flinch. She pulled a small pouch from her side, coin from her last raid. A peace offering. A bribe. Whatever worked.

Osmond glanced at it, gently pushed it back into her hand. "Maren keeps me fed. Your coin's no good here."

Keothi stiffened. "Where is she?"

He shifted. His eyes drifted over the water, on the verge of diving in and vanishing. "Untouchable. Leading the King's forces now. Burning down rebel towns."

Keothi blinked. Her throat went dry. "Wait. The King's forces?"

His silence was answer enough.

"...She commands them?" she pressed, voice lower, tighter.

A nod.

"Let me guess," she said, tone sharpening. "The King gave her a new name."

Osmond's gaze snapped to hers. A silence stretched, taut and dangerous. "You don't understand."

Keothi stepped in, eyes locked. "Try me."

Osmond's hands fidgeted, rubbing salt into his trousers that weren't there. He glanced over his shoulder, then leaned in, words were a guilty prayer.

"They call her Commander of the Shieldmaidens."

Her stomach turned. A sour taste hit her tongue. Not Maren. That name belonged to a firelit memory, not a butcher's sword. A laugh, distant in memory. A boot on her chest. Blood in her mouth.

No. Not her.

"Groa!" Keothi said, the name ripping free before she could stop it. Too loud. The docks skipped a beat as heads all turned towards their direction.

"Shhh!" Osmond hissed. "Are you trying to bring the Shieldmaidens down on us?"

He backed away a step, his hand drifting toward his belt, where a knife might be.

Keothi's hands curled into fists. "I know that name," she muttered, fighting to keep her voice from shaking.

"Everyone does," Osmond spat. "What do you want with her?"

"...Truthfully?" she exhaled. "I'm not sure. But I think I found more than I came for."

He turned without another word. "Forget my name!" he called, halfway to the dock.

Keothi watched him go. No hesitation, outrunning the ghost he'd just unleashed.

Groa. Maren. The same bastard. Why did Mother send me chasing this?

The question burned, sharp with betrayal and bitter regret.

From behind the crates, a voice slithered out, low, velvet-wrapped steel, every syllable deliberate.

"Three scratches brought you here. That's not a coincidence. That's an invitation."

Keothi spun, IronMaw instinctively shifting at her back.

Red hair caught the dying light like flame. Boots whispered commands against the wood. The woman stood with all the patience of a predator who'd already chosen where to bite.

Her eyes didn't watch, they calculated.

Keothi's gut twisted. The blade of recognition cut deep. "Three scratches?" she echoed, wary.

The woman stepped forward, smile slow and scalpel-sharp. "Don't be coy. I'm Vexa." Her voice dipped, suggestive and dangerous. "You joining me or waiting for the ground to rot under your feet?"

Keothi bristled. "If you're with my Mother, I'm not interested in your brand of help."

She turned toward the edge of town, ready to follow the edge of the sea back to the comfort of the woods.

"Careful." Vexa's voice sharpened. "You keep walking like that, you'll convince the world you're not worth finding."

Keothi didn't stop, back against the visitor. "Tell my mother I'm doing just fine. The cave suits me."

Vexa's boots clicked once. "Some of us stayed in the fire. Some of us burned and didn't scream."

Keothi let out a bitter breath, too tired for games. "You keep adding kindling, eventually, you forget what the flame cost."

She stepped into the treeline.

But Vexa didn't move. She just watched. "Groa remembered your name." Her whisper floated behind Keothi like ash.

Keothi's jaw clenched. She kept walking, deeper into the trees. Till a full bodied sprint took her into the forest.

The silence tried to close behind her, but it couldn't swallow Vexa's words.

They lingered like a blade left buried.

Chapter Thirty-Five

Hunted & Haunted

The bear cloak taunted her, a silent, furry accusation. The cloak was a reminder of her mother's warmth and protection, but also of isolation and abandonment. A fresh wave of resentment ignited, tightening her jaw.

The cave's cool air didn't smother her rage. It made it hiss, slow, mean.

"If Mother wants to pull me back into her lies, she's gonna need more than a vixen in boots."

The cloak slipped from the jagged rock and hit the floor.

"Oh good. Lay down and play dead. Just like old times." Keothi sneered, pressed into the cave wall.

IronMaw rested heavy and patient across her lap. She drew a sharpening stone, dragging it slowly against the edge, a sharp defiance.

Sharpen your toy, sharpen your tongue. Which one has your loyalty?

"I don't have to take this from a pile of fur."

She hurled the stone at the cloak, landing with a soft thud.

Cue the dramatic rock toss. Very tragic. Would repress again.

She pushed the gate open and stepped into open air. Sunlight bathed her, too warm and too gentle for the fire under her skin.

She sank onto the stone lip of the cave and pulled the letter from her vest.

Mother.

The handwriting hadn't changed. Smooth as silk, thick with discipline and duty.

Keothi remembered the oak table. The way her mother's fingers guided hers across ink-stained parchment.

It's important, she'd say.

Keothi curled into herself, legs pulled tight, the letter clenched in her fist.

The threads, Bryjna's touch, burned. A choked sob caught in her throat. Was it longing, or the echo of abandonment?

Was this what grief felt like when mixed with fury?

She stood too fast. Grabbed her cloak. Took IronMaw. Action. Escape. The only answers she truly trusted.

"Time to hunt."

The sun bled out behind the trees, painting the sky in hues of orange and purple. She returned with nothing.

Sleep was a cruel ghost that night. Thoughts betrayed her. Memories struck without warning. Even exhaustion offered no escape from the endless assault of her own mind.

No matter how far you run, you'll need to choose.

"This path is mine. I climbed the mountain. I didn't run it. I chose the Hunt. I chose this cave."

You could go back to Spoon.

"Spoon deserves someone whole. Someone who doesn't turn kindness into ash."

And yet you miss her anyway, don't you?

"Gods, that's enough!" She howled into the trees, her voice shredding the silence.

She stumbled backward, clutching her head, trying to tear the questions loose. The raw sound ripped through the forest, leaving only her own torment echoing.

Ah yes, scream at the trees. They'll listen longer than most people ever did.

The days passed, failed attempts at distracted hunts and raids continued. Her body ached, but her mind remained a battlefield of broken logic.

The gate was ajar, leaning against the cave. *Of course you'd forget to latch it.*

She dropped low, muscles coiled, IronMaw humming on her back. The forest stilled.

"Another raccoon? If it's after the jerky again, it's getting the business end of my axe," she mumbled to herself.

She eased open the twig-braided gate, stopping cold.

Warm fire. Roasted meat. Boots kicked out beside her bedroll like they belonged there.

Vexa.

The red fox herself, lounging like a smug sin in silk and ash. A squirrel roasted on a spit, dripping fat into her fire.

"Hungry?" Vexa smiled, calm as a snake on a warm rock.

Keothi drew her axe. "I swear to every dead god, if you touched my packs..."

"Relax." Vexa turned the spit. "You're not that interesting."

Keothi glared, eyes cold. "You don't belong here."

"Neither do you. But caves don't judge." She gestured to the fire. "Sit. Or snarl. Doesn't matter."

Keothi turned, ready to walk.

"Your mother's on her way."

She grabbed Vexa by her bursting corset and yanked her close.

"That daughter's gone." The words cracked under her fury. "Let her bury someone real." She shoved her back hard.

Vexa barely staggered. "You think you cornered the market on pain?" Vexa rose, the fight folding inward. "You think she didn't fight? That she didn't try?"

Keothi's jaw flexed, her chest heaving. "She failed."

"Don't slam the door before you know what she was trying to protect you from."

"Protecting me!? She didn't protect me from anything! She threw me to a fucking madman and tied the bow herself."

Vexa leaned against the wall, all her edges tucked away. Quiet. Deadly. "You're not the only one who screamed, Keothi."

That one landed.

She turned, tone low enough to scrape the stone. "What do you know of the silent scream?"

Silence stretched between them. The fire crackled.

"I was a Keeper." Vexa's tone dipped into something dark and quiet. "I know what it takes to erase a voice."

Keothi's blood turned to iron. "You know nothing about me."

"I know they silenced your scream and you kept screaming anyway."

Keothi's fists shook. "Groa called me the longest scream. A fucking legend in silk."

Vexa nodded. "That's what they do. Call it '*refinement.*' Cut you clean until there's only two ways left to stand. Vessel or Maiden."

A long silence.

Keothi broke it. "What does that have to do with my mother?"

Vexa didn't blink. "That's not my truth to bleed."

Keothi laughed once, hard and hollow. "Everyone's truth, no one's answers." She threw her arms out. "You want to deliver a message? Go ahead. The cave's listening."

Vexa brushed past Keothi, towards the braided gate. "You weren't the only one screaming. You're the only one still pretending no one hears it."

Keothi whipped around, but Vexa was already gone. Footsteps buried by the forest. Not even a leaf crunched under her foot. Keothi stayed, refusing to chase after.

Smoke curled from the squirrel. The silence pressed in again.

But now, it wasn't empty.

Now it listened.

She grabbed the braided gate to shut it, but it collapsed inward with a sad, pathetic crunch. The flimsy barrier she'd once trusted to keep the world out crumbled, wet parchment folding and tearing in the wind.

Her hands clenched. Her shoulders shook.

She dropped beside the fire with a grunt, staring into the flames. They still refused to provide answers.

The squirrel sizzled on its stick. Mocking her. Smug in its silence.

She yanked it off. The heat barely pierced through the battle hardened palms and hurled it through the cave mouth. “Take your damn squirrel!”

The night pressed in. Heavier than fire. Heavier than silence.

Heavier than she could carry.

Soft horse-neighs drifted on the wind.

Campfire smoke, *not hers.*

A constant reminder she wasn’t alone.

She began shoving supplies into her packs, rough and mechanical. Every move jerked with frustration and a desperate need to flee.

“Haunt me? Fine. I’ll find a new home. I’ll leave first thing in the morning.”

Why not now?

“You know why! It’s not safe to travel the roads...” A flimsy excuse, even to her own ears.

Right. Darkness. Real scary. Says the cave-dwelling axe-wielder.

“Bears are harder to kill than soldiers,” she snapped.

Mmhmm. And squirrels are terrifying. Better toss another one into the void.

She curled onto her bedroll, cloak behind her.

Back turned.

Walls up.

Still listening.

Every rustle, every distant sound from outside, held her captive.

The night didn’t offer comfort. Only cold questions and thicker silence.

At first light, Keothi threw her pack over her shoulder. She stepped out into the world. One last glance at the soot-stained cave she’d called her own.

One step.

Two steps.

And stopped.

She collided against someone who shouldn't have been there. A familiar, clean aroma that cut through the lingering smells of the forest. A scent from a lifetime ago.

Bryjna stood there, frozen mid-step, breath trembling in the cool air. For half a heartbeat her hands twitched forward, then stilled at her sides, as if touching might scatter the moment. A presence she hadn't seen in years.

"Mother."

The word cracked something in both of them. Keothi's own throat closed tight. No anger came, just a freezing, full-body clench. Her heart hammered against her ribs, a frantic drumbeat against the stillness. She stepped sideways, out of reach, an attempt to create distance from the overwhelming presence.

Bryjna's lips parted like she might speak again, but only a breath escaped. Steadying herself, she said, "Keothi..." Her voice cracked, raw with a mother's relief and pain. "I can't believe it."

"Believe it or not, I'm alive." Her tone sharpened. "And I'm leaving."

Bryjna smiled softly, "I've been imagining this moment for far too long." Her hand settled on Keothi's shoulder, trembling against the pack and cloak. "Please. Talk to me. I'll leave after. I swear it."

The rage boiled up. Too fast. Too familiar. "You going to call off your lapdog first?"

"Vexa will leave. If you'll listen."

Keothi dropped her pack with a heavy thunk, the fight draining out of her shoulders. "Fine. What do you want?"

"Can we sit?"

Keothi scoffed. "Soot doesn't belong on dresses. Pretty sure that includes dirt and mud."

Bryjna was already lowering herself to the earth, grace be damned. Her movements were slow and deliberate. "By the time I woke up to what was happening, it was too late."

Keothi rolled her eyes and dropped beside her. "Alright. Give me the sob story. So I can live peacefully in exile while I hunt for my disgraceful husband."

Bryjna sighed, tears threatening to spill. "The isolation started within the first two months. Then Vorik struck. Captured all of us." She wiped at her cheeks as tears won the war of restraint. "Your father went missing. Borin… I don't even know."

"It's been almost four years, Mother." She gripped the fabric of her vest to keep her hands from curling into fists. The last memory she had of Bryjna was a flash of chaos. Her mother disheveled, screaming at the captors as they dragged her away.

Bryjna sat now with her legs stretched out, fingers drumming softly against her knees. Streaks of grey threaded her hair. The years had marked her, quietly but undeniably.

"They forced me to help with the transition. Lives were threatened. Vorik swore my family would be spared." Bryjna's gaze dropped. "I stayed in contact with Spoon. She watched over you. Then, a year later, her message came, saying you were lost. Broken." Her voice cracked. "I fled. Found help. Built what I could. But by the time I was ready to break you out… you'd already escaped."

Keothi sighed, trying to listen, to understand. See it from Bryjna's perspective. *Maybe you weren't the only one.*

"I've been building a resistance," Bryjna continued. "Turning Keepers into spies. Gathering intel on Vorik. I think we're close. But…"

"Not close enough," Keothi said.

"Exactly. We may have found your father's location. We could use your help."

Keothi's laugh was low, humorless. "Yeah, of course. Leave me in exile till you need me."

"My dear Keothi…" Bryjna's voice softened. "I'm not here because the rebellion needs you. I'm here as a mother needing her daughter. I don't care who you became. You survived. And you still burn like fire. That's all I ever wanted. That's all I ever feared, you losing that fire."

That stung.

Keothi's hands dug into the dirt. Something raw curled tight in her chest, but it refused to roar. It just sat there, stupid and soft.

"Mother. I don't know. It's..."

"It's difficult, I know. I'm not here to stop your exile. I wanted to see you. Tell you how very sorry I am for everything. I simply hope you'll let me walk beside you for a while."

Bryjna rose slowly. "I didn't come alone. I brought Spoon. I hoped she could say what I couldn't." She stepped toward the cave mouth, stopping where Keothi's sanctuary met the wilds beyond. "I'm needed back at the Sanctuary. Spoon and Vexa leave tomorrow. Please... join them."

She lingered a heartbeat longer, as if she might say more, then turned. As quickly as she'd arrived, she was gone, and the silence she left behind carried the weight of the world.

Good.

She poked the ashes of the campfire. Dirt and ghostfire burned in her chest. The air Bryjna had left behind felt heavier somehow. Keothi's body didn't know what to do: fight, flee, or call her back. She let the silence press against her ribs until it hurt.

Admit it, you missed her.

"I didn't." She sneered at the dead flames, ready to argue with the voice in her head. A soft knock at the cave mouth cut her off.

"Keothi." Spoon slipped inside and settled beside her.

Keothi leaned into her before she could think better of it. The warmth in Spoon's presence dulled the edges of her rage. "You shouldn't be here. You don't need someone broken."

Spoon smiled, poking her side. "I don't see someone broken. I see someone hiding. Someone swinging an axe to keep people away."

A reluctant smile tugged at Keothi's mouth. "What brings you to the rough outdoors?"

"You. As always." Spoon brushed a hand through Keothi's hair, then wrapped an arm around her shoulders. The space between them settled into something comfortable and familiar. Leaving Spoon had been hard, but seeing her again was somehow worse. The time apart had carved more hollowness than she wanted to admit.

"She's using you, ya know? Weaponizing you to bring me to her side."

"Bryjna wanted to take Satira and me to her hideout for safety." Spoon tightened her arm around her. "She didn't come for the rebellion. She came for you. I made sure of it."

Keothi's jaw tightened. "Then why does it feel like she only shows up when she needs something?"

Spoon didn't flinch. "Maybe she's still learning how to show up. The same way you are."

Keothi buried her face against Spoon's shoulder. The tears came hot, unguarded. "How do I even begin to change my view of her?"

"The same way she'll have to change hers. By learning and listening. Through showing up."

Keothi kicked at a loose stone. It hit the cave's wall with a thud.

Spoon's voice softened. "Scars don't need forgiveness. They need to be seen."

Chapter Thirty-Six

UNLEASHED FURY

Keothi hadn't planned to sleep. She never did anymore. Yet with Spoon beside her, tucked beneath the bear cloak, the voices went quiet. For once, even the forest didn't dare whisper.

She woke to damp air and aching ribs, the scent of bear fur and moss thick in her nose. Sunlight crept through the mouth of the cave in slats.

Keothi watched Spoon's chest rise and fall. Something melted in her own chest.

How could she still sleep in a shattered world?

She didn't understand the quiet curled inside Spoon. She craved it. Softness was a luxury she couldn't afford.

Spoon kicked lightly, one leg twitching free of the cloak in a lazy sprawl. She mumbled, sleep-drunk. "...not the spoon drawer... it bites."

Keothi huffed a quiet laugh.

She tucked the bear cloak under Spoon's chin, rose to her feet, and padded out into the waking hush of morning.

Vexa was already there. Cross-legged at the base of a tree, slowly whittling a stake sharp enough to pierce gods. Her expression: unreadable. Her hands: steady.

Keothi sighed and sat beside her without a word.

Vexa didn't look up. "You always wake up like a storm pretending to be human?"

Keothi rubbed at her face. "Thought you were leaving."

"We are. Spoon and I. You coming, or you still chasing ghosts in the trees?"

"I might catch one someday," Keothi muttered. "You'll find other fighters."

"This isn't about skill." Vexa tossed the finished stake into the dirt. "This is about what he broke."

Keothi turned her head. "What broke for you?"

Vexa's gaze steady on the fire like she wanted to climb inside it and disappear. "They told me it was time to breed," she said finally. "No ceremony. No choice. Just... duty."

Her voice cracked. Not loud, but enough for Keothi to hear something splinter underneath. "I carried her. Felt her move. Knew she was real. And the day came... they took her before I could even see her face."

Keothi said nothing. She didn't have words for that kind of wound.

Vexa went on, quieter now. A whisper barely holding shape. "I gave her a name. Keepers aren't allowed a name, but I whispered it while I bled: Vexa."

She looked at Keothi, eyes sharp and shining. "So when Bryjna cut the leash and told me to be free, I didn't choose a name. I stole hers back."

The silence wasn't empty. It was bursting.

Full of everything Vexa had never been allowed to say. "I couldn't save my daughter. I bleed to make sure Bryjna has a chance to save hers." She stood slowly, eyes locked on Keothi. "Don't mistake her quiet for weakness. That woman's grief could drown kingdoms. And she still got back up."

Keothi didn't speak right away. She stared into the fire, nails biting into her palms. Vorik's voice echoed in her skull, velvet over razors. *You are Yrsa.* She exhaled slowly, like the rage might cool if she let it.

"He took everything, but not my name." She met Vexa's eyes, flame catching in her eyes. "I'll carve the ones he stole into his fucking spine."

The fire burned low between them. Vexa didn't speak again. She didn't need to.

Keothi sat in it, the story, the rage, the terrible understanding.

She wasn't the only one bleeding.

When Spoon finally stirred, they broke camp and loaded the horses, morning mist curling from the grass. A nearby garrison waited on their route, once a border post, now crawling with Vorik's Blades. Vexa had orders to reclaim what knowledge they could.

They rode until the sun burned high, the mountain dwindling behind them. The forest thinning to wind-swept fields. By late day, the garrison rose ahead, its walls dull beneath the light.

They tied their horses to the tree's edge and settled in. Keothi stayed restless. Her eyes never stopped. She scanned the place: high palisades, an open gate, guards pacing in a steady rhythm like a silent war drum.

Her voice came low, controlled. "Tell me what I need to know."

"There's an office, second floor in the back. Stacked with parchments. It's said to hold war orders. Names. Maybe even maps."

"How many are being sent to Hel?"

Vexa flinched. Her lips tightened, the way people do when they realize they're dealing with a different kind of monster. "Quiet gets us further."

"IronMaw doesn't wait. It's fed, or it feeds."

Vexa blinked. "...Your axe?"

Keothi smirked. "You've got your ghosts. I've got mine."

Vexa sighed, shaking her head. "Can we at least try not to sound the alarm? Maybe recruit one?"

"The gate'll stand for you. Me? I'll make them scream."

Vexa sighed, pressing the bridge of her nose. "I'll ghost. You do you, Barbarian."

"I'll whistle twice if someone comes," said Spoon.

Keothi lowered the hood over her eyes. IronMaw hung to her side. The axe buzzed with a bloodlust not entirely hers. It wanted names. It wanted reckoning.

Better a weapon that wanted blood than one that doubted her.

Without a word, she vanished into the underbrush, moving with the quiet precision the Shieldmaidens had drilled into her, sharpened by months alone and hunting caravans.

Keothi stepped into the pale spill of light before the gate. She stood tall, owning the path forward.

Two guards flanked the gate, their eyes dull, half-bored.

"Halt! Who goes there?" one barked.

She bared her teeth, a grin gone rabid, and loosed a low, feral growl. It deepened with every step, a war drum made of bone.

Come to the front, watch your front, ignore your back. Noise was a gift. Let them chase it.

Guards scrambled along the wall. Torches lifted. Shouts rose.

The two at the gate gripped their blades tight.

"The Bear hunts. The axe judges. The gods?" She grinned. "They bow to me!"

An arrow thudded into the dirt at her feet.

She didn't flinch. A simple smile formed. "Time to bleed."

As the guards scrambled at the front, Keothi vanished to the rear. She climbed the wooden wall, gripping old fraying ropes that groaned under her weight. At the top, she vaulted over and dropped low into a crouch.

One glance. Two towers. Left and right. She darted left.

Inside, a bow and quiver sat abandoned. She took them, notched an arrow, and peered into the courtyard.

Shouts splintered in the air. "The Bearbarian! She's come for us!" Fear cracked their voices.

The arrow buried itself in his spine mid-sentence. He dropped, bones splitting like dry bark.

A sentry paced the catwalk nearby. She sprinted low, fast. Tackled him sideways, bow slamming into his temple. His head hit the planks with a hollow thunk, and he slumped.

"There's your one, Vexa." Her breath barely shifted. "You're welcome."

She rifled through his gear with practiced hands. A dagger, a short sword. She took the dagger, disappeared into her boot like smoke.

Below, a soldier barked orders.

She dropped.

IronMaw led the fall, and her landing drove it deep into his chest. The crunch echoed. The runes along the haft flared red, heat coiling through her grip.

She rose. Two blades, two throws.

Two thuds. Two bodies dropped, steel humming in their throats.

Four more turned.

Their eyes widened. They didn't see a woman. They saw a myth made of blood and bone.

Keothi crouched low. Grinned, feral and wide.

She charged. "She moves like smoke, and we're supposed to fight that?"

Steel met steel, then shattered. Their swords broke in their hands, useless as splinters.

No match for the barbarian.

The earth turned slick with blood. IronMaw glowed like it remembered every kill it had ever made and was celebrating.

Words were wasted on the dead.

IronMaw sang and bone joined the chorus.

Keothi turned toward the fortress doors, oak and iron. They loomed.

A young recruit stumbled out of the barracks, sword trembling in his grip.

He couldn't be older than Spoon.

Keothi raised IronMaw, and stopped. "Run," she muttered. "No one taught you how to bleed right."

For a breath she waited, enough for the boy to bolt.

She stepped through the doors once the boy tore through the courtyard. Her voice was sharp as grinding steel. "Drop your sword. Or meet your Makers in Hellheim."

She stepped inside. A fire burned. Meat on the table. A Keeper pouring wine. Smiling.

"The stairwell," she said, eyes flicking toward it. "Upstairs, Mi'Lady."

Keothi nodded, moving toward the stairs.

At the top stood a thick, broad-shouldered man, sword drawn, shield ready. He banged his shield, a declaration of war.

Keothi barely blinked. "Terrifying."

He charged, shield first.

She didn't have time to brace. The collision sent her flying.

She hit the stairs, bounced, and cracked down on her back. The impact slammed the breath from her chest, her ears ringing like struck iron.

He didn't pause. He stomped down the stairs after her.

Keothi scrambled to her knees, IronMaw in her grip.

The sword came down, caught on the haft of her axe.

She growled and drove her boot into the man's groin.

He doubled over.

The Keeper moved, swift and sudden, and whacked him across the head with a frying pan.

He collapsed on top of Keothi in a heap.

She gagged, half-buried in stink and sweat. Blood thick on her tongue.

"That's going in the saga songs," she muttered, brushing hair out of her face.

The Keeper blinked at her handiwork, allowing a shy smile to escape. "He... had that coming," she said.

Vexa strolled in. "Done bloodying the place?" She offered a hand and helped Keothi to her feet.

Keothi rolled her shoulders, still catching her breath. She looked to the Keeper, curiously. "Thanks."

"She's one of ours," Vexa said. "The rest? Scattered. Some ran for the trees, others are still searching."

The woman nodded once. For a flicker, Keothi saw no fear in her eyes.

She leaned in, voice hushed but steady. "The office is unlocked. Try not to bleed on the maps."

Keothi grunted. "To the office, then."

They moved through the fortress until they found it, quartermaster's den, center of command. The desk stood thick and immaculate, carved with authority. Shelves groaned with books, maps, and ledgers.

Vexa dove into the drawers, fingers fast and practiced. "Not here. Nothing. Useless..." Her fingers stopped. "Here."

Keothi kept to the doorway, eyes sharp.

She held up a bundle tied with red string. "We're done here. Time to vanish."

They slipped from the fortress and found Spoon waiting at the edge, horse reins in hand. Vexa mounted without a word. Keothi helped Spoon up behind her.

Spoon studied her. "Everything alright?"

Keothi didn't answer. Just tightened the saddle straps.

"I'm not afraid of the ferocity," Spoon murmured. "You don't need to hide from me."

Keothi nodded. "I know, Spoon." She sighed, softly moving Spoon's foot into the spurs. "It's one thing for you to know the rage inside me. Another to see it."

Spoon's hand brushed against Keothi's, briefly. "Don't hide it. Not from me." She smiled softly. "You earned your name. Rage and all. Let the rest of the world flinch."

Keothi wanted to protest. Wanted to argue that rage was ugly and dangerous. But Spoon? She made space for monsters. And wasn't that love, in its strangest shape.

Keothi wiped her brow, left over blood from the recent battle. "I'll try. You're all set." Vexa had already moved ahead. "Think we can trust her?"

Spoon looked and nodded. "Yes, we can trust her. Bryjna has strong instincts." She giggled softly, "Look at me. She took a chance on me, right?"

Keothi chuckled softly, patting the horse. "Yeah, you have a point. Let's go before we're left behind."

Chapter Thirty-Seven

The Mountain Breathes

The mountain yawned black as coal, its ancient breath stirring dust and memories in its bones. From flood chamber to snow-crowned peak, it had learned how to live again.

"This way," Vexa said, voice low and steady, swinging off her horse.

An old mine cart sagged on the rails inside the entrance, rust flaking in scabby sheets. A ghost of industry, silent and waiting.

The tunnel swallowed them in darkness. Dirt crumbled from the ceiling with every step. Wooden support beams groaned under the weight of forgotten years. The air smelled of damp stone and secrets.

"What is this place, Vexa?" Keothi asked, her voice hushed as if afraid to wake the mountain.

"Miners pushed too far. Collapsed the whole lower level. We don't go down there unless we have to."

Torches along the walls flared to life, one after another. The light flickered, hesitant as a shadow poised to flee.

The tunnel spat them out into a yawning cavern: a great wooden lattice of walkways webbed across the vast flood chamber. Far below, a black lake churned. In its center, a waterfall plunged from the stone ceiling, white and roaring, eternal. The sound drowned thoughts. The air glittered with mist. It smelled of iron and ash and old grief.

Home or maybe a grave.

People moved with purpose in the vast space, their footsteps and murmurs weaving through the cavern, a quiet current threading between shadowed pillars. Between tasks, silence hung heavy, as if words could break something fragile

Following winding tunnels, the group came upon a carved-out chamber. Bryjna stood there, engaged in quiet conversation with a Keeper.

"Keothi." Bryjna's face drained, then she surged forward, arms outstretched before the word fully left her lips.

Her mother pulled back, a soft smile on her face. "How was the journey? I hope it was uneventful. There's an increase of activity on the roads."

Keothi's gaze lingered on the chamber walls, on the makeshift desks and the quiet murmurs.

"It was uneventful, except for the raid Vexa led us through." Keothi rubbed the ache in her back, chuckling wryly. "Got knocked down pretty hard."

Bryjna gasped softly. "We have a medical ward, please have them take a look."

Keothi nodded, "I'll stop by. Tell me about these operations."

Bryjna drew herself up, the weight of her armor settling. "We've been taking in anyone who stands against Vorik." Her voice softened, pride flickering in her eyes. "Giving them new names, a safe place to start over. If they're not ready to change, we don't force them."

Vexa stepped forward, clutching a stack of worn documents. A sly grin tugged at her lips as she glanced between Bryjna and Keothi. "Guess who's been busy."

Bryjna's eyes lit up. "Excellent. And the contents? Have you had time to sort through them?"

Vexa shook her head slowly. "Not yet. But it's top priority."

A silence fell, heavy with unspoken promises.

Bryjna gave a small nod, her gaze steady. "Keep me posted, will you? And help them settle in."

Vexa's grin deepened. "Follow if you can keep up."

Before they stepped out, Bryjna paused and said softly, "Keothi, I'll catch up with you once you're settled. I want to hear everything, really hear it."

Outside, the mountain breathed, alive and watchful.

It was no longer a place of ghosts.

Steam curled from forges. Bread rose in clay ovens carved into stone walls. Children's laughter echoed off mine-scarred walls. Fighters drilled until sweat soaked the dust.

This wasn't a kingdom. It wasn't a camp.

It was something else.

And somehow, she was part of it now. A vein in the stone. A whisper in the forge's heat.

Keothi stood outside her room, fingers curling around the iron latch. From the shadows, Vexa's voice softened.

"Stay sharp. We'll be back before you know it."

Spoon's laugh, low and steady, drifted behind her. "Don't let the silence swallow you whole."

Vexa's footsteps faded, Spoon's followed, until only the quiet hum of the forge remained.

The latch clicked shut. Alone again, Keothi sank onto the bed, its unfamiliar softness swallowing her whole.

Inside, the space was spare: a bed, a dresser, four stone walls and the scent of soot and purpose.

Keothi sat on the bed and shifted. It creaked under her weight. The bed felt too soft, unfamiliar, like sinking into empty air.

A small window let in the sun.

It should be a door. Easier for hunts and runs.

She'd lost track of how long she'd lived in that cave. Months surely. Moltrune the leaves were turning. The snow settled. The flowers bloomed. The heat was unbearable, but the mornings are beginning to cool.

She glanced left, then right, fingers twitching at her side. The silence pressed in, thick and uncomfortable. She mapped the tunnels to the nearest exit in her mind.

Too long. Too far. What kind of sanctuary has no proper escape route?

She stared out the window. Beyond, the world breathed wide and wild, sunlight filtered soft through leaves, birds weaving songs into the breeze, carrying the fresh scent of pine and damp earth.

Behind her, the room yawned shut. The door stood ajar, but what lay beyond was a cage. Shadows pressing close, tight walls closing in, a noose of suffocation. The stale, musty smell of stone and forgotten things clawed at her senses.

I shouldn't. But I could. There's a pickaxe stuck in the hall. Unmoving. Waiting.

Her eyes twitched. She rose.

The chill from the stone walls followed her, breath woven into the metal's cold skin.

Veiled Keepers drifted, ghosts of the mines. A child darted through them, laughing, untouched by the hush.

He skidded to a stop in front of her and held out a teddy bear, offering it to her.

She knelt with a giggle, taking it gently as if sacred. Holding it out, she made it run and jump over invisible lands.

"Bjorn! Come on, you've got your studies." A woman called.

Keothi handed it back. He bolted, disappearing into the crowd of Keepers.

She found the lonely pick axe a few doors down. She tugged on it, freeing it, leaving a wound in the Mountain wall.

Keothi thumbed the rough handle and took it back to her room. With a practical grip and swung it into the stone rim. Dust puffed up like forge ash, cracks spidering outwards.

A door. A breath. An escape.

A knock.

Noise disappeared. Her breath matched the swing.

Tap. Inhale. Strike. Exhale.

The rhythm of her other life took over.

"Eh?" Keothi asked, eyes locked on the stone, aiming her next swing.

"Really?" Vexa's voice slid through the bottom of the door like smoke. "Redecorating with a pickaxe?"

"It had a hole already." Another swing, pausing mid-swing. "I'm...fixing it."

Vexa stepped inside, slow and deliberate. She didn't just enter rooms, she claimed them. "You're not fixing. You're fortifying." She dropped onto the bed without permission or ceremony, arms crossed.

Keothi didn't answer. The pick struck again. Stone cracked, dry and satisfying.

"Don't you have documents to study? Secrets to pry?" Keothi asked, not looking.

"Watching you rage is better than half the reports I've got," Vexa said. Her voice dipped low, suggestive, but laced with something sharper. "Makes me wonder what I could do with you on your knees."

Keothi huffed. "Yeah, try another room. That's not happening."

Vexa smirked, leaned back against the wall, legs crossed like a queen on a crumbling throne. "Don't worry. I don't make a habit of taming wild things."

She watched Keothi swing again, slower now. Breathing deeper.

"The tunnels are prone to collapse," Vexa added after a beat. "Not a threat. Just... architecture."

Keothi paused, breath hitching. Sweat at her temple. The stubborn patch refused to break.

"Even the mountain resists you," Vexa murmured. "That has to sting."

Keothi turned, eyes dark. "You want something, or are you here to admire the damage?"

"I want to understand why you're breaking the one safe place we've got," Vexa said, standing now, her tone finally shifting into something real. "What is it? Guilt? Restlessness? The silence making too much noise again?"

Keothi stepped away from the wall and knocked on the stone. "This one? Solid. Won't budge." Knock. "This one? Hollow. It'll cave if pushed. I'm carving a path out. A backup."

Vexa narrowed her eyes. "Escape plan?"

"Exit strategy," Keothi corrected. "If we're overrun, if the tunnels collapse, I refuse to be trapped. I need space to run. To breathe."

Vexa took a step closer. Not threatening. Calculated. Intimate. "You really think that hole will save you?"

"I think it's better than waiting to be trapped. Again."

Silence bloomed between them. For a moment, Vexa didn't speak. Just studied her.

"I know what it's like to live where your only power is the direction you fall. And what it costs to change that."

Keothi blinked.

Vexa turned to go, but stopped at the doorway. "When you're done rage-digging your trauma tunnel," she said, almost gently, "war room's waiting. Bring your axe. Bring your spine." She gave a faint smirk over her shoulder. "And Keothi?"

"What?"

"If you ever want to know what I'd do with you on your knees..." Her grin turned wicked. "You'll have to ask nicely."

She vanished into the dark.

Keothi swung again. Harder this time.

She left the room without ceremony, chalk-dust smearing her hands, sweat streaking through the grime on her arms. Tiny chips of stone clung to her hair. She didn't bother brushing them off.

Her boots struck the carved steps hard, loud, her own little war drum echoing down the corridor. The deeper she descended, the more the silence pressed against her ribs. Heat thickened with every level, the weight of it clawing at her lungs.

She wandered the cavern halls and found a larger chamber. Even here, her mother's perfume lingered in the earthen walls. Brynja sat on the edge of her bed, handkerchief pressed to her nose.

Keothi tapped on the door, "Mother."

Brynja gasped, dabbing at her eyes. A smile formed, fragile as parchment. "Keothi, dear. Sit." She patted the bed.

Keothi hesitated, then lowered herself onto the edge, shoulders hunched, eyes fixed on the floor. The silence remained between them as Keothi managed the courage to speak.

"It wasn't simple."

Brynja slid an arm around her, drawing her close. Keothi let her head rest against her mother's shoulder. "Keothi, it wasn't simple for any of us."

Keothi's voice dropped. "Tell me about the letter. How did you find me?"

The silence deepened, broken only by the hearth's sigh. Brynja rose, crossing to a vanity. From a drawer she pulled a stack of letters, bound in ribbon and sealed with red wax scored by three scratches. She placed them in Keothi's lap.

Keothi thumbed through each one.

"Reports came. Whispers of a bear tearing through the woods, caravans ruined, Blades scattered. I sent word to every Keeper I could reach, had them ride with caravans until one crossed your path. And in Saltvik... I placed the one person I trusted, waiting to find you, to track you, and send word the moment you appeared."

Keothi tore one open, the same as she had received. "Mother..."

Tears streaked Brynja's cheeks. She placed a hand against her daughter's face. "I told you, I fought. I tried. But what can one woman do against a Kingdom? The Berserkers were all I had, and even they were scattered, pressed into Vorik's ranks." Her voice broke. "Keothi, I don't expect you to forgive overnight. But please... stay. Give me a chance. Together..."

Keothi cut her off. "Together we will reunite our family."

Chapter Thirty-Eight

The Last Voice I Forgot

The war room was a sharp contrast, tidy, orderly, smothered in old parchment and recent urgency. A large square table commanded the center, layered in scrolls, cracked leather bindings, and ink-stained plans.

Vexa looked up from a mess of maps, brow raised. "Done breaking walls?"

Keothi shrugged. "A couple more good whacks, clean up some of the dirt. It'll be good."

"What about a door?"

"I'll weave a gate like the one at my cave."

Bryjna walked in out of breath.

"You mean the one that crumbled?" Vexa stood, gesturing toward Bryjna. "Your daughter decided digging a door into her wall was a strategic design choice."

Bryjna chuckled, "Honestly, that makes sense."

"That last gate only crumbled because of a cruel trick from Loki," Keothi responded.

"What do you mean that makes sense, Bryjna?"

"When she was little, she was very restless. She asked if she could have a door in her room. I told her no, for obvious reasons. But once she was older, I made the window bigger for her."

Keothi looked at Bryjna curiously. "You knew I hopped out of my window?"

"Mothers know and see more than children give them credit for." She shrugged. "Now, to the important matters. Vexa, what do we know? Hopefully good news?"

Vexa moved a document toward Bryjna."That depends on how you want to take it. We have a location."

Bryjna's face went pale. She dropped the parchment, one hand clutching her chest, the other covering her mouth. Her legs gave way and she sank to the ground, trembling. The weight of three years' hope and heartbreak crashed down, and she rocked slowly, arms locked around herself.

Bryjna whispered, "He's alive. He's really alive?"

Keothi knelt beside her, hand resting lightly on her back. "Father."

Bryjna broke into a whisper. "I once had a nightmare that his voice would be the last sound I forgot."

Keothi's breath caught. "Vexa, what else? What's missing?"

Vexa's brow furrowed. "They're moving him. We've got a full moon cycle to reach him."

"Where is he?" Keothi asked.

"The Ancestor Chambers."

Keothi's blood chilled. "The family mausoleum. What's the plan?"

"Tomorrow," Vexa said crisply, already scanning another document. "We leave at first light. A scout's confirming he's alone."

She hesitated flipping to another parchment. "But the fortress was too easy. We walked in. Documents were sitting out. No resistance. No alarms...Something's off."

That twist in Keothi's gut wasn't doubt. It was instinct, coiling tighter.

She leaned in to Bryjna and whispered, "I swear, Mother. I'll bring him back to us."

She left, the weight following close behind.

The weight followed her out of the war room. It curled under her ribs, pressed heavy in her boots, sat sharp on her lungs. She walked fast, faster, but stillness was waiting to smother her if she stopped.

Stone corridors flickered past. Keothi had no destination, only motion. Standing still made it harder to breathe.

She was about to get her family back. Ready or not and they wanted her to wait. To plan. But planning didn't keep her from shaking.

A doorway pulled her up short.

Inside, three veiled Keepers knelt, shadows carved from ash. Faces hidden, hands gentle on their knees, their bodies still as statues. Only the faint rise and fall of their veils betrayed breath.

Keothi's knees ached at the sight. Phantom bruises bloomed behind her eyes. Her spine locked straight, stiff, obedient. Her body remembered commands her mouth had long forgotten.

The ghost of the veil clung to her face. Her chest hitched, breath snagging as though the fabric had slipped under her ribs.

Another Keeper appeared from the shadows, just as veiled, just as silent. "Come."

One of the kneeling Keepers rose without hesitation. No sound. Head still bowed. Hands folded like a prayer that never ended. Her steps were soft, weightless against the earth. A ritual of breath and silence.

A hand slipped into Keothi's, soft and certain. Only then did Keothi realize how cold her fingers had become.

"I know, Keothi." Spoon.

Keothi shivered. "Why?"

"It's what they know." Spoon said, a blanket and a flint at once.

Her eyes stayed fixed on the Keepers. "It's strange. Revin kept me from seeing this... but I feel it. A ghost I didn't invite. I feel cursed."

"Even Revin can't block what your body remembers." Spoon tugged on Keothi's hand, "If it's too much..."

"I feel trapped. I can't breathe." The ghost of the veil clung to Keothi's face, each breath snagging against it, her chest tightening as if the fabric had found its way beneath her ribs.

"Then follow me."

They twisted through narrow halls until an archway broke open ahead.

Sunlight spilled in, cutting through the darkness.

Keothi stepped out. Out of the hole. Out of the dark.

She tilted her face to the sun, eyes closed. Breathing.

Keothi dropped to the grass. Spoon joined her, cross-legged and patient.

"I'm turning my room into a cave. Think they'll mind?"

"Do they have a choice?"

Keothi chuckled, raw, but real. She pulled out a small chunk of iron. "I pulled this from the wall. Would you like it?"

Spoon grinned, plucking it from Keothi's palm. "You pulled it out and thought of me?" She turned the iron in her palm. Sunlight caught in its rough edges, scattering light across her fingers. A soft smile tugged at her mouth as she studied it. "This means a lot. I'll keep it. Always."

She placed the iron into a pocket sewn into her dress. A hush settled between them as they watched clouds drift and birds soar. Spoon leaned into Keothi's side, and Keothi wrapped an arm around her.

"Question, Spoon. What happens if my father is moved?"

Spoon sobered. "We can guess. Vorik's pride is wounded, you're out there ruining things. He'll use Halvar as bait."

"And if he's bait, it's both our deaths."

"Likely."

"Vorik believes I'll charge in like a fool."

Spoon didn't argue.

"And Vexa wants to wait until tomorrow, waiting for scouts."

"It's not a terrible idea to lay out the land prior." Spoon shrugged softly.

Keothi dug her heels into the dirt, falling backwards into the grass. "We need to leave sooner. Something is off. We need to catch them off guard." The clouds drifted freely in the skies. "If we all go, it'll slow down the rescue. It'll give the enemy a heads up." Keothi sighed. Spoon sat in silence, letting Keothi work it out. "Will you hate me if I go alone?"

Spoon tilted her head, finally speaking. "Truth?" She smirked. "I was waiting for you to tell me."

Keothi exhaled, laughing softly. "I'll need a map."

Spoon grinned and conjured a sheaf of parchments. “You mean these?”

She pointed toward the horizon.

“Go get him, Keothi. Show them you can’t be caged.”

Keothi folded the map. “Thanks, Spoon. Truly.” She stood and aimed for the horizon.

I’m coming, Father.

Chapter Thirty-Nine

The Hollow & Haunted

At the village's edge, the Ancestor Chambers waited.

Keothi crouched behind a tree, scanning the path. No voices or torchlight. Just a crumbling arch, half-eaten by ivy.

One rune crowned the stone, a symbol: Remembrance.

Beyond it, a mouth of darkness waited.

Keothi crept forward. The gate groaned in protest as she pushed it open.

These tunnels had haunted her since childhood, a place where stories were remembered, and faces erased.

Her mother once spoke of her great-grandmother, the woman who waltzed barefoot into an enemy camp, declaring, "Return him, or I'll outlive every one of your sons and piss on your legacy." She left with her husband in tow.

The stairs led down into damp silence. A lone torch hung on the wall. She struck flint and steel. The flame caught.

Light spilled across old statues and faded plaques, the village founder... a blank-faced figure beside her father.

Is that meant to be me?

She paused at the statue of Halvar. Her breath hitched.

"Father," she whispered. "I'm here."

She bowed her head and muttered a soft prayer under her breath. She pushed forward, deeper into the tunnels.

Rats skittered ahead. Water dripped in slow, cavernous rhythm.

A scrap of parchment caught her eye, brittle, ancient.

Killed them, it read. Nothing else.

It made her skin crawl.

The tunnel narrowed. Cobwebs clung to her face. The air thinned, sharp as memory.

Her mother had been loud in these tunnels, even in silence. Their love, hers and Halvar's, had been a language louder than war drums.

Keothi's stomach knotted. This wasn't about reuniting them, it was about facing the man who'd promised her to a monster. She didn't know if she wanted to embrace him or demand answers. Maybe both.

The stones clutched at her boots, greedy and damp, wanting her bones.

Still, she pressed on.

Scraps of food. A gnawed apple core. An empty bowl.

Her chest tightened.

Maybe her mother's absence was the silent scream Keothi swallowed.

Her mother moved in silence. Keothi, in storms. But the fire came from the same place.

The great-grandmother's story pressed heavy on her back as she reached the oak door.

Iron bars.

Whimpering beyond.

A voice rose, familiar and not, poison on the tongue.

"Coward. Laying there, drowning in your own filth."

She pushed on the door, it opened with ease.

In the far corner, Halvar curled into himself, a broken thing. Above him, a shadowy specter loomed, dripping with scorn.

"You killed them, Halvar. Every last one. The weight's all yours."

Keothi watched, carefully, silently. She placed a hand on the axe, unsure if she should strike. Unsure what she was looking at.

"You handed your daughter over to a monster. For what? Some strangers? Your so-called people? That's what heroes do, huh? Real leaders? Father? Chief?"

Halvar raised his hands, shielding himself

"Lalalala," the voice mocked, "Keothi's dead. Bryjna's dead. And it's all your fault." It crept closer, a predator circling. "Meet your champion: Halvar the Hollow!"

The man huddled in the corner sobbed, the figure continued without mercy.

Keothi stepped forward, her eyes scanning the grim reality of the cell. No bedroll, no bucket, no hole. Just rotten food, an unsettling stench, and stale water.

The creature whipped around, a jagged grey mask cracking like brittle ice. Its eyes glistened, not mirrors, but shards reflecting a fractured self.

Keothi recoiled not from seeing herself, but from the ghost that face had become. That mask belonged to someone she'd long buried.

"Ah, there she is! The bear-slayer who refused to stand by her broken father. Come to save him, have you? Does he deserve saving?"

Keothi's eyes slid past the sneer, landing on the slumped figure, a man hollowed out, not the proud strategist she remembered, but a shadow.

"Father?" Her voice barely a whisper.

The creature's cackle shattered the silence. "The man you seek? A disappointment. Once head of the family, now the reason there's nothing left."

Halvar whimpered, trembled. "Please... no more games. You're not real. You're dead."

"Leave him! He deserves this. Guilty, guilty, guilty. A man who once led armies, now can't even lift his daughter off the floor."

Keothi stepped forward, unblinking. "Alright. That's enough out of you..."

Her fist broke across the creature's face. His face molded around her first, something soft and sickening, guilt recoiling from light.

The mask caved inward with a dull crunch. "Ow! Rude! I'm helping him see. He needs to understand the consequences."

"That mask doesn't scare me. I've worn worse." She dropped to her knees, laying a hand on Halvar's dirt-caked arm. Once muscled. Now wasted. "Father," she whispered. "I'm alive."

He shook, slowly lowering his arms. "K..Keothi?"

She smiled softly, "Yes. I'm here."

"No, no, no. Just another trick. Another illusion..." He wavered in his state. "He killed you and Bryjna. Kept me alive. To torment me... now...." He buried his face back into his arms.

Keothi pried his arms open, and wrapped them around her neck, pulling him in. Forcing him to feel her. Forcing him to recognize her not as an illusion, but real.

"See? Look at him, Keothi. He won't face the shame of what he is. All hail the King of Cowards..." It mimed a drum roll. "Halvar! You trusted a brute, a snake, the enemy and you got your two people killed. Did you really love them? Or was it all a great grand lie!"

He let out a breath, the tension in his body relaxed. His arms wrapped around her.

"If I weren't real, you couldn't feel me. Couldn't hug me."

She tightened her grip, refusing to let him slip away into whatever fog had kept him here. Her cheek pressed hard against his shoulder, the coarse fabric biting her skin. Beneath her hands, he was all bone and tremor, as if the walls had been chewing on him for years. Let him feel that she was solid. Let him feel the heat in her blood. If she had to crush him to make him believe, she would.

"Oh, Keothi...I'm so, very sorry." He cried, the tears burning hot and real. "Please, don't be a cruel joke. Please be real..." His voice hitched, hung thick in the air.

"I'm here and we're getting you out."

It watched closely, continuing its taunts and tear downs. "Aw, he's learning boundaries. How adorable."

Keothi stood, facing the creature. "I know you," she said. "You're the voice that whispers people into thinking they're not worth saving. You seep in through cracks and call it truth."

Her smile was soft, almost pitying. "I had a voice like that, too. You know what I did with it?"

"Trembled? Obeyed? Let it gnaw you hollow? Turned into that?" It jabbed a finger at Halvar, curled and shaking in the corner.

Keothi tilted her head. "No. I named it. I called it out." She shrugged. "Now Negative Nancy is just a pest."

She knelt beside her father, taking his hand gently in hers. "Name it, Dad. That's how it loses its grip."

"Lies!" the thing spat. "You were always the weak link, Halvar. They pitied you. They smiled while you failed!"

His breath hitched. Doubt clung like mud, but... Keothi was here. She had found him.

His fingers tightened around hers. Voice rough and shaking, he whispered, "Downer Dan."

The creature shuddered, but didn't vanish. "You think a name can stop me? I feed on shame, on doubt. On you!"

"Good," Keothi murmured. "And what's Downer Dan?"

She kept her eyes on Halvar, ignoring the flailing thing entirely.

"You think... think... a name is going to, going to, lie! Halvar the Hollow!"

Halvar slowly unfolded, a man shedding a skin. His voice wavered, but held.

"A festering wound that talks too much."

He staggered upright. "I deserve this. But I will fight. I will take back control. And together..."

He looked at Keothi. "We'll kill Vorik."

Echoes cut through the tunnel, shouts, boots, the war drum of pursuit.

Keothi turned, IronMaw in hand, a fierce and determined warrior. She grinned. "Time to get out of the hole."

Halvar growled, "And bury anyone who tries to drag us back."

A dry voice carried down the corridor. "Time to toss the idiot some food."

A softer voice replied. "What do you think that black creature is?"

"How the hell should I know? Keeps him broken. Easier to control."

They both laughed, their boots splashing in the stale water of the tunnel. Armor clinked in rhythm, a cruel, familiar song.

Keothi whispered, urgent. "Father."

Halvar nodded and raised a finger to his lips.

She slid to the side of the doorway, IronMaw ready, breathing shallow.

The door creaked open.

"Back, old man! Don't try anything," the guard barked, holding out a bowl of crusted bread and a bruised apple toward Halvar.

As the guard reached to toss the food, she seized his arm and yanked him in. Slamming the door shut with her back. She locked the axe's haft under his throat, bracing hard.

Outside, boots skidded. Thud thud thud.

The second guard kicked at the door. "Open up, old man! There's only one way out of this!"

With a savage shove, she sent the guard crashing into the wall. He collapsed, lifeless and still.

"Come on, Father. We need to get out of here."

From the corner, Downer Dan sneered. "He doesn't deserve mercy. He's part of it. He let it happen, didn't he, Halvar?"

Keothi pointed to Halvar, then to the door. Block it.

They switched.

Keothi planted her feet in the center of the cell.

"You're trapped," the hallway guard jeered. "Two ways out. You lose either way."

She raised one finger.

One...

Two...

Three.

Halvar threw the door open. Keothi exploded forward, ramming her shoulder into the guard's chest. They both crashed to the ground.

She headbutted him. He went limp. Her own head throbbed.

"Come on, Father. We need to get out of here."

They ran down the tunnels, Downer Dan followed, glee echoing off the walls. They moved up the stairs, past the story-less statues. Torches lit the forest ahead.

Sword on shield. War drums rolling through the trees.

"Yrsa!" Groa's voice cried out. "Give up, and you might survive."

Keothi froze. "Is there another way out?"

Her father scrambled to think, still weak.

Dan whispered into the tunnels, "Ah, the sound of legacy crumbling in the forest."

Keothi hollered from the shadows, "Groa! Long time no talk. It's been a while, how have you been? Well, I hope." She pointed down the hall, hushed, "Maybe we can trap them in the tunnel."

"You've been making things difficult for King Vorik. Choose wisely."

The name.

"Maren, I know the truth. You were broken like me!"

Another taunt by Dan, "She fights like she still believes she's worth saving. How cute."

A low, bitter laugh from Groa. "Maren? I remember that name. A weakling. Not broken. Reborn." She paused. "Ladies! Yrsa refuses to accept the truth. Refuses to conform. Move in!"

Halvar pulled on Keothi's shoulder. "Back to the cell, we'll pin them in."

Keothi and Halvar scrambled back into the tunnel. They ran to the cell, slammed the door shut. Their tomb sealing them in.

Downer Dan chirped, "Ah yes. Nothing says safety like locking yourself in a room that used to be your cage."

Footsteps marched to one beat. Their torches ignited the tunnel, roots bursting into flame, racing ahead of their footsteps.

Keothi braced her back to the door.

He muttered a prayer to Tyr, kneeling beside the guard's unconscious body. "Forgive me," he whispered, slipping the dagger in the man's hand.

A moment of hesitation. Steel to heart. One clean strike. "May you find Valhalla."

He joined Keothi, bracing the door. Sword in hand. His eyes bled guilt, apologies, and love.

Downer Dan grinned, not helping. Just watching. Feeding on Halvar's pain.

"This family reunion brought to you by bad decisions and unresolved trauma." He paused for a sly second, "Also, big fan of the sound of generational failure marching up the hallway."

This time, Halvar punched Dan in the face.

Chapter Forty

UNEXPECTED ALLIES

The march neared. No Groa, just Dan, cutting slurs in her place. An insidious hum in Halvar's still-fragile mind.

A tidal wave of Maidens slammed into the door. The stone reverberated. Wood broke. Flesh slammed into it with fierce fury. The sound was deafening, primal.

Keothi and Halvar barely held the door; every muscle screamed, tendons taut beneath the strain.

Each kick rattled their arms, threatening to tear joints from sockets as the door bucked and trembled, a living thing fighting to contain the storm.

"Father! We need to do something!"

Pale. Bleeding. Terrified. "We open it a crack, split the wave. You think you can hold that line?"

"Do you think you can handle the door?" Keothi countered, her eyes scanning his weakened frame, assessing the risk.

Dan hissed, "She's fighting for you? Pathetic." He curled from the shadows.

"No other options!"

Halvar yanked it open. The ancient oak groaned, then swung inward, enough for the torrent to begin. The door opened into a funnel of death, a narrow corridor where they could turn chaos into a killzone.

The flood came. A brutal rush of bodies and flailing limbs. Maidens propelled by their own momentum and the pressure from behind. Death wedged itself in the gap, bone, blade, and panic crammed tight into that narrow throat of stone.

IronMaw dropped. Spines shattered. Blood sprayed.

Keothi was a whirlwind of motion, her axe a blur of devastating force. Each swing was a precise, lethal arc, aimed for the quickest, most efficient kill. The screams were guttural, cut short.

Bodies piled in the hinge, limp and leaking, forming a gruesome barricade that bought them precious seconds.

IronMaw did the talking now. Each blow bought them inches. The axe sang its bloody song, a rhythmic thunk and wet snap that drowned out thought.

Keep swinging.

Her arms burned, but the adrenaline was a cold fire, driving her onward.

Screams split the dark, the dying cries of those who had come to cage them.

"Behind!" The Maidens cried, their ranks dissolving, faces contorted in terror as a new threat emerged.

Feral war cries echoed back, deep, guttural. Not the King's disciplined soldiers, but something wilder. Older. The kind of roar that rattled bone and stirred blood. Keothi knew it instantly. Berserkers.

"Push!" Halvar roared. "Break through or die in the jaws!"

Keothi carved space. IronMaw relentless, creating a narrow, bloody path through the press of bodies.

Halvar cleaned up, his recovered sword flashing, eliminating any lingering threats, his movements stiff but gaining grim efficiency.

Wet crunches. Slipping steps. Blood in her boots.

"How many more will die before you call it your fault?" Dan snarled.

Halvar felt a sudden chill, a phantom weight on his shoulders, making his already strained muscles burn worse.

"Keothi!" A voice, familiar, misplaced, cutting through the din of battle, a lifeline thrown from the chaos.

Arms rose. Blades dropped. The surviving Maidens, suddenly outnumbered, hesitated, their resolve shattering.

Through the carnage stood a man. Beard of thorns. A jagged scar on his cheek. His presence was commanding, radiating a hardened, battle-scarred strength.

Keothi froze, heart stuttering. Barnaby here? Against all odds. She shoved the thought aside and swung again.

"Barnaby!?" The haft of Keothi's axe caught a Maiden's temple before Iron-Maw crashed down in a brutal arc.

Barnaby's sword stuck through a Maiden's side. He pulled it out, blood flying out, painting the tunnel walls sticky and warm as his blade sang through the air. "Follow us, Bear-Slayer!"

Keothi looked at the fleeting Maidens.

Barnaby barked, "Leave them. We move."

Over the corpses they went.

Halvar's legs trembled; he stumbled over the bodies, fingers clawing at the cold stone for support.

Keothi brought his arm over her neck, bracing him. "Come on, Old Man. Valhalla has to wait for you!"

Halvar chuckled, accepting the help. "It's been too long since I've needed to fight this hard."

Dan cackled, skipping behind like shame with a leash. "Trauma bonding already? How adorable!"

And behind Barnaby, the forest spat out ghosts. Grizzled, glaring, forged from bark and blood. Men chasing the honor of Valhalla. These were not simply allies, but a force of nature, embodying the untamed spirit of the wild, their eyes burning with a fierce, ancient pride.

Torches lit the sky, war drums filled the forest, and pounding hooves rushed toward them. The King' army was terrifyingly close, a relentless pursuit that thundered through the night.

The group ran in the opposite direction. Horses tied to trees, waiting. The sight of the horses was a jolt of hope, the promise of swift escape.

Barnaby rose behind her, "Grab a horse!"

Keothi saddled onto one, pulling Halvar up on it. His body was stiff, still trembling, but he held on tightly. She kicked its sides and it took off.

Downer Dan floated beside them, a banshee grinning like a favored guest at an execution. His ethereal form seemed to dance in the wind, a morbid herald for their potential doom.

The wind sliced. War drums hunted. Hooves pounded. Survival was all that mattered.

She didn't know where Barnaby had come from. Didn't care. All that mattered was that he was there.

The torches dwindled behind them, fireflies of fury, swallowed by the trees. Roots clawed up, old bones warning them back. Branches erased their tracks. The forest closed in, both refuge and snare.

They rode hard into the night, fleeing the hunt.

Darting down roads, skimming rivers, anything to scatter their scent. Only when breath caught and hooves faltered did they slow to a trot.

Barnaby rode up beside her. "You alright there, Runt?" He grinned wide.

Keothi laughed, breathless. "Where the hell did you come from?"

He shrugged. "Saw the bastards on the move near Home. Figured they had you boxed in."

"That's putting it mildly. Where are we headed?"

"Away," he said, deadpan. "Direction's optional."

Keothi snorted. "I know a place. Trust me?"

"Lead the way," he said, already turning to follow with the rest of the Berserkers behind him.

Hours blurred, the sound of pursuit finally fading behind them.

They rode to the Keeper sanctuary. The thought of the mountain's embrace, the hidden depths, now seemed less like a cage and more a refuge.

Vexa stepped from the shadows. Not angry. Not cold. Controlled.

"Do you know how hard it is to build a rebellion from whispers and half-truths?" Her voice was velvet soft, dangerous. "You stir the hornet's nest and call it courage. It's recklessness with a death toll."

Keothi slid off the horse, helping Halvar down. "He's alive. That's all that matters."

Vexa's gaze flicked to Halvar. She exhaled, slow. "You're lucky that matters to me too."

Her eyes found Keothi's again. This time, something older, rougher lurked behind them.

Barnaby stepped forward, giving her a slow once-over. "Want to call me Daddy and have your day ruined?"

Vexa took one slow step forward, eyes locked on him like he was something beneath her boot. "Try it, and I'll wear your beard like a trophy." She turned her disgust on Keothi, eyes like knives. "Don't mistake my relief for approval. I've buried too many because someone '*had a feeling*.' You want to bleed for the cause? Good. But if you get one of mine killed pulling stunts like that, I will gut you before the enemy gets the chance. And gods help me... I'll be happy doing it."

Keothi opened her mouth, but before words formed, Bryjna emerged. Her presence didn't just break the tension, it shattered it.

Halvar was already off the horse, stumbling forward on instinct, eyes locked on her, refusing to blink.

Vexa brushed past Keothi, whispering low: "Try that again without the miracle ending, and I'll make you wish you stayed in the cave."

Bryjna and Halvar's arms found each other, magnets snapping home.

Vexa didn't wait for applause. She disappeared into the mountain without a glance back, the echo of her warning sharper than any goodbye.

He let out a wail, raw, ragged, threatening to split bone, and collapsed into her. His knees gave out. Bryjna caught him as if she'd trained her whole life for this fall.

They clung together, touching and kissing, hearts refusing to believe the other was real, drinking in the presence they'd feared lost. The gritty feel of dirt and blood on their hands as they held each other.

"Halvar," she whispered, cradling his face in trembling hands. "Is it really you?"

Her fingers mapped the gaunt lines and time-etched scars."I see your light... but your smile, your real smile, it's gone. And your eyes, gods... they've sunk so far. What did they do to you?"

He could barely meet her gaze. His lips moved, but it took a moment for the words to find breath. "You're not a dream?" His voice frayed, low and wrecked. "They told me you were dead," he whispered. "Said there'd been a raid. Said you and Keothi never made it out."

Tears spilled, hot, silent. "I mourned you. I broke. I..."

She pulled him in again, one hand pressed firm to the back of his neck, holding the world together. "No," her voice hitched. "I had to find you. Even when they stopped saying your name. Even when they called me mad."

His whole body shook.

"I waited," she said.

He kissed her shoulder. Her collarbone. Her temple. Reverent and desperate.

"Even without you, you were always with me," he whispered.

Together, they said, "To the edge of the map and beyond."

Dan rolled his eyes, voice low and cutting, "Look who's all warm and mushy again. Bet you forgot how messy this always gets. Don't trip over the ghosts you left behind."

The men dismounted and began unpacking: mud-slicked, bloodied, and alive. Their tired movements, the quiet relief on their faces, told their own story of a desperate escape.

Keothi said, "Settle in, Barnaby. This wasn't a rescue. It was the first move."

Chapter Forty-One

REFUGE & REVELATION

The mountain belched warriors drunk on victory and lust, their war cries drowned beneath the slap of thighs and ale against stone. They gathered at the roots of the Mountain, sloshing ale beside the underground lake, fires snapping around them.

The flames, as always, offered no answers.

Her parents were in this mountain. Breathing the same air. And she wasn't ready. Forgiveness was a foreign concept. Simple, they said. But not to her.

Barnaby stumbled next to her. Beard foaming with ale. "Runt! You should be celebrating! We narrowly escaped the horde. Cheers!" He clanked his mug against Keothi's.

Keothi chuckled, "Cheers, Barnaby." She took a soft sip. "You showed up just in time. Where did you even come from?"

He took a long drink. "I saw the army. And your poster. Didn't need either to know it was you. When Bryjna's people started moving, I knew I'd find you in the thick of it."

"My Father was imprisoned there. I can only guess for three years." She shrugged, taking another drink.

"He'll recover. He's stubborn as a mule, twice as hard to knock over. He'll come out kicking."

Cheers erupted behind them as Trond was lifted in the air and tipped upside down into an ale barrel. Keothi's stomach clenched seeing him. He had survived. Her gaze lingered a heartbeat too long before she spoke.

"Yeah." Keothi hesitated not wanting to ask, but needed to. "Where's Elara?"

"In Valhalla." He didn't flinch, taking another long swig.

"Want to talk about it?"

He shrugged. "She stood up. They pushed her down. What's there to say?'

Keothi shrugged and lifted her mug. "To Elara, may your perfect smile shine through the war." She took a drink, and followed it up with the perfect Elara-smile she was taught so many years ago.

Barnaby laughed and followed the drink. "She would have been equally impressed and hated this mountain. It's too cold and too rough. She preferred the warmth and spice, people who talked back."

Keothi chuckled. "That's why she put up with you. Cause you talked back?"

He shook his head. "Na, it's why she liked you. Appreciated your dulled tongue. We were arranged sure, but we grew into each other. She used to say I'd die with a sword in one hand and a lie in the other."

"That sounds like her."

"First sip for the fight, last sip for her."

"Cheers to that," Keothi took a sip.

"I have to ask, Keothi. That fiery redhead." Barnaby tilted his chin toward the edge of the clearing. Vexa stood there, tankard in hand, surrounded by three men too drunk to notice the warning in her stare.

Her eyes were cold as daggers. Her gaze flicked from the loud, posturing men to Keothi and Barnaby. One sigh. One raised brow.

Keothi snorted. "Vexa? She's too much for you. Looks like a damsel in distress, though."

Barnaby smirked. "Elara'll never be replaced, but if a damsel is in need..."

He leaned back, chest out like a half-drunk forest nymph auditioning for a hero's downfall. "Let her steam. Let her ache for my loins, just a little longer."

Keothi chuckled, shaking her head. "Good luck with that, Barnaby."

Vexa rolled her eyes, turning back to the swaggering fools around her.

He nodded toward the campfire-scarred men weaving half-true war stories. "Join in, Keothi. Take your pick. I'm sure they'd be honored."

Keothi scoffed. "I'm not looking for company. Rage makes a better pillow than regret. Bonus, it doesn't expect you to chit-chat through the quiet."

He sipped again. "What about Spoon?"

That earned him a punch to the shoulder, more forceful than playful. "It's a bond I could never repay," she muttered.

"Fine, fine." He rubbed his arm. "Just saying, grief's a full stomach that never empties. Better to eat something sweet before the end."

"Sure. Eat enough desserts for us both before the world ends."

Barnaby rose with a wink, "There's also Trond." Before words and punches could be thrown, he left Keothi to her fire and ale.

A roar went up behind her, two shirtless fools now trying to murder each other with joy. Coins passed around a circle, men taking bets on who would win. Within the circle of watchers, Trond stood. Eyes on her, instead of the fools.

She buried her gaze into the mug of ale. A soft hand settled on her shoulder, pulling her from the amber liquid. Keothi didn't flinch, leaning into it before she realized.

"Spoon."

A soft giggle confirmed. "Keothi."

"You didn't get into trouble, did you?"

"Nope, I'm too innocent and sweet to get into trouble. Told them you went hunting." Spoon smiled faintly. "You've been hunting. I've been listening."

"You're too kind."

Spoon fed the fire a fresh log. "Not kind enough." She lowered herself beside Keothi. "You might want to check on your parents?"

Keothi sighed. "Yeah. Maybe. Or I could pretend they're still lost."

"You could. But, is that what you want?"

"I hate you, Spoon."

"I know." She chuckled, warm as the fire.

Behind them, Barnaby leaned up against the wall near Vexa. He rolled up a sleeve, pointed to a scar.

Vexa sipped slowly, one brow lifted, the look of a woman deciding whether to step on a spider or keep it as a pet.

Keothi let out a slow breath, knowing she couldn't watch the tragic story of Barnaby getting crushed by the Vixen. Her own tragic story needed attention, and her parents were center stage.

"Where are they?"

"They're in there. Waiting for someone to admit they still need them."

"What do I even say?"

"Nothing. Leave your rage out here and listen."

Keothi snorted. "Gross."

She stood, muscles aching, heart heavier still. She wandered down a side tunnel lit by flickering sconces. Her parents' shadows danced, nervous hands across the stone.

She paused outside a half-closed door. A warm glow spilled across the ground, brushing the tips of her boots. She took a breath, steadying herself, trying to gather the nerve to enter.

Bryjna's voice came first, cautious and tender. "Are you sure you're okay?"

Halvar replied, "No, I'm not. But I'm better now that I'm with you."

Something flickered behind them, a smear of shadow, not quite human, not quite gone. It clung to the corner of the ceiling.

Dan's dry voice sliced the moment. "But are you, Bryjna? Are you sure? This man ripped apart your world."

On the ground, their shadows leaned together, a silhouette of old, broken love trying to stitch itself whole.

"You do look like hell," Bryjna said gently. "We should get you patched up and fed."

A chuckle from Halvar. "You always did have a thing for the skinny, haunted types."

Dan, unimpressed: "Guys, I'm right here. You don't have to ignore me..."

Bryjna shook her head. "When is your shadow going to disappear, darling? Will it be like last time?"

Keothi's stomach dropped. This has happened to him before? And Mother knew? The revelation was another unspoken lie, another fissure in the fragile reunion.

Of course they knew. Of course it was another thing they decided she was too fragile to hear. Or maybe they were too ashamed to admit it.

"I hope so," Halvar said. "I broke the moment your name stopped echoing in the halls."

Her hand met his cheek. "You vanished, and so did I."

"Gods, Bryjna," he whispered. "I missed you. I tried. I'm so... sorry. For everything."

"Oh, sweetheart." Her voice rasped. "We both tried. We were too late."

A silence stretched between them. "Keothi? Will she ever forgive us?"

Bryjna said, softly. "I don't know. I've been giving her space. I think that's what she needs."

"All of us," he said, and released a breath that had waited years to escape.

Keothi looked back at her parents, seeing the shape of a family hovering, still unfinished, still aching.

She pushed on the door. The hearth crackled with fresh wood, warmth flooding the room. Her parents sat on a couch, fingers entwined. Her father was a fragile, living corpse. He held a glass of wine. Her mother barely moved, seemingly afraid to scare away a baby bird.

Dan floated around in the shadows. He was thinner than before, grief dissolving.

Keothi took a deep breath. "Mind if I sit?" This wasn't the time for rage, isolation, or disappointment. This was a moment to connect.

Hopefully.

Bryjna patted a chair, with a soft smile. "Please."

Keothi sat. "I didn't think we'd ever sit together again... not with a hearth between us, instead of a battlefield."

Laughter filled the room. Smiles spread. A fragile, almost disbelieving sound, breaking the tension, a brief flicker of joy.

Bryjna's hand rested on Keothi's knee. Halvar's joined hers, rough and trembling. They leaned forward and pulled each other into a quiet, clumsy hug. The embrace was hesitant, awkward, a physical manifestation of years of unspoken pain and longing. It was a silent apology, a desperate clinging to what remained.

They let go. The hearth cast flickering firelight across their faces. The dancing flames painted shifting shadows, making their expressions hard to read.

"I didn't mean to eavesdrop. But. I need to know. Downer Dan. You've seen him before?" Keothi asked, disbelief twisting her voice.

Bryjna chuckled under her breath, a brief, knowing glance flicking his way. "Yeah, it happens on occasion."

Halvar's voice came slow and steady, as if each word carried weight.

"It happens when emotions are heightened. They're too much for anyone else to carry. The kind that breaks you open and reforges what's left."

Halvar raised his glass toward Dan.

Dan tilted his head, a smile spreading like an oil slick. He tasted Halvar's vintage pain.

Keothi chewed on her bottom lip. "I had a shadow. Revin. She helped Spoon. They freed me."

Bryjna spoke, rough and low. "You were never meant to carry this alone."

Keothi folded forward, elbows on her knees. "When I close my eyes, I still see her. Watching me from a mirror that's not there."

Halvar's eyes widened. "Borin was right. You did see your shadow." He sipped on the wine. "How long's she been with you?"

Keothi shrugged. "The first time she showed was at the Mountain Race."

"And you never thought to tell us?" Halvar asked.

"What was I going to say? 'Hey guys, I know you want me to be Miss Perfect, but my reflection is smiling back at me'." She chuckled, "You would have exiled me for sure. A shameful daughter."

Bryjna squeezed Keothi's hand. "You really think that's what we wanted?"

Keothi pulled her hand from Bryjna's, standing abruptly. "I had all the expectations! Etiquette, obedience, strength. It all weighed on me. It was too much! If I didn't meet them... it was exile. It was a curse. I was too much for you two."

Too much. Dial it back.

Halvar spoke, "Keothi. Please, we're trying to understand. You could never be too much for us."

"The one time I tried, you got on a ship, and prepared my wedding." She sat back down. She sighed, "I'm sorry. It's still too much. Painful."

Leave your rage out there and listen.

Bryjna wiped away a tear. "I know. I wish we could change the past, but. Please, give us a chance."

Keothi nodded, "For Spoon, I'm trying."

Halvar took a sip, "Trying is all that we can do."

Bryjna's smile wobbled. Her eyes were puffy, but soft. She reached for Keothi's cloak, fingers thumbing the fur at the collar. "I'm glad you found it. I wanted you to know how incredibly proud I was..."

The words caught her off guard. She'd imagined them a hundred ways, in a hundred different lives, but never here. Never like this. Something tight in her chest refused to give way, not yet.

"It's served me well, Mother," Keothi said, voice low.

The fire popped. Keothi looked up and sensed it before she saw it. A new current in the room. The hairs on her arms rose, a shift in the air that told her of an approaching power, something ancient and knowing.

A figure leaned in the doorway, head cocked like she'd heard the music shift before anyone else. "Three points. Makes a shape again. Shame about the shadow limping behind it," Satira said.

Keothi smiled softly. "A welcome strange sight."

"Or that this room?" Satira mused. She drifted along the edge of the space, smoke curling at the corners. When she stopped in front of Dan, she sniffed once, deeply. "Not tonight. The air's wrong."

She turned back, sharp as a hinge. "You three." Her bony finger traced an invisible spiral. Then she licked it, frowned, and sniffed again. "You three. You're humming with tension so thick it's chewing the walls. Meet me tomorrow night. I don't care if you limp or bleed there, arrive."

Halvar raised his wine. "As you say, Satira."

Bryjna sighed. "So long as it fits the Keepers' schedule."

Keothi looked between her parents and the witch of the woods. "So... no choice, then?"

Chapter Forty-Two

PROVE IT

"You want me to do what now?" Barnaby and Vexa fell in step on either side of Keothi as she climbed the mountain corridor. Refugees pressed aside.

"We need to challenge someone," Barnaby said, as he fidgeted with his hilt.

"Who and why?"

Vexa lifted a scroll. "Barnaby has reported on a barracks. He's concerned about who's inside."

Keothi stopped in the middle of the hall, grabbing both of their shoulders to halt them in place. She crossed her arms, a refusal to move. "Can you two not dance around the topic? I have enough dancing with Satira and my parents at night. Satira and my parents have already exhausted me and it's only been two nights."

Vexa exchanged a look with Barnaby before speaking. "Blades. Vorik's forces. There's a garrison and the reports are indicating they're recruited from other villages."

"Recruited." Keothi sighed, pinching her brow. "Let's move."

Barnaby and Vexa again didn't move. Once Keothi noticed the absence of following footsteps, she turned around. "We're not done yet."

Barnaby cleared his throat. "They can manipulate sound."

"Really? That's the big concern? I feel like forced recruitment should take priority."

"It's more than music," he said. "They can make their armor ring across a valley or march in total silence. Like the Maidens in Irevandor."

Vexa continued, "We need this place to rescue the false recruitments, but also to learn more about how they work their armor. We can't afford an ambush, but we also don't know if it's the maidens or both the maidens and blades."

"So we move to this garrison, I challenge someone of their choosing, we take the barracks and gain information."

"Yes," said Vexa.

They slipped through the crowd of refugees toward the war room. In the war room, Trond and Bryjna leaned over a map, fingers tracing ridgelines.

"More good news?" Keothi asked, setting IronMaw on the table.

"We're trying to locate Vorik," Trond said.

"Father should know. He's been there before."

"He met one of his commanders in a different city. It's not his home."

"Let me understand this." Keothi poured herself a glass of wine. "Blades singing with armor and the snake's hole is missing?"

Vexa cut into the barrage. "We're concentrating on the barracks first. Trond, keep the squads moving and pushing past the mountains. Can you also inform Satira that mandatory fun time is put on pause? Keothi is needed in the field."

Bryjna rubbed her chin in thought. "I'll handle Satira."

Keothi glanced between the dynamic, unsure of what was missing from the group. A familiarity of comfort flowed between them.

Bryjna smiled warmly and moved to Keothi. "Barnaby and Trond have been running the Berserker's in our absence. Doing what they can to hold our home together."

"We've been communicating through codes and letters," Barnaby said, moving next to Trond to analyze the same routes.

"Right. When do we leave?"

Vexa let out a short, disbelieving laugh. "Last time I told you the plan, you washed the place with blood. The second time you went off on your own."

"And it worked..."

Barnaby cut in, his fist clenched tight. "You almost died trying to save one man. That was noble. If you die now, Keothi, you don't get to finish this. You don't get to make Vorik pay. You don't get to lead us out of this mess. Is that what you want?"

The room grew quiet. Keothi's jaw tightened. She lifted IronMaw from the table, letting the weight steady her. "Tell me when we move."

She didn't look back. The tentative warmth of the last few days was still too heavy to carry. She needed the open air, the wilderness where thinking didn't feel like treason. Keothi moved down the hall, the war room's lamplight shrinking behind her.

A hand on her shoulder pulled her back, halting her in midstep.

"Fireheart."

Her pulse stumbled. "Trond. Glad to see you still breathing."

"That's all? Are you planning to avoid me forever?"

"As long as it takes."

The silence pressed in. His hand stayed. Her parents had left her; he'd promised he never would. Promised to be her shield. Promises broke easily in the fire.

His soft breath brushed against her neck. She was back in the rabbit field, his hand guiding her aim. The tension he carried weighed on her.

"You promised to be a shield." She pulled against his hand and he let go.

"It's true. I wasn't there when you needed me," he said softly. "I'd give anything to undo that. All I can give now... is Vorik."

"Then prove it." She vanished into the tunnel, dragging the silence with her. He stayed behind, still her shield, but one she wan't ready to carry.

Chapter Forty-Three

Legend in Blood

A weathered stone garrison loomed over the misty hills, its jagged silhouette cutting a bleak figure against the pre-dawn sky. The air, thick with the scent of damp earth and coming rain, carried the faint, metallic tang of unease.

Hooves thundered against dew-soaked grass, a rhythmic drumbeat of anticipation and dread as Keothi's forces approached.

Steel clanged in the yard, sharp, relentless, the harsh symphony of an army preparing for battle, blades testing stone, armor shifting.

Sweat and dust thickened the summer air, a gritty haze that blurred faces, leaving only grim determination.

Crows wheeled across the brooding sky, Odin's gaze, cold and unblinking.

Vexa leaned close, voice low as the wind. "Bearbarian, recruit, not slaughter."

Keothi sighed, IronMaw humming against her spine. A familiar comfort.

Killing would've been easier.

She stepped forward, just beyond the reach of drawn arrows. "The Bearbarian has arrived! Send out your strongest man to face me! Slay the Legend in Silk, and our forces will leave! Fail, and we take the garrison."

Silence shrouded the yard. Steel fell silent. Every eye pinned her, measuring, gambling, praying they weren't next.

Keothi spoke again, steady and cold. "Save the lives of your boys and men."

A voice rang out in response. "We will send a challenger! Give us your word, if you fall, your forces will leave!"

The ranks behind Keothi hammered swords and axes against shields, echoing their fierce agreement. A deafening chorus of metal, a primal roar of assent, shaking the very ground, leaving no doubt about their commitment.

The gate swung open. Slowly, reluctantly, revealing the silhouette of a formidable opponent.

Keothi flung her cloak aside. IronMaw hummed to life in her grip. The red runes blazing, casting an infernal glow.

A towering man in full armor stepped forward, halberd and shield in hand. He was a wall of steel and muscle, his helmet obscuring his face, making him an anonymous force of defiance.

Vexa watched the garrison. "Are you sure you don't want armor? Or a shield, at least?"

A hunger flashed behind Keothi's eyes. "Those who carry shields are the ones planning to get hit."

Vexa crossed her arms, eyes narrowing. "Ten coppers say she breaks his shield before he makes her bleed."

Barnaby snorted. "You're on, but if she bleeds? I want double if she still wins."

Vexa smirked. "Oh, she'll win. I just want to see if he cries when she takes his kneecaps."

They circled. Dust rising. Eyes locked. The air crackled, tension thick enough to cut with a blade. Every step, every breath, deliberate. A silent language of strategy and threat.

The crowd pressed forward, boots grinding stone, breath held. The crowd and crows were hungry for blood.

"The Bearbarian hungers," Keothi sneered. "The axe judges. The Gods bow only to me."

She dug a heel into the dirt and charged. IronMaw held low, a blur of red runes and gleaming steel. She lunged like a whip of muscle and metal, aiming for his ankles.

His shield slammed down. A wall of iron, blocking her blow.

She rolled, a blur of rage, and came up snarling.

His halberd swept where her head had been. Missed by heartbeats.

She struck the shield.

It shuddered. The wood groaned against the force. Metal bent, but it held.

He surged with his full weight. Pushing the shield towards her chest, making contact.

Pain bloomed through her ribs. She staggered back, breath ragged.

He was strong, no question, disciplined too. Yet, tenacity roared louder than pain.

Keothi regained her ground, planting her feet. A grin broke through the dulling ache. Pain was proof she was still in the battle.

"Good," she said, spitting blood. "I hate killing amateurs."

He slashed low, followed by a quick arc high. Each arc was clean and efficient. His halberd belonged in his hands since birth.

She leapt, barely cleared the bite of steel. IronMaw answered.

One strike. Two. Sparks danced with every blow.

Sparks flared. Steel shrieked. The air rang with the stubborn heartbeat of war.

She roared, a guttural, soul-deep sound, and came down hard.

The shield exploded sending a storm of splinters outwards. The wood and metal shrieked.

The crowd gasped, stepping back as fragments rained around them.

He dropped the wreck, his fear finally showing through the slit of his visor. Now it was just the halberd and what was left of his pride.

They clashed. Sidestep. Stamp. Slash. Roll. Exhaustion began to settle in Keothi's bones. Her muscles burned with the dance of steel.

The halberd found her thigh, ripping against it. White fire erupted.

Her leg buckled with her breath.

He came in fast not missing the opportunity. Another slash, against the ribs this time.

A searing line of pain. She dropped hard, the dirt greedy beneath her.

No. Not here. Not now.

She snarled, rolled back, shoved herself to her feet. Blood dripped like rust from open seams.

IronMaw rose, humming, trembling in her grip, knowing the fight wasn't over. The sound that ripped from her throat wasn't human. It was survival made noise. She brought it down, aiming for the halberd this time instead of an opening.

The man wasn't expecting. His response delayed. The halberd snapped under the crash of the axe. It split like brittle bone. He stumbled, shock cracking through his mask of calm.

She didn't hesitate. A boot to the chest. A clean, brutal shove.

He hit the ground with a grunt. The armor betrayed him as he tipped to the side to stand back up. He flipped his halberd around, as Keothi lunged towards him. IronMaw glimmering in the afternoon sun.

He shoved the jagged haft toward her like a makeshift spear. Defiant, even in defeat.

The crowd held their breath.

She didn't hesitate. One final swing. IronMaw crashed down.

A sick, echoing crack. A silence born of awe.

He lay still. Eyes wide. The halberd dropped from his fingers. IronMaw released him with a wet squelch. Blood soaked the splinters, thick and dark, painting the dirt like war paint.

And behind her, just beyond the ring, rose the roar of war: the clash of blades, the thunder of shields. A chant filled the world. "Bearbarian! Bearbarian! Bearbarian!"

The forge of the world roars once more.

But for this heartbeat?

Only her.

IronMaw's burning runes dimmed, it was sated. For now.

Barnaby, low: "Well. I owe you ten coppers and a kneecap."

Vexa grinned. "Told you. Legend in silk, legend in blood."

The crowd's roar collapsed like a wave dragged under. What remained was breath and rust and awe.

Keothi stepped through the gates, limping. Blood trickled from her wounds as they passed the large oak doors. A shadow made of defiance and dust.

The garrison didn't lower their weapons because they were told to. They lowered them because they saw her.

Boys, too thin. Men, too tired. Every one of them holding weapons they no longer believed in.

The silence wasn't peace. It was an aftershock.

One squire locked eyes with her. Raised his chin. His sword hit the ground a second later.

Behind her, the wind rustled banners. Inside her, the ache screamed. She did not flinch, but something was wrong.

Not in the way the garrison sagged, or the way the Blades stared.

But in the quiet itself.

It wasn't just silence.

It was waiting.

White-knuckling IronMaw, Keothi limped through the haze, following the thick, metallic air that pulled her deeper into the garrison. The axe felt heavy, thrumming with a strange, unnatural pulse, guiding her toward something unseen.

Barnaby and his squad moved with ruthless precision, disarming the men, forcing even the boys to their knees. No exceptions. No hesitation. They stripped the last scrap of defiance from the surrendered.

Vexa fell into step beside her. "You got hit."

Keothi smirked, tearing her sleeve and knotting it around the wound. "Just a scratch. Tell me about the Blades."

"When Keepers give birth, the child's destiny depends on gender."

A soft groan escaped Keothi. "Great. Why is it that all destinies are tied to what's in our pants, Vexa?"

Vexa stopped mid-stride and bent over, laughing. "Keothi, I love your mind."

"Oh good," Keothi muttered, grinning. "Glad I can be your entertainment. You done laughing, or are we talking?"

"Right, right." Vexa wiped her eyes, still chuckling. "As Vorik takes villages, he recruits volunteers."

"Let me guess. Women become Vessels and the men go to the Blades to die."

"You nailed it."

Barnaby joined them, wiping soot from his brow. "Thin crew in there. Malnourished. Could take time to bring them up to strength."

"Do what you can," Keothi said.

Trond burst from the Keep, wild-eyed and panting. "We've got a problem."

She snapped to him. "What is it?"

His gaze darted to Barnaby. "Another altar."

Keothi frowned, gut twisting with unease. "Altar?"

They nodded in unison. "Come on, Keothi," Barnaby said, already moving.

The stench hit first—rot, blood, unwashed bodies battling the wind. Berserkers moved among the Blades, gathering their weapons and gear.

The garrison's thick timber walls stood strong, weather-worn but well-kept. A walkway lined the perimeter; below, scaffolding braced the basics. They reached the Keep, but veered left, toward the chapel.

Keothi shoved open the door.

The pews stared back. A congregation of wood and silence, waiting for judgement. At the far end, an altar loomed. Wrong in shape. Worse in presence.

"Barnaby?" she asked, but her voice was already trembling.

IronMaw pulsed against her spine. Each step forward felt ritualistic, her feet slow, deliberate. The silence wasn't peaceful. It was *too still.* Too *complete.*

Not holy. Not safe.

Something was pretending to be sacred and wearing its skin too tight.

At the center stood a single rod. Up on it: a mask. No ropes. No hooks. Just hovering, watching the quiet chapel waiting for another offering. Or a warning.

Its white surface was smooth. The eye holes weren't holes at all, but it still watched her. A still, malevolent thing that pulled the air inward.

It didn't feel foreign. No, worse. It felt enthroned.

As if it had built the room around itself.

At the mask's edges, names scorched into the metal. Around the altar: scraps of clothing, folded with military precision. Small glass jars filled with hair. Each labeled in the same perfect script.

As she stared, patterns emerged—etched into the mask, faint at first, then clearer, spiraling inward with no true beginning or end.

You will be loved when you are no one.

Keothi's gut turned. The mask felt ancient, predatory, coiled. Not power alone, purpose. It wanted something.

It had always been here, waiting.

The Mask twitched.

Just a flicker. A glitch in reality.

A blink too long. A breath too short.

Her knees locked. Her body froze.

For a moment, she thought of Sigmantis.

No. Not him. Something colder. Hungrier. Something worse.

No name. No shape. Just the feeling of being prey.

Not a grief-shadow like Revin. Not a whispering weight like Dan. This was different. This one didn't mourn.

It hunted.

IronMaw rose without her permission. The runes lit up like they'd seen a ghost and decided to bite it. The axe swung.

CRACK.

The altar split. The sound tore the air and something deeper than stone screamed.

She wasn't alone. Something had seen her through that mask.

Now it knew her name.

This wasn't a victory. It was a declaration.

A hand gripped her shoulder. Steady. Firm. Too warm to be death.

Keothi flinched. "Spoon."

A dry voice, "No. Vexa."

Light rushed back. Sound returned. Her pulse thudded in her ears. The world had seams again, but they didn't match.

Reality snapped back like someone forced the wrong piece into a puzzle.

A halo of blood ringed her boots.

"Vexa, right. That altar," she said, throat tight. "It wasn't..."

She couldn't look away. The mask lay in shards, but the dread hadn't left.

It lingered. Clung to her bones, refusing to release their prisoner.

Vexa eased her down to a pew.

Keothi felt unstitched like the room had come apart and barely sewn itself back together.

"Or maybe," Vexa said quietly, "maybe you got hit in the head too hard."

Keothi didn't answer. The words stuck to her skin like ash.

You will be loved when you are no one.

She tore a scrap of tunic from the pile on the floor and wrapped the mask carefully. No bare contact. Not worth the risk.

Even in shards, it pulsed, like it remembered being whole. A heartbeat with teeth.

From the door, Trond and Barnaby stood watching quietly.

Trond sat next to Keothi, a soft hand on her knee. "They've been occurring more often. This was the first time one was broken though."

Keothi forced herself to focus. "Do we know anything?"

Trond shrugged, "Only that if we hit a village or a garrison, one is bound to be somewhere."

Keothi leaned forward as Barnaby and Vexa joined them. "You'll be loved when you are no one," she repeated. The sentence scraped against her spine like teeth. "Maybe Satira will know. Or guess. Or lie well enough to sound like the truth."

The shards shifted against its containment. Enough to keep her skin crawling and her nerves unsteady.

Chapter Forty-Four

TO RIVAL THE GODS

Deep in the mine shafts beneath the sanctuary, the stone walls held their breath, cold and damp as a grave. The sharp bite of poultice herbs battled the stink of sweat and pain. The air itself seemed to vibrate with lingering echoes of pain.

Someone moaned in sleep, another whimpered for a mother long dead. Broken prayers tangled in the silence, rising faint, like desperate smoke from the cots lining the narrow chamber. Each breath in this place was a conscious effort, filled with the collective agony of the wounded.

Spoon sat at the edge of a cot, wringing out a threadbare cloth like it owed her answers. Her hands were steady, the kind of stillness that comes from holding it together with the last frayed nerve. She hadn't stopped moving since they left. Not really. Her exhaustion had etched into the lines around her eyes, yet her movements were precise.

The mask's presence twisted in Keothi's satchel, a hateful hum pressing against her ribs. It hadn't moved, yet the air buzzed around it, alive with malice.

Keothi was led to a wide chamber lined with cots and bandages, a tomb for the barely living. She set IronMaw on a stand beside her cot.

Spoon dragged a chair close, voice raw as she threaded needle through torn flesh. "Keothi… you weren't supposed to get hit."

Keothi gave a breathy, bitter laugh. "I know. What can I say?"

The needle wove in and out. Spoon's grip tightened on the thread, tugging harder than she meant to. "You won't get hit again. That's a start." The cloth scraped harshly against the skin.

"Ow! Spoon..." Keothi winced, face pinching.

"You need a little roughness in your life," Spoon teased, but the tremble in her hands betrayed her. "Now hold still."

A newly recruited ShieldMaiden slipped in quietly. "Spoon, training this afternoon."

"I'll be there," Spoon said, without looking up.

"Training?" Keothi asked.

Spoon shrugged without looking up. "I need to learn how to fight. Can't hide under a cot forever."

"Your spirit," Keothi warned.

Spoon's warm hand brushed Keothi's cheek. "You're sweet. But you don't survive war if you don't wield a sword."

Keothi sighed, lifting her arms despite the stretch of fresh bandages. "Let me train you, then."

Spoon shook her head, beginning to wrap the wound again. "You'll go easy on me."

"Of course I will..."

"Ingvild won't."

Keothi scowled. "I don't like it."

"And I don't like you going feral." Spoon stood, brushing her palms on her apron. "Sometimes we have to compromise." She offered a smile, kind but unreadable. "Take it easy, yeah? I'll come check on you later."

Keothi dropped her arms, sore and raw. "Don't work too hard."

"I never do," Spoon nodded toward the far wall. "But... looks like you've got a visitor."

Keothi followed her gaze to Satira, standing still as a statue, eyes sharp as blades. Without a word, she crossed the room and stopped in front of Keothi.

"Grab the satchel, now."

Spoon's smile was polite but guarded. "Satira."

Keothi frowned, "You alright?" She picked up the satchel and held it out.

Satira yanked it open and froze. Whatever she saw inside drained the air from the room. Her gaze snapped to Keothi. "Follow." She turned on her heel and strode toward the tunnels.

Keothi shot Spoon a look. "This isn't going to end in screaming, is it?"

"Only one way to find out," Spoon said, already moving to another cot.

Keothi followed Satira through winding tunnels into the dug-out cavern used for family gatherings.

"It's been itching for a mouth since you found it," Satira said at last.

The moment her fingers brushed the leather, the satchel twitched, alive. The flap gaped, and a dry whisper coiled into her ear, warm as breath: "They'll never understand you. But I will."

Satira's face tightened. She flung the satchel to the ground. It struck with a metallic clang, spilling splinters of carved bone and rusted clasps.

"What is it?" Keothi asked, voice tight.

Satira didn't answer. She swept the fragments into the fire and tossed the satchel in after them. "It wants something: identity, silence, attention. Some curses act like children."

From a hidden pocket, she drew a pouch of gray herbs. She tossed three pinches into the flames, each falling as ash. "Three for flame, one for ash." She snapped her fingers, spat into the fire.

The satchel screamed, not in sound, but in pressure. The air clenched around them. The fire flared blue-white, shadows bending in impossible directions. Keothi's knees buckled under the weight of it. Her ears rang, her skull ached. The silence that followed struck harder than the sound.

Satira's hands trembled as she straightened. "He may have found a spark to extinguish. But I've set the barrier."

"Who?" Keothi's voice barely rose above the settled silence.

Satira stared into the flames. "Virell."

Halvar and Bryjna stood in the door, Dan at their side.

His fingers shoved into his ears. "That was one way to wake up..."

"Satira?" Bryjna asked.

Halvar sank into the chair like he'd been hit. "We thought Virell was just a word. A story."

Satira's gaze went distant, as though tracing runes only she could see. "When the gods slew Ymirr, his Shadow lingered. It split in two. One half was Nyrr, blessing the few who could bear the weight of their own shadow. She gave them sight beyond the mask, and with it, a weapon the gods could not touch: the truth of who they were."

The fire popped. Shadows on the cavern wall seemed to lean closer.

"They gathered those blessed by Nyrr, and built Moltrune. Not to rival the Dwarves. To rival the gods. Every hammer strike said the same thing: Look away, or remember what you've tried to forget." Satira's mouth curved in something too sharp to be a smile. "And gods... hate being reminded of their mistakes."

Her voice lowered, the weight of it pressing close. "But the other half of Ymirr's Shadow was Virell. Where Nyrr gave form, Virell gave erasure. He promised safety with order, love in stability. He whispered that it's easier to be no one, easier to wear the mask. And the longer you wear it, the more you forget you ever breathed without it."

Bryjna leaned forward, voice barely louder than the embers snapping in the hearth. "My father warned of his reach. I thought it was a simple winter tale to keep us entertained."

"Erasure isn't a story," Satira said. "It's a hand over the mouth. A weight on the chest. What did he tell you?"

Bryjna swallowed. "That Virell would lay a black blanket over the world. Suffocate it. His voice could slip into the mind and turn your own senses against you, make you beg for the mask."

Satira nodded grimly. "And now he's building again. Inch by inch. The shrine Keothi found?" She glanced at the fire, eyes sharp. "That's not just a shrine. That's his forge."

From the shadows, Dan said quietly, "Once he plants one, it never stops growing."

Satira didn't look at him. "Virell doesn't retreat. Every time he's forced back, he leaves something behind to keep his grip. They don't go quietly. They leave masks behind."

Keothi's eyes shifted to IronMaw, leaning against the doorframe. "If Moltrune's forges made weapons to buy the gods' silence... then what does that make IronMaw? I forged it there."

Satira crossed the room. She stood close to the axe but didn't touch it at first, breathing in like she could smell its history. Then she traced a single finger down the haft. Her shoulders tightened. "Keothi... this thing isn't alone."

Caution threaded through her words. "After I forged it... a spirit appeared. Said he was my uncle."

Halvar froze. His head lifted slowly, eyes narrowing. "Kern. My youngest brother. He... didn't come back."

Keothi's breath hitched. "Why didn't I know?"

Bryjna's gaze dropped to the floor. Her voice was barely a whisper. "Because we didn't know how to tell you."

Halvar's jaw worked as he stared into the fire. "Borin, Kern, and I found IronGrove together. Three brothers went in. Two came out."

From the shadows, Dan's voice curled like smoke. "Always leaving your loved ones behind."

Keothi's mouth tightened. "Shadows. Uncles. What's next, a secret sibling in a closet?" The joke fell flat. Her gaze dropped to the axe. "Uncle Kern. I met him. In the forge."

Halvar straightened, sharp and sudden. "You what?"

"I faced Sigmantis," Keothi said, her throat dry. "Kern appeared. Said he was my uncle. After I forged IronMaw... he vanished. Into the axe."

The weapon shifted as if it had heard. It tipped and hit the floor with a metallic thud, the sound ringing too long in the air. A single rune flared blue, cold light crawling over their faces before fading like breath on glass. A faint vibration hummed through the floorboards.

Satira flinched, fingers twitching, but stayed silent.

Halvar stared at the axe. “Kern... inside the axe?”

Keothi nodded. IronMaw shimmered faintly, a low thrum rising in the room.

Satira spoke at last. “That’s no relic.” She let the silence stretch before she said the words. “It’s a god-slayer.”

Keothi’s breath hitched. “And?”

Satira’s gaze locked on hers. “It chose you.” A breath held. “And it has a purpose.”

Keothi’s words came out brittle. “Do I get a say before the gods show up with an eviction notice?”

“Only the Fates know,” Satira said, almost kindly. “And they’re not speaking, dear.”

Chapter Forty-Five

TAMED & TAMING

With each swing, the stone yielded. She was turning a window into a door. Every bedroom deserved a way back to the wild.

A soft knock at the actual door made her pause, breath catching.

Spoon giggled, slipping in. "Still at it?"

Keothi nodded. "Raids. Recruits. Reports. War waits for no one."

Spoon shut the door. "I saw something unexpected. Barnaby and Vexa."

"They're commanders. They talk." Keothi knocked a clump of stone loose.

"Sure, if talking involves tongues."

The pickaxe paused mid-swing.

"A bursting corset with metal and furs. Tongue."

"Great, now I need to wash my brain."

"I know!"

"Maybe we should make Mother and Father separate them." she muttered, then chuckled. She turned back toward the hole in the wall and resumed swinging. "Spoon. Tell me a story."

"A story?"

"Yeah. A story, something I don't know. Haven't heard."

Spoon shrugged, "Alright, once upon a time there was a Princess named Allandrea."

Keothi looked over her shoulder and glared. "Not a bedtime story. Something about you." Another swing, buying a moment. "You're always grounding me, lifting me. I love you for it. But you can't just be Keothi the Tamer."

Spoon laughed. "But I enjoy being Keothi the Tamer." She pulled her legs into herself. "Alright. I remember when I was really little, I snuck outside. The air was cold. The sky was clear. No one was around. Not a soul, not a breath."

Keothi leaned the pickaxe against the wall and crawled toward her. She rested her head on Spoon's lap.

"I unclasped the veil and took it off. For the first time. Outside of my room." Spoon touched her throat, memory flickering in her fingertips. "I thought the stars would be dim, but they were sharp. Real. Not softened through gauze or secondhand stories. There was this cluster, kind of shaped like a bear. I didn't know the name. But it burned behind my eyes, it saw me."

She glanced toward the hole in the wall, squinting, trying to spot those stars despite the afternoon sun flooding the room.

The words softened. "Years later, I was working at an astrologer's home. Saw maps of the stars. I asked the astrologist about it. That one, it's called Ursa Major. The Great Bear. And then the Keepers started calling you Yrsa..."

The name hit like cold water down Keothi's spine. Spoon's fingers never stopped stroking her hair.

"...When you found the bear cloak, I knew. The bear saw me. The bear named me. When I saw you, I knew I was meant to help the bear." Her gaze glanced at the hook where the cloak hung.

Keothi's vision shimmered. Moisture blurred the edges. Her heart thudded in her ears. "Spoon..."

Spoon smiled down at her. "It's something I've never told anyone. I didn't plan to. You've tamed me too, you know. I'm not just your support. You're mine."

Keothi exhaled. "I'm standing because you reminded me how."

Spoon poked her stomach. "Sisters forged in the fire, learning how to be human together." She giggled. "Now. Door, or nap?"

Keothi smiled, eyes heavy. "The door can wait. I can't move right now."

The afternoon slipped by in a soft blur, time folding quietly around the slow scrape of wood and whispered breath.

As the last hinge clicked home, a distant murmur drifted through the hallway, a familiar voice carrying the urgency of duty.

Spoon glanced toward the door, a flicker of concern in her eyes. "Satira's waiting," she said softly.

Keothi exhaled, reluctant but resolute. "Another Cuddle Cult Check-In. Satira insists it's healing. I think it's emotional hazing with snacks." She pushed herself upright. "Save me? Please?"

Spoon giggled. "There's no saving you."

Keothi stepped into the shadowed corridor leading to what awaited.

When Keothi arrived, ear intact, her parents were already there with Satira. Dan hunched, looking weaker with each passing day, while Halvar's frame had filled out again, muscle threading back over bone.

"Sorry I'm late," Keothi said, pouring herself a glass of wine and settling beside her parents. "I was building a door with Spoon. So, what's the next myth we're about to learn?"

Bryjna and Halvar chuckled.

Halvar said, "Oh? Building a door with Spoon huh?"

Keothi rolled her eyes. "Oh god, not you too..."

Bryjna shook her head. "Come on you two. No bickering."

Satira smiled, "The dark cloud is lifting between you three. Means it's working. Shall we continue?" She glanced toward the shadowed corner where Dan lounged and muttered, "He still hasn't left you, has he?"

Halvar followed her gaze. "Nope. Doesn't seem too keen on leaving either, but he does seem to be weaker."

Satira drifted through the room, fingertips trailing like a half-forgotten thought. She paused at the table, swirling a cup of wine, then jabbed a bony finger into Dan's chest.

Dan flinched."Hey! You old bat!"

Satira's laughter rang sharp as shattered glass. "You left pieces of yourself behind, Halvar. This ghost found them first."

Dan shuddered, memory biting deep. "Don't you have a coffin to crawl back to?"

The flickering sconces threw shadows that writhed and stretched along the cracked walls. The air thickened, laced with burnt wood and old regrets.

Satira's shadow peeled from the floor, remembering itself into form, stretching along the beams before gathering into shape. Limbs, neck, eyes.

"Noema," Satira breathed.

The shadow-woman hovered a foot above the ground, wringing her hands like a worn cloth. She cracked her neck with a dry snap, cocked her head toward Dan, and sneered. "Oh, we're doing this again? Who's the guilt-rag this time?"

Satira gestured with flair. "Noema, meet Downer Dan."

The air shifted, sharper with shame that had nowhere left to hide.

Satira shrugged. "She's not a toy. Noema helps me see, speak to Fates, find patterns. She's... useful."

Keothi shifted in her seat. The formation of the shadow unsettled her nerves. "Revin said she's gone but not forgotten before leaving."

"We all have different shadows, Keothi. A spectrum. All loud in their own ways. All helping us to remember."

Dan stared, wide-eyed and deathly still.

Noema circled him, voice a sultry croon. "Freya's cat's got your tongues. Don't worry, she always gives 'em back eventually."

Satira asked, "Let's sit back and watch, shall we? Anyone bring snacks? Dried berries? Moth jerky? No? Should I summon a Keeper for snacks, or is that a war crime now?" Satira dropped onto the couch with a sigh. "He's all yours."

Noema's gaze sharpened to Halvar. "This might get messy. Cry if you must. Scream if you have to. Hold nothing back. Otherwise, it stays. Own it. Understood?"

Halvar nodded, loss for words.

"When did you first appear?" Noema pressed, circling Dan like a predator.

"When I want. Shoo. Go burn in the sun," he muttered.

Noema's eyes didn't blink. "Halvar."

He swallowed. "Time blurred in the cell. Hard to say."

"Tsk, tsk," Noema tutted. "I said, don't hold back."

Halvar sighed, fingers twitching against the couch's rough fabric. Bryjna's hand found his, warm and steady.

"I was replaying the first night away from Keothi... on my way to Vorik."

"Choices," Noema said softly. "Tell us what you faced."

Halvar sipped wine, steadying himself. "Do we really need to do this here? Anywhere else?"

Keothi's voice was soft, "I can leave if it helps."

The room seemed to close in as Noema's voice filled every corner, sharp and unyielding. "The wound must be faced if you want this shadow gone. Once you bleed, Dan fades. But if you avoid him, you're never free."

Dan hissed, "Nice speech. Got any delusions of grandeur to go with it?"

Noema smiled. "Now. Where were we? Ah, yes. Speak."

Halvar's breath caught. "I was on the boat. No wind. Men weary, drifting. I smelled charred bone. A bowl, floating. A candle lit. No hand to place it. No voice to claim it. Then the wind screamed. The sea turned black."

Dan leaned in, voice a priest's whisper at a funeral: "One who worships the Old Gods chooses silence. Do you believe, Halvar? Or is it all pageantry in warpaint?"

He leaned in, swallowing hard before he spoke. "Keothi... don't blame your Mother. It's me."

He closed his eyes. "Vorik's summons came, final kiss to Bryjna. Brief. I thought I'd be back for dinner. I went to the fields, to his tent. But he wasn't there. His soldiers knocked me out, dragged me to the Great Hall where I saw Borin in his own battle." He took a moment to catch his breath. "Keothi fought harder than I did. I should've..."

Tears burned down his cheeks.

Dan snorted, the sound like bones knocking. "They needed a storm. You gave them a drizzle."

Bryjna pulled Halvar close, fingers threading through his hair, lips brushing his temple, her own eyes glistening.

Dan circled them slowly, voice soft and cruel. "They carved their prayers into stone. You brought parchment. You always break when it matters."

He continued, sharper and spit-hot. "You knew he wouldn't play fair. And still you stepped in, wearing your dignity like armor. It broke easily. Just like you."

He turned his gaze to Keothi, slow and deliberate. "And her? Carrying your silence like a second spine. She screamed once. With a plate. Bet that crash never left your ears."

Halvar recoiled, shaking.

Dan's voice dipped lower, almost kind. "Tell me, do they know how loud you scream in dreams? Or how well you smile in daylight?"

He snapped, full venom: "You handed your spine over like a gift-wrapped apology. Every breath you take is one more Keothi has to carry. You don't get to cry."

Noema's grin was a blade. "Enough. You've said your piece." She waved a hand.

The shadows stilled. Dan froze, mid-sneer.

Noema stepped between Halvar and Dan. Shadow wings unfurled, war banners hung behind her. Her voice dropped into the language of every mother, midwife, and monster who'd stared down a man's pain without flinching.

"Halvar. Back to now. Name five things you see."

Halvar pulled from Bryjna's hold, blinking. "Candlelight flickering. Cracked wood on the table. Bryjna's worried face. The stain on the rug. Wine glass."

"Four things you can touch."

He rubbed his hands on his pants. "The rough fabric. Couch cushion. Keothi's hand. Cold glass."

"Three sounds?"

"Fire hissing. Satira's soft breath. Dan's low growl."

"Two smells."

"Smoke. Wine."

"One taste."

"The bitterness of wine on my tongue."

Noema's voice softened, centuries behind her words. "You're here, Halvar. Safe enough to face this."

Dan muttered, trying to stir.

"Say it. Say it loud. I'm here."

Halvar choked. "I... I'm here."

"A step forward. But you need to mean it."

Keothi squeezed his hand. "Father. I failed too. The night after meeting Vorik, I thought of killing him in his camp. I didn't." She exhaled slowly. "Sigmantis told me to learn from the past and try again. We're here. Together. That's what matters."

Bryjna's hand clenched Keothi's, forming a circle.

Dan twitched, stuttering.

Keothi's voice hardened. "We'll bring him to his knees. Put him on a pike. Together."

Halvar squeezed their hands tight. "I'm here."

Dan hissed like boiling oil. Noema's smile was cold steel.

"You're not guilt. Not truth. You're a wound wearing a crown. Your time is done."

Dan flickered, fading.

"Keothi," Noema said gently, "tell your father what you see."

Tears glistened in Keothi's eyes. "A man who walked into a trap, but still tried to crawl out. My father."

Through sobs, Halvar unfolded himself. "I was set up to die in silence. But I didn't. I'm here. I name the pain."

Dan howled, an echo fading into nothing.

"And this is why," Noema whispered, "you're free to stand."

Halvar rose from Bryjna and Keothi's grasps, wiping away the tears. He faced Dan in defiance. "It's not Dan I fear. It's what I gave him to say."

Dan's shape twisted, unraveling into a swirl of ember and ash, before disappearing in a gust that stirred the dust. The air shivered, haunted by the smell of burnt sage and sulfur. The aftertaste of something finally driven out.

Noema turned to Satira. "May I sleep now?"

Satira nodded. "Thank you. Now we focus on his lesser interruptions."

Before disappearing, Noema smiled at Keothi. "Honey, your shadow is deeply in love with you. Take care of yours. You've got a special one."

She melted into the floor, leaving silence in her wake.

Chapter Forty-Six

THE RED WATER FLOWS

Boots pounded dirt, kicking up dust. Trees blurred past. The sky hung cold, pale as bone. Breath steamed in the air, ragged and fast.

Keothi glanced over her shoulder. Halvar was doing everything he could to keep up. He'd put on weight, muscle, not fat. The old strategist was back in his prime. No longer a prisoner, he was the man from the stories: shield-wall breaker, a greying battlefield wolf.

"Come on, Old Man! Keep up." She jogged in place, heart pounding, beads of sweat trailing down her cheek.

He chuckled. "I have to go easy on you, make you think you're something more."

Their morning runs carved out space before the day's orders came crashing in. Halvar commanded the refuge's soldiers. Bryjna handled the spy network. Keothi? She sat in the middle, pulling strings that set off battles, decisions, raids, a deadly symphony where every tremble had consequences.

Was this leadership? Pull one string. Watch the world twitch.

They reached the ruins. A long-forgotten field, rediscovered by accident, claimed by routine.

Jagged stones jutted from the earth, broken teeth, remnants of some long-forgotten fortress. Pillars leaned like drunk sentinels, half-buried in the soil, runes worn to scars.

In the center, they knelt side by side, each bracing a hand on one knee, shoulders heaving. The quiet that followed pulsed. They stretched in shared silence.

Joints cracked, muscles bent. Pain flickered through each movement, but they didn't flinch. They'd bled through worse and they would again.

Keothi leaned IronMaw against a crumbling wall. A trunk and two shields waited nearby. She opened it, tossed a war hammer to Halvar. He caught it with ease.

She followed with a shield. "Ready?"

He twirled the hammer. "Born ready."

She picked up her own. "Let's dance."

His hammer came down. She raised her shield just in time.

He didn't wait anymore. He pressed.

She shoved back, pivoting. Swung at his side, easy block.

"Come on, girl. You can do better than that."

"Thought I'd go easy on you."

He laughed deep and hearty. "How else will you learn?"

Another blow hit her shield. She staggered.

"Hits happen. That's why we shield, not because we're weak, but because we're not done standing."

Another swing. No time to reground.

A smack to her thigh, calculated, not cruel.

She limped to the side. Lunged. Brought her hammer down toward his shoulder.

He stepped aside with ease. "If you can hold your own against a hammer, girl, you can dance around anything else."

"I'll dance on your grave, Old Man!" She slammed her hammer into his shield.

He used the momentum to shove her back. Came in hard with another blow.

"Use their weight against them. Control the field."

She lifted her hammer, eyes lit with fire.

A sound split the world. Low, distant, climbing like smoke through ribs. Not a call, but a curse. A war horn. Every bone remembered what it meant. War had found their doorstep.

They met each other's eyes. Together they said, "The Mountain."

Keothi dropped her hammer and shield. She snatched IronMaw from where it leaned against the crumbling wall, the axe instantly familiar in her grip.

Halvar kept his war hammer and shield tight in hand.

They ran toward the Sanctuary, but the forest betrayed them. Blades stepped from the trees, silent as spiders, fangs already drawn. One licked his teeth, tasting blood before it spilled.

Father. Daughter. Charged.

Halvar's hammer folded the soldier's skull, one hit, one silence. Keothi's blade tore across another's chest, a searing line of red.

Steel flashed, a sword arced toward Halvar. His shield caught it with a sharp cry. He shoved forward, the soldier stumbling, falling to the ground. The hammer came down with a crack.

Slice. Slash. Bodies hit like broken branches.

IronMaw screamed. Metal met metal. Wood splintered under fury.

An arm snaked around Keothi's neck. She dropped low, twisted beneath the arm. Legs snapped tight in a lock against the attacker's neck.

The attacker sailed over her shoulder, crashing to the ground behind her. She rolled. Rose, only for judgement to fall. IronMaw to chest. Bones broke as breaths ended.

Screams. From the mountain, raw, human. Ripped from the core.

The air thrummed with distant war. It had begun.

They sprinted toward the mouth.

At the forest's edge, the air pulsed with screams. Blades and Maidens danced in the dirt, cutting down anyone who moved: ally, enemy, refugee, child. No one was safe.

Bryjna, sword and shield. A force of her own.

Vexa with a rapier, slipping through shadows and allies.

"Shield wall!" hollered Barnaby.

"Spears!" A second order.

Faces blurred. Blood painted the dirt.

Maiden. Blade. Keeper. Refugee. Death didn't care who they were.

A wave broke, splitting the world like an old scar.

Keothi's heartbeat stuttered, then broke. The air turned brittle, stretched thin, ready to snap.

A soldier lunged from the brush.

IronMaw swung, carving him down in one brutal arc.

She saw them. Across the clearing.

Past smoke. Past bodies.

Spoon. Groa.

Keothi stood at the forest's edge, too far to stop it. Close enough to see every detail.

Groa's hand gripped Spoon's hair, dragging her upright.

Keothi and Spoon's eyes locked. Her eyes fierce and steady. Already accepting her fate. Ready to say goodbye.

Groa smiled. A predator with prey.

A message. A trophy. A warning.

"A gift for the King. Your heart, as promised." She leaned in. Whispered something only the dying would hear.

Spoon flinched, but she did not look away.

The blade slid in slow, cruel, and deliberate.

Halvar broke ranks, roaring her name, but the spear wall held him back. Bryjna didn't move. Shield at her side as if she'd forgotten what it was for.

One step. Two. The world bled.

Groa yanked Spoon back. A puppet returned to strings.

The blade buried, forcing it clean through Spoon's frame. Hilt to spine. Blood soaked the cracked earth.

Spoon shuddered as the foreign object pushed through her.

IronMaw howled, but distance made her useless. Rage had no reach.

She whispered my name when I couldn't.

Held me when my hands shook.

Named the grief in my gut before I could speak it.

Even when I forgot it, she remembered my name.

Not Spoon. Not her.

Keothi roared, something animal, something broken, and sprinted. Her ribs barely held her together.

Spoon met her gaze, still fierce and unafraid. She touched her own chest, a silent farewell.

Keothi's hands were already bloodied. Rage was faster than grief. She had no words, only IronMaw.

Slash. Dash Swing. She carved a path in blood. Each blow a promise. A refusal of acceptance.

Groa blew the horn, victory notched in blood, her smirk a knife across memory.

Retreat.

And retreat the enemy did.

Groa pulled the sword free, kicking Spoon into the dirt. She ran into the woods, swinging at refugees. Not a care in the world. Her mission had succeeded.

One body. Two bodies. Not enough will earn the blade.

Keothi slid, knees scrapping the dirt. Hands moved under the dying woman. Keothi pulled Spoon into her chest. Pressed her hands to the wound, trying to hold the pieces in.

Blood slipped through her fingers, warm and impossibly swift.

"Don't cry for me," she mouthed. "You were always enough."

The light behind her eyes flickered.

Keothi's breath hitched. Her hands shook. The world blurred. Time froze.

She rocked Spoon to her endless sleep. With a bloodied hand, she closed her eyes.

Vexa came running up, behind Keothi. A hand on her shoulder.

Keothi recoiled. She laid Spoon down to the ground. "Watch her."

"I will," Vexa said, voice low. "Release the Bearbarian."

She stood, IronMaw roared with her. They weren't done. Even the axe grieved, singing fury into each blow as she gave chase to the fleeing enemy.

Groa vanished into the underbush.

Halvar. Bryjna. Barnaby. Vexa. Trond.

All eyes watching. All eyes wide. Drenched in sweat, blood, and terror.

She turned, faced the forest, vanishing like smoke, fury and grief given form.

Bryjna called after her, "Keothi!" But the wind swallowed the name.

She ran into the forest. IronMaw was feral.

My turn.

Retreating enemies were nothing more than sliced hogs on Yule morning.

You took her. I'll take everything.

She chased the fleeting army. Cutting down stragglers without pause. Hunting the dregs of the army, left none behind.

Until the hill.

Groa. Maren.

Not running. Simply waiting.

Maidens encircled Keothi. Swords and shields were drawn, forcing Keothi to halt her assault.

Groa emerged from the shadows. Blank-faced. No weapon drawn. Only the faint echo of a scream in her eyes. "You brought this," she said. Two voices. Hers and something else. Older and more hollow. Rot behind silk. A puppeteer behind old flesh.

Keothi raised IronMaw.

Groa tilted her head, eyes cold as winter ice. "How many more before you break?" She pulled her sword and stepped forward. "Let's end this, Yrsa!"

"I am Keothi of the Shadowforged. Remember it when you fall."

Groa charged. Keothi met her.

Sword on axe. Shield and boots. Grief on rage.

Their old sparring burned beneath the chaos.

Groa's lessons twisted in Keothi's fists, ghosts rising to kill their maker.

No rules. No mercy. Only blood, memory, and rage.

Groa's blade thick with Spoon's blood. Keothi's heart thick with the loss.

They danced. One disciplined. One primal.

Groa's hilt cracked against her skull. "You still drop your left shoulder."

Keothi staggered backwards, spit blood at Groa's feet. "You never showed me how to survive without her."

IronMaw's ember runes turned white. Keothi struck. The axe ripped through from cheek to chin, peeling skin from muscle, leaving a red, ragged grin. Blood sprayed in hot arcs.

Groa staggered, laughing through the torn ruin of her face. "You think I need this face!? When you are no one, you need nothing!"

Two voices louder now: *"End her."*

The Maidens swarmed. They didn't come to save Groa. They came to die for her.

Keothi turned IronMaw in a fury. Each swing a scream. Each kill a refusal.

Still they came. Still they died.

Groa slipped behind them, bleeding, leapt onto a waiting horse. The horse vanished into trees like smoke through leaves. Dragged by madness and loyalty.

Keothi didn't stop. As long as they came, she swung.

Another wave thundered from the Sanctuary. Refugees poured from the trees, ragged and burning with vengeance.

They crashed into the wave of Maidens.

Keothi's axe sang, carving through chaos.

As long as they fought, she fought.

Every swing pulled a string. Every corpse, a consequence.

Bodies carpeted the forest floor.

Only when they stopped coming did her knees hit dirt. IronMaw thudded beside her. Blood in her mouth. Ash in her lungs.

Her head fell back and she screamed. It was mourning, sharpened into a promise.

The stench of iron drowned the pine.

IronMaw pulsed, still hot, still hungry. It hadn't had enough.

The bear's claws had torn through her like bark under steel. Keothi still remembered the sting of ground herbs rubbed raw into the wound, screams echoing off stone when the water hit. The sleepless nights, the pain in every breath.

She would take the claws again. The burn. The nights screaming into stone. She'd bleed until there was nothing left—if it meant Spoon could wake, just to hear her take one more breath.

Not on a pyre.

Not waiting for the Valkyries to carry her away.

Chapter Forty-Seven

EMBERS OF GRIEF

Spoon lay on the pyre, arms crossed, an axe nestled in her hands. Flowers boxed her into eternal sleep.

Keothi laid a hand on hers, for the last time. “Freya, Field-Mother. Take the one who never lifted a sword, but carried me all the same. Let her into your field, your garden, your fire. Let her rest among those who fought without being seen. Let her be held. Let her be honored.”

She bowed her head. “Spoon. You stepped into the light. You saw someone trying to hide and never looked away. Follow the Valkyries. Let them take you home. I’ll hold your hand again when the embers cool.”

Children laid grass charms by the pyre. Bryjna spoke the old words. Her voice hitched. Someone played Spoon’s favorite song on a chipped flute.

Keothi didn’t hear it. Her ears rang with a silence only she could hear.

The air stank of crushed lavender and forge smoke. Some flowers were fresh and wild-picked. Others wilted. Spoon hated beige. She would’ve laughed.

Someone pressed a torch into her hand.

She lit the kindling and watched the fire take her.

She stood as the flames rooted deep.

Only then did she feel someone beside her. Bryjna. Eyes rimmed red. Silent. A shared ache. Wordless. Old.

Ash twisted into the sky, carrying Spoon beyond reach. Keothi didn’t cry. Not then.

She didn't move until the last ember died. When she was more smoke than skin.

Days later, a forge rose in the mountain's root beside the underground lake.

Not a refuge of peace, but of repetition.

The clang of iron. The hiss of steam. The breath of bellows. Anything to drown the silence Spoon left behind.

Uncle Borin's hammer fit her hand like memory. The rhythm returned.

Ingots from forgotten mines.

Metal never stopped moving.

And neither did she.

I can't stop. If I stop, I'll shatter.

One sword down. Another waiting.

Each blade a promise of another destined execution.

Hollow hands. Hollow work.

Dull edges. Newborn blades.

Weapons waiting for meaning.

When the mountain asked, Keothi answered.

Cinder fireflies danced.

Her breath matched the bellows.

The forge didn't care if her heart was broken. It demanded heat. Pressure. Repetition. She gave it everything.

Rage. Grief. Silence.

The cinder fireflies bit back, leaving soft burns on her calloused hands. A flicker of relief.

The fire answered with pain she could touch.

A pain she could name. Grounding her, bringing her back to life. For only a moment.

Until the pain faded, cooling, iron in the air.

The soot drawer of her mind creaked open. She used to hide feelings there. Now it was empty and mocking.

No sign of Vorik. Or Groa. Or Borin.

No vengeance was offered. Just the echo of her own breath.

What was the point of vengeance, when the one she tried to protect was already gone?

Spoon had died without a blade.

Keothi had survived with blood on hers.

It wasn't balanced, but punishment.

All her strength, all her fire, none of it had saved her.

That truth clanged louder than any hammer.

Years training to kill monsters, and she'd missed the quiet ones.

Spoon had protected her not from blades, but from silence. Still, Keothi lived. The cruelest kind of theft.

Bryjna and Halvar tried. Food. Words.

Vexa at the door with raid talk.

Barnaby begged for the Bearbarian to return. Tales of her fury were already legend.

She didn't answer.

She kept hammering.

Reports piled.

Shrines to Virell multiplying.

Blades made of ordinary iron couldn't pierce the new barriers.

Still, the forge called. Still, the fireflies danced.

Halvar left roasted roots and lamb on a carved stone plate.

Bryjna brought honeyroot milk. The kind Spoon made long ago. She used to serve it scalding hot. Said it forced people to slow down and taste it.

Keothi didn't touch it.

The food grew cold.

A moth drowned in the milk. Wings were still twitching when she found it.

She didn't flinch.

Just cleaned it away.

The mug stayed.

This wasn't exile. Not punishment. Just the consequence of surviving.

Steel wasn't enough. Not when the enemy was god-shaped. Not when the war lived in minds, not muscle.

Vorik. Identity Slayer.

Groa. Spirit Slayer.

Still, the hammer rose and fell.

Then one calm evening, the anvil singing its song, Trond came to the forge. "We found them." Keothi didn't look up. When she finally did, he was already gone.

The words remained, an offering she couldn't take.

I will slaughter them both.

She sat on the stool, IronMaw across her lap. Unbloodied since Spoon. The whetstone scraped the blade. Sharpen the executioner's axe.

A soft meow. An orange-striped cat sat at the edge of the forge, watching.

She didn't look up. The axe shimmered in forge light.

Another meow. This time the creature brushed her shins, demanding attention.

The whetstone froze. Keothi looked down.

Before she could react, the cat leapt onto her lap and curled atop the axe head. Vibrations rippled through its furry body.

The axe had never felt so heavy.

Her arms, never so tired.

Her fractured heart, so full.

"I can't stop. If I stop, I'll shatter."

The cat didn't move. It knew it belonged.

She almost pushed it away.

Almost.

But she didn't.

Couldn't.

Instead, she cried.

Not a flood.

A slow leak.

Her heart cracked. Leaking in silence.

Her shadow stirred.

Peeled from the floor. Rose from the soot covered boards.

Revin wrapped silent arms around her, held her and her tears.

The cat.

Her shadow.

Her breath.

Keothi exhaled.

She knew what the message was. And this time, she accepted it.

To kill,

To finish the war,

She first had to grieve.

Not burn.

Not break.

Just feel.

Chapter Forty-Eight

BRASS & STEEL

"Keothi..." Vexa stopped mid-stride, staring at Revin. The forge hissed behind her, smoke curling in the firelight. "Hold up. Who's that? Is that..."

Keothi paused mid-swing, hammer raised. She glanced between them "Right. You two haven't met. Revin, Vexa. Vexa, Revin."

Revin sat on the wall, legs crossed, silent as ever. She waved like she'd just been let out of a box.

Vexa scoffed, waving back. "Yours is quieter than your dad's. Creepier too."

Revin tilted her head, gazing at Keothi.

"What brings you here to the forge? More attempts to pull me to the sun? To take walks?"

"Keothi, we're just worried about you... but it seems you're finally moving forward if your shadow is here."

"Revin."

Vexa sighed, leaning against the forge pillar. "Alright, Revin. Either way, glad to see you processing the event from several months ago."

"Should I keep working, or is there an actual reason you're here?"

"We found them."

"The squad that had fallen from the rock cliffs?"

Vexa shook her head. "No, not yet. We still have scouts out searching. We found Vaelriker."

Keothi slipped the burning blade into the barrel. Steam hissed up like a warning. The molten iron coiled around the names, strangling Keothi's throat. They found the city. Finally.

She steadied her grip, because if she didn't, she'd start breaking steel instead of forging it. "Give me the brief."

Revin floated over, grabbed a tin cup, and handed it to her.

"Everyone's gathering in the war room." Vexa moved to Keothi who remained staring into the barrel. She squeezed Keothi's shoulder. "We have them. It's real."

Keothi gripped her hand, the tremor giving her away. The quiet hum of the forge and the mountain breathed for her. Flashes of Groa's blade and blood played in Keothi's mind. Plans of how to make Groa pay. Memories of Vorik's serpent smile haunted her.

Revin's eyes flicked toward the hammer, then back to Keothi.

Keothi's breath hitched. She forced it down with a swallow that scraped like rust. "Let's go."

Vexa scrunched her nose. "First? Maybe bathe. You reek like boiled leather. Seriously, when's the last time water touched you?"

Keothi chuckled, pulling herself from the swirling oil. The cat stretched in the forge's corner, blinking at them. It settled near the kiln. Down here at the roots of the mountain, it was cooler. The kiln provided necessary warmth for the creature.

"New cat?" Vexa raised a brow. She kneeled down, stretching its ears. "Are you replacing us?"

Keothi sipped the water, cooling her dry throat. "Never. Ember's the new resident of the forge. I'll wash up and join as soon as I can."

Vexa lingered a moment longer, watching Revin with curiosity.

Revin politely nodded. Whatever passed between them, Vexa seemed satisfied.

Trond stood outside the war-room door, pacing until Keothi came into view. "Keothi, minute?"

Keothi and Revin stopped. "Yes?"

"Revin, right? Vexa told us."

"I don't think Revin is why you want to talk..."

Trond exhaled through his nose. From his pocket, he pulled a small, worn button. Golden, dull with time, but unmistakable.

Keothi froze. Her eyes locked on it. "Trond..."

Trond held it out, resting in his calloused palm. "It was in Spoon's bag. None of us touched it. We figured... when you were ready, you'd want it."

Keothi plucked it from his hand. Her fingers trembled. She closed her fist. The edges dug into her palm, grounding her. Tears threatened, but she blinked them down. The button still smelled faintly of skin oil. Her thumb rubbed the groove worn smooth by Spoon's hand. An object meant to silence her.

The thought of Spoon keeping it ripped through Keothi's ribs.

"If you need anything..." Trond started, but the rest stayed unsaid.

Revin stepped closer, laying a quiet hand on his shoulder.

Keothi swallowed, throat burning. "Thank you, truly." She looked at the button one more time, then turned. "Come on. Seems like we have some good news, finally." She pushed through the war room doors.

Revin and Trond stood in silence, watching the door shut like it could seal the past behind her. Neither followed, not yet. She had taken the button and that was enough.

Conversation died the moment Keothi stepped inside. Bryjna, Halvar, and Vexa stood waiting, tension thick in the room.

"Let's not waste any more time. Hel is waiting. Where are they?"

"Here," Halvar said, pointing to a map on the table. Keothi moved over to it, looking at it.

"Didn't we already look there?"

Trond and Revin walked in. "We did. We just weren't looking at it right."

Keothi watched Revin float in. A soft frown formed before she replied. "What are you talking about?"

"Have you ever heard of zodiacal light?" he asked.

Keothi raised an eyebrow. "Sounds poetic. Try again."

Vexa spoke. "Light scattered by dust in the upper atmosphere. Right before dawn, or with a full moon. You can't always see it, but from the right place, it makes hidden things visible."

"And the squad saw it?"

Revin's expression didn't change, but her pacing slowed. Her fingers curled at her sides, quiet tension rising in her posture.

"From the peaks. They followed it. And there it was." Vexa grinned, crossing her arms. "The city."

"We don't get it," the Berserker muttered. "From one angle, it looks like a fortress...sharp, clean, perfect. From another? Like the stone bent sideways. Like it shouldn't hold together."

Another Berserker continued. "From the west, it looks carved by hands. From the east, like it shaped itself. Like the stone remembered something it was never supposed to be."

"I don't care how it hides. I know who built it. I know what waits inside." She looked up from the maps, glancing around the room, meeting everyone's eyes. "We're going."

Revin stayed to the edges, but her eyes tracked every detail spoken like they were blades.

The room remained quiet and still for a long moment until Vexa broke the tension. "We have scouts gathering information. Barnaby is gathering the forces. We're moving in four days."

Trond said, "Scouts say the eastern slope gives us cover. If we're quiet, we can get within striking range before they even know we're there."

Halvar said, "Now that we've seen it, we don't need the light. Just a straight line and the will to walk it."

Revin paced the room, staying in the shadows. She stepped forward, as Keothi remained silent. She pressed a finger against the maps.

Vexa said, "It is not confirmed Groa or Vorik are in the city. But, we can confirm we haven't found them anywhere else."

Keothi stepped away from the table without another word. The weight of her choice pressed into the floorboards as she passed.

Revin followed silently. No one stopped her.

The door shut behind them. The map trembled in their wake. The only thing left behind was the certainty of someone who'd finally seen the place her nightmares pointed her toward.

Chapter Forty-Nine

THE THEATER OF WAR

Villagers lined up. Soldiers, smiths, seamstresses, each pressed their palm to a blade they might never lift again. A war camp born of desperation and stitched with hope.

The camp sprawled across the fields like a rising graveyard. Grunts of sparring soldiers met the rasp of whetstones, sharpening more than just blades. War campaigns had grown significantly as lost and broken souls flooded in by the dozens.

It was strange to think, beyond the ridge, Vorik and Groa slept under their god's shadow. Vaelriker lay buried in the peaks, the cliffs clenched around it like fists.. The rebels camped along a valley slope, tucked just out of sight of the watchtowers. No roads, no guides, only rumor and chance led them here.

No one agreed on the walls. Some swore they pierced the clouds. Others said no higher than twenty feet. Either way, there would be blood getting in.

Keothi strolled the rocky fields, studying the faces behind the sacrifices. People of all flavors willing to stand up to Vorik and Groa. They were willing to lay down their lives to speak their truths.

Their lives all depended on Keothi. The weight was hers alone. The pressure hollowed everything.

Wild boar roasted above campfires. Ladles stirred the day's rations. The air was thick with the mingled scents of meat, sweat, and something sour beneath it all, fear dressed in bravado.

Past the training dummies, lute songs danced with the ring of steel.

One tent stood shamelessly open to the world. Keothi slowed, struck by equal parts curiosity... and terror.

Barnaby knelt in nothing but his drawers. Vexa stood over him, radiant in a purple garter belt and corset, one heel pressing into his shoulder like a queen claiming tribute.

He spotted Keothi and beamed. "Join us Barbarian! One last ride before we storm Valhalla!"

Vexa didn't blink. She yanked his beard gently, but with purpose. Her voice flat as slate. "Eyes on me."

Keothi barked a laugh. "I thought you didn't tame wild things, Vexa?"

Vexa shot a glance Keothi's way. "He needed a lesson." She looked down at the meat puppet kneeling before her. "Close the flap, would you?"

Revin closed the flap, rubbed her eyes, and shook her head like she'd just seen something illegal in three different dimensions.

Keothi nodded, "Yup, blinded. Spiritually scarred. Let's go find my parents."

They moved through the camp. Blades were being sharpened, gods whispered to, drinks passed around like charms against the dawn. Not everyone bore the war like a funeral march.

A few warriors laughed too loudly. One stared at the fire like it held his death. Another sharpened her blade until her fingers bled.

At her parents' tent, Halvar stood outside, Bryjna's hand in his. He was smiling. She was smirking. Teenagers about to break curfew, they slipped inside and pulled the flap shut behind them. Some things were best left to one's imagination.

Keothi shook her head, "Guess we're not going there."

Revin collapsed in protest, flat to the dirt like a dying flower.

Keothi kept moving. The camp pulsed with life, steel on stone, skin on skin, laughter like a spell against the dark. People were living, even with death squatting on the edge of the horizon.

She watched, and felt no ache. Only peace and joy for each individual.

Let them dance. Let them joke. Let them find each other in the dark.

They chose how to spend their last day, not in fear, not in angst, but in pure, chaotic joy.

She was here to move through it.

"Let's go talk to the gods," she said, eyes on the sky. "Maybe they have answers."

At the edge of camp, a circle of stones scorched with charcoal and tears was laid out.

She knelt and pulled the brass button from her pocket, running her thumb across its worn edge. It was simple in all the ways. No one knew why Spoon had kept it, but Keothi understood.

Keothi looked up at the sky. Two crows cut across the sky. Black wings, wide and watching.

"All Father. I see you. Provide me the wisdom and strength to be the executioner. Welcome all who fall into Valhalla. All except my two enemies."

She kissed the button. The dirt crumbled cool and dry over her fingers. A small grave for a veil, and the girl who wore it.

An old crone's hand rested on hers. "The Gods listen. They provide direction."

Keothi smiled, "Satira. Good to see you again."

"Good to see you in the sun."

"War has forced me out."

"Don't make it seem so grim." She chuckled, kneeling down beside Keothi. "Flood the world with your question, Deary."

Keothi sighed. "What are the Fates whispering to you?"

"Ah, we fear the unknown, don't we? We beg the Fates to pluck a string, to tell us which way to go. But that's not their gift."

"So, they only speak when it matters, when the choice is laid bare?" Keothi pressed.

"You miss the point, Keothi. The bird in the cage forgets it can fly even when the door is open."

"But I do feel suffocated."

"That's not the Fates. That's fear. That's grief. You're walking with the living, but buried in your own bones. The Empty isn't silence. It's everyone else living out loud. You're just starting to join them."

"Legend in Silk," Keothi chuckled. She scooped up a handful of dirt. Let it fall, grain by grain, into the wind.

Satira left her in silence.

Keothi remained, kneeling. Around her, the war camp bristled, laughter, music, steel on steel. For a breath, the world was alive. Unburdened by expectations, rebellion, and war.

She stood slowly, brushing dust from her palms, and began walking back toward the camp. The button's grave behind her. The crows were long gone. But the sky was still open.

Hoofbeats interrupted the somber moment. Screams sounded from the camp below. Frantic and feral.

She ran.

In the center of the camp stood a horse, drenched in blood, frothing and wild-eyed. A torn banner clung to its flank. Virell's sigil, shredded.

A boy slumped in the saddle. Shaggy clothes. Blood crusted every seam, stiff and blackened. And over his face, a white mask. Sewn on. Silver silk threads pierced through the skin. Each hole dripping with blood.

He fell, hitting the dirt with a thud, shaking.

Keothi dropped beside him, pressing a hand to his shoulder.

His voice was a breath, barely sound, muffled by the mask. "Tarnheim."

An arrow shrieked through the air.

Straight into his chest.

He went still. The crowd of soldiers turned towards the horizon, scanning the edges. Looking for the threat.

Keothi's gaze remained on the boy. The arrow's feather fluttered in the wind from his chest. Her fist closed as the message was clear. "This was for me." Her voice was steady. Dangerous. "I don't know what's in Tarnheim. But we ride. *Now.*"

Barnaby didn't hesitate. Two fingers to his lips. A sharpened whistle cut through the fears. "Mount up! We ride fast!"

Shrieks tore the sky. Smoke strangled the clouds. Death was coming.

This was a first. The army of Unmasked had, until now, been raiders. They ambushed caravans, struck trading outposts. They liberated garrisons and forts. Villagers had poured into the mountains, chasing a life beyond the King's oppression.

This wasn't that. This wasn't freedom. This was a calculated difference.

The horse's hooves barely touched the earth before launching forward, reins snapping like whips. It was fast, but not fast enough for Keothi.

Barnaby and his men rode behind her, carved from bark and bleeding myth, their eyes locked on Valhalla.

Tarnheim burned. Screams echoed between falling beams.

Maidens in ceremonial paint and soldiers in armor slashed through the innocent. No mercy. No message. Only slaughter. Chaos had descended like a curtain on a stage.

Keothi's squad charged into the maelstrom. Axes flew. Swords flashed.

Save the villagers. Save the village.

Keothi vaulted from her horse, IronMaw already mid-swing. A body split open like rotten fruit.

Something was wrong. The atmosphere twisted.

What's the play here?

A masked soldier screamed and rushed her blindside. A blade burst through his chest before she could turn.

Barnaby stood behind him, slick with blood, grinning. This was his playground.

"Watch your back!" he called, already turning toward his next kill, someone fresh to send to Hel.

Keothi didn't move. Her fingers clenched around IronMaw's haft. The world compressed. She was moving, but it didn't feel like her body. Her soul had taken a step back to watch.

It felt rehearsed. The dying knew their cues. The living knew when to strike.

Feral men, battle hardened and half-mad, clashed with trained soldiers: disciplined, efficient, devout.

All willing to die.

Die for King Vorik.

Die for Virell.

Die for Ancestors.

Die for Honor.

One destiny called to them all: Death.

Another faceless enemy. Another thud of IronMaw. Another name she'd never learn.

If that's the case, then why this carnage?

A masked soldier bowed before striking. A child was handed forward like tribute. The screams were too rehearsed.

This wasn't a raid. It was theater.

This wasn't a battle.

It was a ritual.

Every scream, a line of dialogue. Every corpse, stage dressing.

Another slash with IronMaw—another soul taken. The weapon trembled in her grasp. Was it IronMaw or her hands?

A child's scream split the iron-thick air.

A soldier raised his blade, already mid-swing.

Revin emerged from the shadows, stepping between the blade and child. A shield made flesh. A shadow turned protector.

The blade struck her chest, scraping across ribs and bone, but no blood poured from her.

The child cowered behind Revin, tears streaking their face.

The soldier's blade twisted in his hand—warping, melting, sizzling against her shadowed skin. It crumpled into a useless hunk of metal.

The soldier stared at it. "What the hell..."

A war axe slammed into his chest. He dropped.

The child ran into their mother's arms, sobbing.

Revin didn't move. Didn't speak. The ruined blade steaming at her feet. She turned toward Keothi.

IronMaw tilted in her grip. Pulled. Pointing, not at Revin. At a hill beyond her.

Keothi looked.

Silence was on that hill. Thick. Eerie. Birds wheeled high above, encircling the world.

Birds? Carrion or witness?

The same pull from the altar of Virell. She moved forward, step by step, leaving the chaos behind.

IronMaw tugged, not at her hand, but at something deeper. A compass spun in her chest, always north, always death.

Keothi crested the hill.

A blackened tree towered ahead, its gnarled branches grasping corpses. A white banner hung from the highest limb, painted with a black mask stretching the full length of the tree.

Beneath it, bodies swayed, decorations. Dozens. Men. Women. Children. Silver silk nooses shimmered in the wind.

Below the tree, a pile of heads. Arranged deliberately. Offerings to the divine. Eyes frozen in fear. Each scalp pierced by a white mask, silver thread biting through flesh.

At the center, atop the pyre, one head bore a dagger through its crown.

An ornate weapon. Amethyst in the hilt. Runes gleamed down the blade.

Her stomach clenched.

Borin's work. His signature technique, the one he swore to teach only her, etched in every inch.

A perfect mask of craftsmanship hiding a prisoner's hand.

Proof he was alive, but bound by invisible chains.

The blade pinned a parchment, its edges curling.

Yrsa,

We all come to crossroads.

I've made my choice.

Now it's your turn to choose:

This destruction, ten fold.

Your Uncle

Yourself

Two walk away, the third doesn't.

I'll be waiting.

-King Vorik

On the back, a map, drawn in blood and still wet.

She turned, eyes on the village below, veiled beneath a curtain of smoke.

Beyond that, the white stitched tents, a disease spreading.

Above it all, the capital rose from the haze.

Five rivers split around the base, their currents vanishing beneath stone grates and re-emerging in silver threads along the walls, feeding the city.

Rings of dwellings and workshops coiled upward in perfect symmetry, streets aligning like ritual lines towards the plateau's crown.

At its heart, the castle waited, carved into the stone itself. Its towers mirrored the points of the star below. From its stone altar, Vorik could see everything: the markets that fed him, the temples that praised him, the forges that armed him.

A god's geometry. A design too precise to be alive.

This wasn't the end. This was the beginning. The infection would spread.

More villages. More death. More lambs to the altar.

Who would be left to mourn?

The message was crystal clear.

This time, she chooses.

Her body, or her mind.

Thousands dead or a single girl hollowed out.

She gripped IronMaw.

The steel stayed silent.

She won't just lose someone this time. She'll be the one carved apart.

Flesh or fire.

Bones or soul.

Body or mind.

Only one walks forward.

CHAPTER FIFTY

THE WEDDING

Keothi lay flat against her horse's back, wind cutting through her hair. IronMaw burned on her spine like a second soul. She couldn't wait. She wouldn't.

This wasn't a rescue or revenge.

This was the moment she'd choose what part of herself could live and what had to die.

The prophecy pounded in her skull, not a whisper but a war drum:

"Fire kindles a shadow.
A bear, cloaked in golden chains,
Screams beneath the weight of silence.
The masked shall feast,
And the forged shall choose."

Maybe it hadn't happened yet.

Maybe this was it.

Live your truth.

And the truth was gutting.

Vorik hadn't just infected her.

He would infect everything.

The serpent had left his hole.

Time to burn it shut.

A church stood stranded in the wasteland, skeletal, gutted, forgotten.

No towns. No life.

The wooden pews lay splintered and rotting. The stained glass shattered.

The roof had caved in decades ago. Yet even decay couldn't mask the stench of ritual.

Vorik stood at the altar, smug as a man with no god.

Beside him, was Borin, gagged. Slumped. Hollow-eyed. The great smith, reduced to kindling.

A white mask banner hung above them.

The smell of Virell lingered on every beam: hunger, silence, a prayer half-eaten.

Keothi dismounted. IronMaw slid free. Her hands didn't shake.

Vorik's smile curled like a blade. "You came. I hoped you would."

"Let him go." She bit down on everything else she wanted to scream.

"Is that how you greet your betrothed?" He yanked Borin up by the hair like a trophy.

Ashes still clung to the altar. Burn marks etched symbols she didn't recognize

He dropped Borin's head, theatrics thick in the stale air. "Choose, Yrsa! Him or yourself!?"

"I choose myself."

Vorik chuckled, a cold, brittle sound. "Then prove it. Drop the axe."

"Release my uncle."

"Tsk, tsk." He wagged a finger. "You know better. You belong to me."

Her jaw locked. IronMaw flared in her grip.

Vorik drew a dagger, cruel, gleaming, pressed it to Borin's throat. "Kneel or watch him bleed."

IronMaw burned in her hands. She held on, breath by breath, trying to stop time. Her fingers cramped around the haft, tendons screaming to hang on.

The void bloomed anyway. She let go.

It struck the stone with a deep, resonant toll. The vibration climbed her legs and settled in her ribs. A sound that mourned her choice.

The sun caught on the axe head. Her reflection, Revin, pounded from within. Fists slamming against the steel, a silent, frantic warning.

With one last, aching exhale, she stepped forward into the silence, unarmed, exposed, but unbroken. Each step peeled something off her: a lie, a legend, a shield.

Vorik grinned, but an ancient hunger flickered behind it.

With a cruel shove, he sent Borin sprawling. The old man scrabbled backward, muffled screams, desperate pleas.

Keothi spoke, voice steady. "What does the coward behind the mask crave now?"

"It's not me." His fingers snatched her cloak, yanked hard.

Her knees hit stone, but her gaze didn't drop. Not this time.

"He waits," Vorik whispered. He nodded toward the banner. "One last feast."

He twisted her braid, forcing her head back.

Steel kissed her throat, parting skin with a cruel precision.

"You're the last defiance. The rot that whispers freedom. Your death will cleanse what's left."

The world narrowed to a single, searing point. Pain flared; the rest of her refused to kneel.

"It's not pain. It's healing. You should thank me."

Her gasp split the silence. She pressed a hand to her throat. The warmth ran through her fingers, unstoppable.

The world tilted. The ground rolled like a wave beneath her knees.

Borin tore the gag away, voice shredded. "No! Don't let him...!" But he was too late.

Vorik raised his arms, eyes wild. "Virell! I have struck down your enemy! Erase the world! We become one!" His laugh echoed, sharp, manic.

Until she moved.

From her boot: the dagger. The one from the pyre. His message. Her answer.

No scream. No warning.

One strike.

Low. Fast. Unseen.

The blade found the artery behind his ankle.

A whisper across skin and sinew.

He staggered, blood coated the church's floors. Vorik fell beside her, eyes wide, hands slick with disbelief. He desperately grabbed onto his ankle, trying to stop the bleeding.

She turned her face toward him, vocal cords exposed. A hoarse whisper. "Not wife. Not weapon. Not yours. Me."

The strength left her. Breath through broken glass.

Her arms fell. Her vision narrowed. Her mind had been the first sacrifice. Now her body was the second. This one, at least, was hers.

She collapsed, quiet, final.

Vorik twitched once.

Then stilled. A final breath escaping his lungs.

Their blood pooled together, spilling over stone.

Betrothed.

Husband.

Wife.

Together in death.

But only she had chosen it.

Chapter Fifty-One

SOFTNESS HAS GONE

F*rom Keothi, for Spoon*

The softness has gone.
Your laugh. Your steadiness.
Your silence that made me braver.

Groa didn't tear down the mountain for me.
She came for you.
Because I let you stand beside me.

They stripped my name.
Then they took you, and with you, my soul.

You guided me through shadow.
When I was broken, bruised.
When I swallowed the scream, you were there.

You steadied my hands
As I faced the unfaceable.

You were supposed to be there when I took the head.
But silence took your place.

The whisperings have stopped.
The space hums too loud without you.

Where are you?
Do the winds carry your laughter?

Tell me you're with Freya.
That she found you.
That her fields opened to you like arms.

How do I face what's still coming, without your quiet strength?
I am paralyzed.
Cold. Angry. Hollow.

Spoon, come back.
I need you.
And you're nowhere.
You were my shield.
The quiet kind, built of knowing glances and unsaid truths.

Love this deep is a forge-fire.
Burning silent
Shaping steel without ceremony

Love isn't always loud.
It builds family.
Offers refuge, creates sanctuary.

And that is what Groa took.
My home. My chosen family.
I carry your voice, a scar I won't let heal.

Chapter Fifty-Two

A Forged Path

Sit with me. You're hurting. Good.

That means you cared. That means you saw her.

I felt it too, the way your chest cracked when she walked into that hollow church, all splinters and silence. She broke me. I won't lie.

But hear me now.

We've built trust, you and I. I won't betray that with comfort, when what you need is clarity.

There were only three choices before her.

Option 1 – All-out war.

Glorious. Bloody. Doomed. Too many would die. Mothers. Sons. The fragile-hearted. And she would live with it. That is no victory.

There's no glory in throwing away a life. Even if it is destined for Valhalla.

Option 2 – The silent blade.

A whisper in the dark. Strike fast, and die slower. No saga. No witness. A shadow's death for one who burned too bright.

Option 3 – Step into the trap.

Strip everything away. Name. Mask. Duty. No one else bleeds. Two lives traded for a world that lives. Accept herself. Fully. Finally.

The path she chose. The only one that left her whole.

She walked into that church alone.

No counsel. No witness. No regrets.

You call it death. I call it truth.

She let the mask consume her. Then rage. Then pain.

But beneath every scar, every scream, every sorrow-tempered breath, she remained one thing:

A protector.

Vorik took her name. Groa took her spirit. But neither ever touched her core.

The only way to lose the mask is to become the one who never needed it. She did.

Then she stepped into the church and pulled the blade.

If you mourn, good. Even gods need to grieve.

If you don't understand, go back. Watch her from the forge onward. Walk with her again. Feel what she carried.

We, those who speak only when truth is clear, have always watched. And I have watched her longer than most. So now, I welcome her to our ranks.

The chains are shattered. The world stirs.

And she rises.

Not as the girl they tried to break.

Not as the legend they tried to tame.

But as the fire they will never contain.

-Nyrr, Silent Flame of the Shadowforged

Keothi the Barbarian

Those who broke her will learn: the fire remembers

And when memory burns long enough, the Flame Ascends.

EPILOGUE

Vorik's skin bulged. Something twitched beneath, as if whatever ruled him was waking up, hungry to crawl free of the puppet.

Uncle Borin stumbled to her side, blood dark on his knees, tears carving lines through soot. "Kindling," he rasped. Each breath scraped like gravel. His wrists bled where rope had chewed through skin.

From the axe's core, a soundless scream burned. Trapped in steel, the shadow begged for war, demanding mercy in blood. The girl died. The weapon didn't.

Somewhere in the deep, where gods once forged themselves from shadow and flame, something answered her name.

Chapter Fifty-Three

— PLAYLIST —

Never Enough – Five Finger Death Punch

Whispers of Warmth – Coded Distress

——□——

Lift It – Endless Tavern

Blodfest – Danheim, Heldom

The Fire – Jax the Bard, Haylie Allcott

Pagan Protest Anthem – Polk County Pagan Market

——□——

Shatter the Silence – Melody Stellar

If Only You Knew – Meraki Moon

Compass – Sail North

——□——

Sorry I'm a Murderhobo – Dominik Witka

Hunt the Sky – Voice Play, J. None

The Iron in her Heart – Mythborne

War isn't Murder – Jesse Welles

——□——

You're Already Enough – Hoshi-zora

—ABOUT THE AUTHOR—

Kessar writes cross-genre fiction for readers who crave stories that are messy, myth-soaked, and emotionally sharp. Neurodivergent and narratively possessed, she explores identity and transformation through fantasy, thrillers, and whatever else the story demands.

She writes from a cluttered desk somewhere on Earth, fueled by cold coffee, too many tabs, and the relentless pull of stories that insist on being told.

Add your Ember to the Forge

Every forged blade needs a witness. If this tale left its mark, let your review help carve the path for the next reader.

Goodreads

—FROM THE FORGE W/ GRATITUDE—

This book was not shaped alone. These creators, friends, and fire-hearted allies helped hammer this tale into being. All through their wisdom, chaos, encouragement, and unshakable belief in me.

The words below are each creator's own, offered here as an invitation.

Fellow Wordsmiths

Kelly Gabriels

Lifelong bookworm and compulsive story spinner of fiction that ranges from light hearted romps to dystopian horror, and refuses to apologize for it.

Amber B

Amber B. is a fantasy author who writes with emotion, intention, and a deep love for the kinds of stories that stay with you.

SR George

An Author Witch who enjoys telling fantasy romance stories.

Robin Alden Howard

Stories that leave a Mark. Inspired by truth. Shaped by survival. Told without apology.

Fellow Shadowforged

Coach Susie | Chaos to Clarity

Thriving with ADHD isn't about fixing yourself—it's about finally seeing your brilliance and building a life that works beautifully for the brain you've always had.

www.ingramcontent.com/pod-product-compliance
Lightning Source LLC
LaVergne TN
LVHW100515110826
845146LV00002B/647

* 9 7 9 8 9 9 4 2 5 4 0 0 4 *